JUST THE WAY YOU WANT ME

Also by Nora Eisenberg

Fiction

The War at Home

Non-Fiction

Stepping Stones: A Course for Basic Writers
Great Writing: A Reader for Writers
The American Values Reader
The Questioning Reader
(with Harvey Wiener)

JUST THE WAY YOU WANT ME

a novel by

NORA EISENBERG

Leapfrog Press
Wellfleet, Massachusetts

Published in 2003 in the United States by
The Leapfrog Press
P.O. Box 1495
95 Commercial Street
Wellfleet, MA 02667-1495, USA
www.leapfrogpress.com

Printed in Canada

Distributed in the United States and Canada by
Consortium Book Sales and Distribution
St. Paul, Minnesota 55114

First Edition

The characters and events in this book are fictitious.
Any similarity to actual persons, living or dead,
is coincidental and not intended by the author.

Library of Congress Cataloging-in-Publication Data

Eisenberg, Nora
  Just the way you want me : a novel / by Nora Eisenberg.-- 1st ed.
    p. cm.
  ISBN 0-9679520-8-5
  1. Fathers and daughters--Fiction. 2. Women journalists--Fiction. 3.
Missing persons--Fiction. 4. Loyalty oaths--Fiction. 5. Labor
leaders--Fiction. 6. Ex-convicts--Fiction. I. Title.
  PS3605.I83J87 2003
  813'.54--dc21

                                                        2003004080

              10 9 8 7 6 5 4 3 2 1

In memory of my father
Alex Eisenberg

NEW YORK CITY
1992

1: Stuck

I WASN'T OLD but I wasn't young. At almost forty, I was statistically smack in the middle of my life, but psychologically, it was clear, I had reached the end of the line. There was David, an unmarried, unmacho man, saying the kind of things you hear mostly in dreams: Let's run away and live happily ever after, you and me. He'd been saying it for months, and each time his eyes got dopey with devotion but his mouth dipped musingly—producing just the touch of irony you want in a man declaring undying love in the last decade of the twentieth century. And here I was, sure he would never leave—not even when my face and breasts collapse, my continence and comprehension vanish. And I wanted to look back into his ardent eyes, smile back a philosophical smile and say, OK, let's give it a shot. But I didn't. Instead I picked a fight.

For weeks I'd been picking fights for the littlest thing. Today's little thing was a fresh pearly spot on the cushion we were sitting on, which we'd just been lying on, making love. David was saying, Come on, Bet, come with me. And all I could think was, What is that spot? Milk from our morning coffee? Cream cheese from our bagels? It could have been anything but I decided it was residue of David—a teeny speck of cum. Go with you? How could I go with you? Look at what you do to couches!

David can almost read my mind, another reason why I love him. Now he said, "Screw the couch. We'll throw it out. We'll throw it out and live happily ever after." He laughed. "Damn it, Betsy. I'm not good at it either. This happiness bit. But we'll try it together. Every day we'll wake up and practice love and loyalty and all of that. Like scales."

I said, "Look, David, if you have to try, what's the point? That doesn't sound like happy. That sounds like a whole lot of work." I hated the wise-ass words jumping from my mouth like toads, but I couldn't seem to stop them.

"Come on, you know what I mean."

And I did, of course.

Again and again, he'd gone over it. He loved me, I loved him. I hated my job at *Big Apple*, the insipid magazine I'd been working at for half a decade. I'd wanted to quit and freelance and now I could. Work was moving him to Guatemala for at least a year, and it would be a good move for both of us. I'd listen and nod away. But then, when I actually had to say, OK, something would happen. I'd pick a fight. He'd say, Everything will be awesome. And I'd say, Twelve-year-olds say awesome. Grow up, David.

I know it sounds bitchy. I usually tend towards kindly and calm—it was totally out of character for me to be barking like a nervous terrier. Barking and barking at dear David with his deep spaniel eyes and soul. Or to shiver when I thought of packing up, closing doors.

"Betsy," David said, stroking my hand. "What's wrong? Really, what's going on?"

But I couldn't say a thing.

David, like most everyone I know, gave up smoking years ago, but lately, with the stress of the move—and my bitchiness no doubt—he'd been smoking again now and then. He lit up now, and his eyes teared up from the smoke and he began to cough. How I hated myself! How I loved him—his dark eyes, wet and worried, his bare chest, rising and falling, his long legs stretched out before him, white and graceful. I wanted to say, You're the best. With *you* I can do it. Move out. Move on.

"Don't smoke, David. Smoking doesn't make you happy," I said instead.

10

"And you? What will you do?"

"I don't know."

"Jesus, Bet. Why don't you know?"

"I don't know why I don't know."

And then, I guess, it all got too much even for Saint David.

"Well, figure it out," he said, standing. "Figure out what the hell's the matter with you. Why the hell you want to screw us up."

Screw up *us*, I thought. You don't separate parts of an extended verb, though of course you do.

And then he was "reading" me again. "And don't even think of correcting my grammar, Bet. In fact, don't even think of saying another word. . . ."

And then he was in his clothes and at the door, saying, "Figure it out, just figure it fucking out."

On a day like that day, when he had an early photo session, David would wake at six, shower, and then dress in the living room so that he wouldn't wake me.

At least that was his intention. Usually I heard him, and usually I wanted to hear him. I wanted to sit on the couch and watch him—the way he put on one sock then one shoe, walking around half shod for a half-hour, the way he spread the newspaper on the floor and read it standing up, the way he rubbed his head into consciousness like a sleepy schoolboy. How much I loved him then—and some slow mornings, like this morning, we'd end up clasped together on the couch, like we were starting out, starting over again—like we were back on my office couch, that first time, becoming best friends and lovers in a single awkward lunge. That first day, with David and me, as soon as the tape went on and my questions began, something came to life, something between us that was stronger than either of us apart. Expressed in our crazy, urgent sex that finally, of course, had little to do with sex.

"What do you think of when you pick a human subject to shoot?" I had asked.

"The face," he said, "Always the face." And he stared at my face, at my nose, actually.

I was used to that. My nose is a big shock in the middle of an otherwise conventionally pretty face. I have high cheek bones, tawny hair that matches tawny skin, full naturally crimson lips, bright green eyes—and then the beak. So I'm used to people staring and squinting, thinking, I know, how much more attractive I'd be with a half inch chopped off. But David's stare was different, like he was seeing through skin and bone and cartilage. I felt uncomfortable and I started to laugh. "The nose?" I said. And then I corrected myself. "The face? What about the face?" I felt my face burn.

"What's there behind the social façade, behind the smile."

"I see," I said. I tried to change the topic. I showed him our view from the fiftieth floor. I talked about the new replacement windows, the sky, the weather.

"An ache. I look for an ache, I guess. It's what I trust in the face, in the person." He wouldn't stop staring.

I covered my face with my hands, squealed an embarrassingly squeaky "oh"—small and sharp, like I was coming. I thought, keep your hands on your face and crawl under the desk. Then I heard David walk over to the couch where I was sitting, felt him pry my fingers from my face, one by one.

But now David slammed the door hard and I felt my heart slam with dread. He was right. I had to figure out what was going on. Or else he'd be gone and I'd still be here. And I'd had enough decades of still here and everyone gone.

So I stood up and began wandering through the apartment, looking for clues. But I felt clueless. It was going to be one of those spooky days, I knew, when you decide to take stock of your life, with no idea of where and how to do that, certain only that there's something wrong and you're running out of time. Could it be the apartment that held me? I had never liked it. The living room with its cramped "dinette" or "denette," depending on what you put in the "convertible space"—as the managing agent called it—for which I was charged an extra $300 a month. A tiny slice of a kitchen, in which a pregnant guest once got stuck. A bedroom on a hopeless shaft. What here could possibly be keeping me?

My mother left my brother, Tommy, and me when we were young—but I still had her rocking chair, which I'd run to over the years as others run to parents. Now I hurled myself on the old oak ladderback, rocking, thinking. I must have been rocking hard, for after a couple of minutes, the chair starting creaking; then there was a snapping sound and suddenly the whole thing collapsed, throwing me to the floor. I wasn't hurt but I was miserable. Lying there, I couldn't escape an intimate viewing of my furniture's pitiful bottoms, the stuffing and springs hanging, the frames and bolts dangling. *You've ruined my couch!* What a joke! Most everything I had was shot and ready to go.

And hadn't I known it for years—somewhere on the edge of consciousness, where knowledge about one's life accumulates like footprints on an old carpet, slowly, carelessly until there it is—heels and toes, smears and soot, dark and inescapable? For years now, every time my brother visited from Africa, where he is a field organizer for International End Hunger, I'd say, Let's go through things! The furniture and papers and ancient clothes. Go through—*Be through*, was more like it. And Tommy, hearing the meaning which I myself couldn't hear, would cry, But it was *theirs*, meaning our parents, like they were royalty and I was a traitor to the court.

I rose, picked up the cracked-up rocker, and then, opening the door of the living room closet, shoved it into the growing pyre of arms and legs, backs and bottoms of dismembered tables and chairs. Twenty-five years ago the best of my parents' furniture was marred and scarred; now half of it had come to this end, the rest just holding on in my cramped rooms. They'd moved on, my parents, to their sorry fates, but their stuff had stayed. Every time I got my coat, the remains of my father's

Morris chair stared out accusingly. Fix me, glue me, Betsy, they seemed to say. Don't forget us.

They'd all moved on but I was supposed to stay, minding all the family stuff and memories. Wasn't that the deal? I looked around. The only things in the place with a future came from David. A tall teak bookcase. A pretty, old, mirrored mahogany music cabinet for his photos. The photos themselves piled high on top.

I picked up a photo. A black boy with a white dog on a broken-down porch, wisteria poking through the broken beams. The boy was in profile smiling at the dog, holding the dog's face forward to the camera, like a proud parent.

I remembered the boy, the April afternoon David and I had wandered up and down the hills of Yonkers. I was doing an article on Westchester homes, and David had been hired to do the photos. On our way back from Scarsdale and some modern mansions, we got lost in Yonkers. David said, Look at that, that Westchester home, snapping picture after picture of dilapidation, neglect, and then here and there some sprig of hope that made you want to cry—lace pressed against windows patched with cardboard, half burnt-out buildings with front doors painted in multiple coats of cheery red enamel. *Big Apple* edited out the Yonkers section, but David won a prize somewhere else for the picture of the boy and sent him the money. The boy wrote back that he was planning a trip to New York City one day and would call. Could David take more pictures? He could bring his sisters and cousins. The whole family was very photogenic.

How could I not run off with a man who befriended eleven-year-old kids the world had discarded? I'd been degraded by enough bottom-line men in yellow ties and trendy black-clad artists to know crumply, earnest David was my once-in-a-lifetime prince. And here I was blowing it—the best, and last, offer to ride my way.

Then the phone rang. It was Maurice, a copy editor from work.

Had I left the proofs in the office? he asked. Could I bring in the dummies?

Dummies. Sure I could bring in the dummies. How fitting—a dummy bringing dummies. I was a dummy—staying a second longer in this dummy place!

We're on our way, I said.

When I arrived Margaret was at her desk working on her Anna Lisa column. That morning her mouth looked particularly tense, as if it had been pinched in worry since dawn. Which, probably, it had.

For Margaret was now Anna Lisa. She'd been Anna Lisa almost half a decade, since the real Anna Lisa Russo died, leaving her to answer the thousands writing into *Big Apple* magazine for advice. "Anna Lisa on Modern Living and Loving" was the name of Margaret's column, and it appeared in each issue with a picture of Anna Lisa just before she collapsed and died on the bus on her way to work. The odd thing was that although *Big Apple* acknowledged Anna Lisa's tragic death in a long article, the column remained "Anna Lisa's" with Margaret, who had been an editorial assistant and occasional stand-in, not so much replacing but becoming Anna Lisa. It always struck me as ghoulish and cruel—the dead Anna Lisa dragged out smiling each week, the live Margaret hidden behind her, speaking through Anna Lisa's red, smiling lips.

Ever since I'd come to *Big Apple,* Margaret and I had been friends, silently appreciating each other's awkward set-up in life. Together we laughed at our boss, Alan Marcus, whose name we privately changed, regularly if not cleverly. Alan Mar-us, Alien Marcus, Alotta Mucous, All Marvelous, laughing, like teenagers, in uncontrollable spasms. We celebrated birthdays together, Margaret and I, indulging each other in Italian silk scarves and French perfume in an office that had settled on black cotton and unisex musk.

"Hi there," Margaret said. "What's happening?"

What *was* happening? I saw David's face, heard his words—Figure it out. My house? My job? Could my job be keeping me?

After my childhood, my work—with its predictable routines and steady if unremarkable salary—had brought significant calm to my life. Was I simply scared to abandon the security I'd never known before? My job might be stupid but it was certain.

Margaret waved a sheet of paper at me. "A woman in Bay Ridge," she said, "says her husband has a glue habit and kicks her when he's high. She says she can't leave because they have four dogs and the dogs are very attached. I guess she has her own 'glue' problem," she laughed.

Generally, when Margaret laughed, I'd join in. But that morning I just couldn't. She suddenly sounded like a noise machine, one of those whirring boxes psychiatrists put in their waiting rooms to cover over the howls inside.

That Margaret was howling or at least whimpering inside, I had little doubt. She lived with her mother, who, instead of dying from rheumatic fever as a child in Cork, lingered on for eighty years, ruling Margaret for more than half of that time with episodes of quick breathing, slow walking, and the threat of her heart stopping. How much longer could Margaret go on with *her* life?

Her mother called a dozen times a day. Alan stood over her and shouted. The worried letter writers told her that without her help and wisdom they'd die. She'd write back to "Bay Ridge," I knew, and praise her honesty and perseverance. Maybe she'd offer her the number of her direct line. The woman would call. Margaret would find her a community mental health facility, a reputable vet. . . . The scripts varied—but Margaret never did. She was there for everyone every day. And then every night she went back to her mother, who waited on the front steps with some sputum or stool specimen in her hands, a scowl on her face. Would she ever escape her servitude? Find a satisfying job, a gratifying mate or friend? Did *she* ever have some sweet, loving David type? And did she blow it?

What was I waiting for? I was an experienced journalist. It wouldn't be hard to get freelance work that I would enjoy more than my work at *Big Apple*. But here I was still hanging in with this stupid job, stupid Alan. How much crazier was it being run around by a crazy old lady, a glue-crazed husband, a herd of hounds?

"The husband says if she leaves she'll have the dogs' deaths on her head. I'm going to tell her to take the dogs and go into pet therapy." Margaret winked at me as if we were in cahoots on a genius plan.

"Cats are easier," I said distractedly.

"Right you are," she said. "But dogs are cozier. My mother wants us to get a dog."

"Margaret," I said, thinking to confide in her. But then I said nothing. What could she tell me? Get a dog, a nice, cozy pooch and forget your problems?

"Hey, what's wrong, Bet?" she said. "You look miserable. Just tell Anna Lisa," she laughed.

I looked at Margaret's bony shoulders. They looked like they could be snapped between two fingers, like chicken wings. I wanted to rush out to Woodside and shake the old woman till she fell at my feet and begged for forgiveness, promised she'd let Margaret go free!

"I don't know what's wrong," I said.

I studied her hair, plain and tame, without a wisp of vanity, and I felt my throat throb. How long till I grew my own gray helmet? Maybe, like Anna Lisa, Margaret would collapse under the weight of everyone's hopeless problems. Then maybe they'd appoint *me* Anna Lisa? And I'd sit, old and invisible, advising others. Then go home at night to the dog and the broken furniture. . . . A picture of David secreted under a tattered cushion.

Margaret said, "Yes you do. . . . You want out. . . . Go, Bet. Get out of here. . . . Before you can't. Before you end up . . . me," she whispered.

And I gasped.

She said, "Listen to Anna Lisa and go!"

And then she laughed, and I held her in my arms so she wouldn't see my face slicked with tears.

Since I was late and my face was probably red from crying, I tried to tiptoe past Alan's office. But his door was wide open and he was staring out from behind his desk.

"You're late," he said, looking down at a watch in either palm. "Sit," he said, pointing to a chair across from him. And I sat.

"How are you, Alan?" I said. But I could see he was happy. He was always happy when I was late. It gave him an advantage all day that fueled spirited door slamming and speeches. But I wasn't being fair. Long ago Alan had stopped that, for long ago Alan and I had stopped battling each other. Or if we battled, we did it subtly. I, for example, spoke in short sentences and avoided Alan when I could, which irritated Alan, who liked to trap me—and a multitude of women—in leisurely talks, leading up to long lunches and still longer suppers, with long stylized stares and strokes.

"Anything special?" I said.

I looked past Alan to the collection of Japanese tea bowls on the wall unit behind the desk.

"We're running out of time with those interviews," Alan said.

I just studied the bowls, the only thing I would miss here besides Margaret. There were ten of them in all, and I knew them by heart, each gently sloped, in colors of flesh or earth, as natural and graceful as a shoulder or the edge of a pond. If it weren't for those bowls, I thought, what happened with Alan probably never would have happened. Indeed if it weren't for the bowls, I might never have come to work for *Big Apple* in the first place. I have no disposition toward either mysticism or collecting, but when I first saw those tea bowls, the very first time I met with Alan, sitting with him in the office, talking about a job at the magazine, I thought: I need those, I need to see them every day. I meant the quiet easy shapes, reassuring calm and certainty forever. Into the future. Into the past.

"I love those bowls," I said.

"So you've said . . . a hundred times. Tell me something I don't know, like when you're going to get to my interview."

Big Apple had a little bit of everything. A little gossip. A little arts. A little politics. A little celebrity profiles. A little fashion. It was a little retro (Anna Lisa), a little hip (Sexy Lexy—a glossary of the latest terms for the latest sexual practices), a little humorous (Cool Cash—a cartoon about a Wall Street brokerage house, with plots mostly lifted from old *Archie* comics). According to Alan, *Big Apple* was halfway between the "pretentious" *New Yorker* and the "pedestrian" *New York* magazine. "Halfway but never middle of the road," he liked to say. "A medley." A mish-mash was more like it, filled with whatever gimmicks and shticks Alan Marcus's hyperactive mind had settled on that week.

But *this* interview would be an all-time low even for *Big Apple*. A double interview: An Israeli and Saudi, each orthodox and devoted to an extreme religious faction back home, were on speaking tours to make money for their respective groups. Alan's idea was to put them together in the same room and have them go at it. Alan was paying them well for the right to print their words: I'm pure, you're corrupt. I live, you die. I tried to imagine the garbage they would hurl at each other.

"It's immoral," I said. "Supporting their fanaticism."

"So bypass the religion and politics. You'll find a way to do it different," Alan said. "The Fashion of Fanaticism. Ishmael's plaid *keffiyeh* versus Shmuel's striped *tallis*. And then, moving right along, one's *tigiyah* versus the other's *yalmulka*. Or do your culture jazz. . . . You *are* our senior culture editor. Let them talk about books. . . . *Koran* versus *Torah*. . . . Jesus, Bets, let them kill each other and get some arty pictures. But just do it," he laughed.

19

How could I have lasted a month here, let alone five years? On top of its editorial cheeziness overall, it was an editorial mess day to day. I was senior cultural editor. But there was no junior editor. So I did most everything for every book or movie story—research, interviews, writing, editing, copy editing. And—big surprise—people kept quitting on Alan, so half the time there was no political editor, or fashion editor, and I was stuck being senior/junior/research/copy editor for half the other departments. I, who knew nothing about local politics or fashion trends, would end up writing stories like "Albanians Claiming Bronx Political Territory" or "New Light Looks for New York Locks," skating on thin ice, my nerves wrecked as the magazine went to press.

The bowls. I couldn't take my eyes off them. Once upon a time I had high hopes for Alan—and my life at *Big Apple*—and it was all because of the bowls. The owner of those bowls, I had told myself when I saw them at my interview, would have to be serene and wise. No matter that Alan's eyes jumped and his mouth ran. The discriminating man who owned those bowls, who chose them and lived beside them each day, would emerge in time.

"Some tea?" Alan said now. "Or coffee?"

"No thanks." Should I have said, yes? I was being more spiteful than I wanted to be—disappointing Alan twice, first by refusing to acknowledge that I'd been late and then by refusing something to drink when I knew that Alan liked to make use of his collections, resigning himself to serving coffee and even soda in the tea bowls.

Alan had many collections, but none besides the bowls were of any consequence. Down the rosewood wall there was a collection of ivory carvings, nervous little figures busy in activity—musicians tooting pipes, children turning tops, old men playing cards, courtesans bowing to the floor. Alan claimed he was building his collection with the help of a fine dealer, but I'd seen him several times at Fifth Avenue gift shops, the kind that claim in their signs to be going out of business but never do, specializing in Italian corkscrews, French lace hankies, Persian rugs, and netsuke—all made in Taiwan.

"Whatever you think of the interview you have to do it. It's part of your job. Understand?"

I heard David, Come. I heard Margaret, Go.

Say, no. Say, no to all of this. Say you're leaving. But I said nothing.

"It's non-negotiable, like getting to the office on time." Alan opened his desk drawer and took out a handful of watches. "Here, pick one. A present. Maybe being clear on the time and date will get you clear on other things. Like the duties of your job."

"I'm not in the mood for this, Alan," I said. "I don't want your presents and I don't want your speeches."

"Timex will be worth something one day," he said. "One or two of these are real beauts."

Timex. Alan would collect anything. In addition to the collection of tea bowls, the netsuke, the sword shields, the old Timex watches, there was probably a drawer in his desk piled thick with old string. This, too, Alan would claim as special. They don't braid it like that any more. That's circa 1960 bakery string, 100% cotton, I imagined him saying. A treasure.

How he went on and on, meting out his judgments, appraising the value of everything and everybody every damned minute. It amazed me, sitting across from Alan that morning, how angry he could still make me!

You're so special, Betsy, he had said. It was years ago—just after I'd come to *Big Apple*. We had drunk too many eggnogs at my first office Christmas party and had ended up in a cab uptown together. Hyper, slick Alan Marcus was about to disappear, and a wise, calm Alan would appear in his place, my drunken mind concocted as we rode up Third Avenue. And so when Alan said he wanted to show me something in his apartment, I went with him eagerly. And when he went into a bedroom to use a bathroom, I lay down on the furry rug, barely conscious, telling myself that peace and wisdom were minutes away. I don't think I thought of sex, or if I did it was only as a step to serenity.

The next thing I knew, Alan was flat on top of me, and I felt something stabbing my back.

"Oh, Jesus, be careful," he was shouting, pushing me over. "That's vintage Fisher Price. It'll be a collector's item before you know it. You're goddamn crushing it."

My head banged on the floor as I rolled, and I saw that "it" was a small red and white bus filled with little figures. I moaned a long, drunken moan of defeat.

That's when Alan said *I* was special, too, a real treasure. I've never been sure if Alan said that because he thought I was sexually excited, rolling on the floor, moaning, or because he caught the disgrace smeared somewhere on my drunken face at being shoved aside and banged on the head to save some plastic bus filled with plastic people.

The bus safe, Alan stopped talking. He took off his pants, put his penis in my mouth, and came in a second. That wasn't supposed to happen, I thought. I don't know what Alan thought. He just pressed my head hard as if it were a door buzzer. I wanted to scream. But I couldn't—my mouth was full. So I just stood up, walked to the kitchen and spat in the sink, in a bowl filled with dried Spaghettios. So there were children, a wife, I thought. I thought about washing the dishes, not leaving the gunk-topped noodles for the wife to clean, but the room was spinning too fast.

"That was very sweet, Bets." Alan said when I returned to the bedroom to get my coat. It was a child's room, I saw now, with toys tossed in each corner.

"Let's clean up!" I said with crazy cheer, as if straightening up the room would erase the crazy mess of a scene that had just occurred.

"My wife will clean it up tomorrow when she and Joshie come from St. Bart's. . . . Just relax," Alan said. Then he closed his eyes and was out. And I staggered down to the street and took a cab back to my empty apartment.

Now Alan said, "OK, Bets. I'm sorry I yelled. OK, the interview is not your thing. But just think of it as a favor, Bets. A favor for an old friend."

But you're not a friend, I wanted to say. Though I understood why Alan thought of us that way. For after that fiasco of an evening, Alan and I ended up spending an evening a week together for four years. *Because* of that evening. Meeting Alan publicly in restaurants, sitting upright beside him on red leather banquettes, clinking moderate amounts of wine in immaculate goblets, later back at my place, playing Scrabble, watching the news, having tea and cookies, like an old devoted couple, I hoped to recover some of the dignity lost that night. That was my logic, at least. I was an unadventurous person, not the least of all sexually, and the fact that I ended up on a floor with Alan's bare bottom in my face, his strange penis on my tonsils, pursued me for years and sent me to more evenings that might set things right. But nothing about the trail of evenings was ever really right. Not the talk, not the occasional tenderness—mostly handholding on my couch—which I sought for restoration of innocence and hope. Only once, Alan tried to make a move. But I looked away, making believe I hadn't seen him pointing to his fly like my grandma used to point to her candy dish as if to say, *Look, take.*

Mostly the evenings were not sordid, just pathetic. Neither of us pushed to cut things off, though. I, not so much because it would have meant more evenings home alone—I had developed considerable skill in that—but because I wasn't willing to admit how poor my judgment was, how fantastical my yearnings. I was still half convinced that the other Alan, the serene man of the beautiful bowls, would reveal himself—that beyond all the yelping and sticky cum, there was a lucid man who could teach me something I didn't know. Alan went on with it, I think, simply to get out of the house. The routine of family life—dinner, bath, story-time—was no doubt uninteresting to Alan, who wanted special things. And so, despite my big nose, modest accomplishments, and obvious conventionality, I was enlisted as a special woman in Alan's vast special woman collection. Other nights, I was sure, held more exotic offerings. I thought of myself as a mid-week blueplate—the date version of Salisbury steak or fish sticks—in a week's line-up of specials.

"It feels good to be close to someone extraordinary like you," he'd say.

Even then, it always made me sad and teary. The claim that we were exciting and excitingly close, that we were entwined in the fascinating intimacies of remarkable personalities. I was plain—and I knew it. And what's more I wanted it. After our mad childhood, tracked by cops and FBI and reporters like we were some mutant species, I'd wanted only that—plain and simple forevermore.

Then, a year ago, I met David. "I've met someone," I said. "I can't make dinner on Tuesdays any more."

"I could switch things around and meet you Wednesdays."

I shook my head.

"How about Thursdays?"

"No good," I said.

"OK. Friday. And one Saturday afternoon a month. You win."

I said, "No good. It's over."

"You're a special lady, Bets, but you're really acting mighty conventional and *yenta*-like. I expect more from you."

"Don't."

"I mean you seem plain, but that's your specialness. But frankly, it's too plain even for you to say, 'No good. It's over.'"

"It's over," I said.

"You work for me," he said.

A threat? I thought. "A threat?" I said.

But Alan shook his head. "I'm a prick but not a bastard. I wish you luck. You're a remarkable woman. I want us to stay close."

Stay close. I thought of the little people in the little bus, squashed close together, and Alan, his eyes closed, clutching them like a sleepy King Kong, saving everyone from a terrible fall into mediocrity.

"Of course," I said. "No problem."

"Actually, that's a boring thing to say, Bet. Boring people say, No problem. Or, No *problema*. You should say more interesting things, especially at a special moment like this."

Now, a year later, I looked across at Alan. A new patch of gray hair sprouted on the left side of his head. I shouldn't be so hard on him, I thought. He was harmless. Maybe even oddly noble. Wanting so much for me, when I wanted so little. A modern-day Midas, casting his glitter on all sorts of junk. I thought, What does it matter as long as you're no longer one of his important pieces? I thought, Just tell him you're leaving. It's really over.

"They're interesting men," he said. "Risk-taking."

I couldn't do the interview. I couldn't do any *Big Apple* interview. The pointless questions and endless answers. This person's new choreography—how it expressed the promise of B flat and cocaine at once. That person's laser sculpture as a critique of antidepressants. Suddenly I wanted to hear no more—of everyone else's crazy ideas and plans. For the first time in my life I had a chance for my own. So what if it was a corny life imagined in C major, a square's square vision. Yes, David. No, *Big Apple*. I opened my mouth to say it. But I couldn't say it. I'm going forever.

Alan said, "You're edgy. Am I right that you could use a little cozy supportive dinner? Are you free for dinner? We could talk some more about the piece. Flush it out." He always said "flush" for "flesh"—and today I imagined him going "flush, flush, flush," like a toilet, on and on and on, gurgling into eternity. Why couldn't I say it, Goodbye, I'm going?

Then I saw her face, the way it used to be, pink and vulnerable, like a peeled peach. Then laughing and as bright red as a baboon's ass.

"I have an interview," I lied. But if I timed my morning right,

I could escape the office by four and make it out to Brooklyn before the rush hour. I suddenly knew I had to see Marie. I'd see her and then maybe I could go.

I stood to leave.

"Surprise me," Alan said. "Make it special and make me proud."

The sky was overcast when I reached the gate and the air frosty.

"Some weather, Miss Vogel," the gatekeeper said, tipping his cap. "Cold enough for you?"

"Miserable," I said. I held myself tight and regretted that I hadn't worn a coat over my blazer. But I hadn't known when I left the apartment that I would be out late, seeing Marie.

"Missus said she got a call this a.m. that her friend would be coming this p.m." He winked.

"Oh, did she say that?" I laughed. "She's a funny one."

He gave me my pass and told me to have a good visit. I walked through the old brass gate and thought how much it hurt even after all these years to hear about the "friend."

The walk to the cottage was down a steep incline and the wind was blowing hard. Making it the hundred or so yards to the bottom of the hill to Marie's cottage took almost ten minutes and all the breath I had. But then nothing involving Marie was ever easy.

Mrs. Zaritsky, the cottage-mate, was on the recliner when I opened the door.

"Tending to toilet," she said, nodding toward the bathroom door.

"How are you?" I asked.

"Considering circumstances as well as can be assassinated."

"Good," I said.

I had once thought that Mrs. Zaritsky was born in Eastern Europe, Hungary or Romania, that this was why she spoke the way she did, but I met her son once at the cottage. His mother was born in Astoria, he said. She used to talk differently. Shortly after they noticed her talking this new way, they moved her from their house on Staten Island to the cottage. An odd reason to be locked up in the cottage compound, I thought—just talking funny. But that seemed to me to be Mrs. Zaritsky's only problem. Unlike Marie.

"Can I incite you in tea?" she said, "while she's tending to toilet?"

"Yes, thanks. It's freezing."

Mrs. Zaritsky stood up and walked to the kitchen on the far wall. Then Marie walked in, not from the bathroom but from the front door. She had on what she often had on—a baby blue quilted robe, an engineer's cap, black basketball sneakers.

I said, "You'll freeze to death going out like that."

"Wouldn't that be swell for you."

"Stop talking that way," I said.

"What do you want now?" she said. "Oh, what do you want now? Tea? Oh, she'll have us in the poor house yet."

I wanted to kiss Marie hello. But I wasn't sure where to put a kiss—her face was covered with cold cream.

"I thought you'd be here later. I was doing my face in the light of the moon. Dolling up so I wouldn't embarrass you." She stuck out her tongue.

"I see," I said, though smearing cold cream was scarcely dolling up, and it was years since Marie had embarrassed me.

"Mrs. Z, you know my friend here, right?"

"We're fraternized," Mrs. Zaritsky said.

"How have you been, Marie?" I said. I dug into my bag and took out a box of Perugina chocolates. "Here," I said.

"I told you she could be decent when she wanted to." She opened the box and took out chocolate after chocolate, raising each to her nose. "But lots of times she's a fucking drag, and a disloyal spy to boot in the fashion of the communist FBI."

"Seems perfectly conscious on my part," Mrs. Zaritsky said.

Conscientious, I thought she meant. I wanted to say the word—conscientious—to say aloud, That's true, I am conscientious, I'm not bad, I come every month or so, I would come more often, I would take you out more often, for good even if things were different. If you were different. If what happened hadn't happened.

Now Marie was taking bites out of different chocolates. "Once she brought me poison fudge. But these are clean of rat and other poisons, which I can almost always smell."

"My son tried to astonish me once but the police prevented it."

"Luckily, I never had children," Marie said.

Mrs. Zaritsky smiled at me. "Here you are." She handed me a cup of clear water.

"Here, Samantha," Marie said, handing me a half-eaten truffle. "See what a good friend I am when you don't bring me your poison fudge or toxic waste meatloaf," she laughed.

I wanted to say, That was goose liver paté and it cost me forty dollars, but I wanted to bring you a treat. And my name's not Samantha. My name's Betsy. And I'm not your friend. But I just sipped the lukewarm water.

"I may be going away for a while," I said.

"Toodle-oo."

"I'll write," I said. "I'll call."

"Don't bother."

"I'll come back to visit."

"Why won't she stop yakking?" she said to Mrs. Zaritsky.

"More tea? We have quantities," Mrs. Zaritsky said, pouring out another cup of water.

I started to laugh. Then suddenly nothing seemed very funny. "Listen," I said, and I heard my voice climb higher and higher. "Please, please listen."

"I'm not your mother, darling," Marie said, "So don't you whimper at me."

And then I was crying, running out the cottage door. Out into fresh falling snow.

In the cab I rocked back and forth. I was nothing to her. Simply a bearer of chocolates and suspect ones at that. Probably Marie could get Mrs. Zaritsky's astonishing son to bring some Hershey bars now and then. Another grand friend of hers. My hurt surprised me, my tears.

It had been years since she had remembered me, years since she had been the old Marie, happy Marie with that bounce of blond curls haloing her head. I sat in the back of the cab and remembered her. She had taught Tommy and me to tap dance, to swim in formation, to write in code. Once, after one of my father's arrests, she helped us write to him in invisible ink: DPNF CBDL TPPO—COME BACK SOON. Which he did. The next time he was arrested she talked of our escaping the authorities by swimming to New Jersey. One night she had us put on bathing suits under our jeans and took us down to the pier. But standing there, facing the dark river, the long dark barges, all three of us began to cry. It was just a thought, forget it, she said. Let's all stop crying by the time I say. . . . She looked around, lost, up and down the river. George Washington Bridge, she called. I got other good thoughts up my sleeve, my darlings. The next time he was arrested, she had already "escaped" to a hospital ward.

I curled up on the taxi seat and remembered what I hadn't remembered in years. Back to when I needed her, back to when she needed me. And I cried and cried on the long drive home. For a speck of me had gone out there thinking she'd be different, a tiny, crawling, infantile speck had actually thought a different Marie would be at the cottage, arms open, calling, Come, my girl. Chocolates for me? Oh, my dear, dear girl. My darling daughter.

The apartment was empty when I got back. David had probably decided to sleep at his studio. Sometimes we slept apart and tonight I was glad. I wanted the matter settled once and for all. There was nothing to stay for. The day had made that clear. Not my mother, not my job, not my furniture, not my apartment. There was nothing to stay for and every reason to go. A new place. New work. David.

How wondrous to have him in my life. With him it felt like the early years when Tommy and I so often had only each other.

We never thought of ourselves as orphans, just child-parents, anticipating each other's every thought and need. You're hungry, Tommy would say. I'd nod. You're tired, I'd say, trying for a parent's knowing, caring lilt. In Mexico, when they took our father on the street and the desk clerk saw it and called up to tell us, we holed up in the hotel and made believe we were not two kids. Arm in arm, we'd march down the Reforma, searching out our dinner, a taco, a mango, *queso fresco* and cocoa buns. Carrying our marketing back to the hotel, dumping it all on the big double bed we'd claimed as our own the night our father left, making our suitcases into walls, our blankets and sheets into the roof of our *casita*, where we ate and slept and played grownup. Making a game of our burdens. Eat this, eat that. Sha, sha, la la. Not to worry, not to worry. . . . Poor children, all alone for a week, Gladys Simon said when she and the others finally sorted out what had happened and came to get us. We had each other, Tommy said. Yeah, I said. They could have been kidnapped, or killed, we heard Gladys whisper to one of the others. And when I started to cry, yielding to my dread for the first time, Tommy whispered, They don't know how strong we are. And we felt each other's muscles. Then we heard them whispering about which of them would take which of us. And we crawled under the bed and wouldn't come out, till they promised us we could stay together forever.

Only with David did I capture any of that closeness. Many knew, I'm sure, about my father, but until David came along I discussed my past with no one. Where's your mother? She lives in Brooklyn, which was true enough. Where's your father? He left when we were young. True enough again. But when or why, I told to David alone, whose dark eyes lured the truth from me.

Until David, I'd given up trying to tell anyone the story. That born in 1952, I met my father for the first time in jail, where he was awaiting sentencing for contempt of Congress, a charge that followed his failure to comply with the Taft-Hartley requirement that elected union officials disclaim association with communists. That my father was never a member of the Communist Party, but that believing the law a violation of his constitutional rights, he refused to sign. And then the next month called before a committee of Congress to explain what he was—communist or not—he refused to answer, except to say, I am an American. Which led to the contempt conviction and two years in the Lewisburg Penitentiary. That he was trailed constantly and jailed for something or other regularly—first for contempt, then for misuse of government property (continuing labor work in prison), then for violating the terms of parole (leaving the country to find work), then contempt again and again—his last contempt citation for declaring to the House Un-American Activities Committee, It's my constitutional right to believe as I wish, to speak when I want, to do what I must to maintain our nation's soul. That out on bail on another charge, weakened and sick, he decided to never return to jail but to live the remainder of his life on the run. That more often than not he touched us and kissed us through the bars dividing families from felons or in dark corners of dark depots in strange cities.

When I was young, on special occasions—a pajama party, or a sleep-out in summer camp—with darkness hiding my face and whispers soothing my mind, I found myself speaking the truth, or trying to. One girl would murmur, My mother, I hate her so, her fat walk, her fat laugh, I swear. Or one would confess that she rubbed her breasts each night in perfect circles so that they'd come out perfectly when their time to come out came, and I would whisper, I have a secret, too. My father is Sam Vogel. But always someone would say, The subversive traitor who wants to destroy America? And I'd say, Oh, no. Oh, you mean another Sam Vogel? someone would say. And I'd whisper, Yes. Another Sam Vogel. The Sam Vogel who died. My father's dead, I'd lie. In an accident, he died in a terrible accident. And the girls would line up to pat my back and I would cry—feeling more isolated and misunderstood than ever.

Until David I never tried again. But now my father *was* dead. I told David how, sick and desperate, he had eventually snuck back to say goodbye, dying from a simple and fatal heart attack on my aunt's sofa. How my father's father, a carpenter, had fallen from a skyscraper, whose thirtieth floor he was framing, to his death, leaving a wife and three children, my father, at twelve the oldest. How at thirteen Sam quit school, roaming the city looking for people to clobber to move the pain in his heart to his hand. At fifteen a carpenter friend of his father caught him dangling a kid from a fire escape, and ordered him to bring the boy down, apologize, and come with him to work. How the image of his father falling through the sky and the knowledge of Herman Rossi's support inspired Sam to become a master carpenter, at twenty-eight assuming the presidency of the New York local of the Federation of American Woodworkers, replacing his daily urge to common revenge with his conviction that a new, just world was right around the corner. How he was in jail half of my childhood, and when I picture his face it is tattooed with octagons—my mind etched with the chicken-wire glass through which I saw him for so long.

And I told David about Marie. The poor Virginia childhood. The ballet scholarship. Escaping the misery of coal country with her flaxen curls and long legs. Twirling into my father's arms at a ballet benefit for Russian war orphans. Then those years when everything changed. No work, no dance, no husband. People following us every day till all she knew was being pursued, local police and FBI agents transforming in her fevered mind into Hitler and Attila and their legions. That she worried too much to let us out in the dangerous world, finally—when Sam was away—locking us in our apartment for five weeks, until our aunt came and took us, and an ambulance came and took her. David even met my mother. We took her out to a picnic at Jones Beach, and he photographed her, catching the ravaged hollows that used to be cheeks, the spinning black marbles that used to be her liquid, loving eyes.

If there were things I didn't tell David, they were things that I couldn't bring myself to think about ever again. The buzz of the courtroom at Foley Square, the gavel striking the wood bench, my father hobbling off in leg-chains. Then outside, the shouts: Kill him, kill the communist-loving traitor. Those are his kids. . . . Grab the kids.

A couple of years ago David and I did a story on an orphanage on Staten Island for the *New York Times* magazine. I knew it would be a sad place, but nothing prepared me for the hushed halls, the children sitting frozen in grim waiting rooms each visiting day, staring at the door for someone, though no one ever came. I'd written, *Shame and dread are the only reliable visitors. Each day they come. And each day the children of St. Barnabas sit beside them, longing for magic.* I got an award for that article, and at the luncheon the presenter marveled at my empathic intensity. Small wonder—I was writing about myself.

"Your father's dead," I said now, out loud in the empty room. "Your mother's mad. Your brother lives on the other side of the globe. No one is coming back. That life is dead and gone. It has been for decades."

I listened to my words, registered their meaning, like they were advice from a parent, or Anna Lisa. And then I went to my furniture closet. I laid out all the broken parts, the arms and legs, the fronts and backs, the tops and bottoms that I'd meant to glue back to where they belonged. One by one, I threw them in a big black plastic bag. Like a mass murderer carrying a sack of body parts, I dragged the bag out to the hall, down to the elevator, through the basement and out to the garbage cans at the end of the alley.

Then I went back upstairs and called David. "Yes," I told him. "Happily ever after," I laughed. And then we hooted and talked dirty for a while, then whispered goodnight, goodnight, and happy, happy dreams.

2: Moving On

WE WENT TO DINNER to celebrate—to an Italian restaurant on West 68th Street where the waiters are mostly chorus boys full of outrageous made-up stories. Madonna is really 200 pounds but airbrushed into shape. They know for sure because she comes in a lot, eats like a pig, and stuffs focaccia in her backpack. John Lennon's ghost sometimes comes in for a drink when the bar is empty and tips terribly. Lauren Bacall left an earring on the table near the sugar bowl and it wasn't even Fortunoff junk—it was just plain junk—a knock-off of a knock-off of a knock-off that you buy in a street bin for a dollar. It's strange that, with all the stories, I've never seen anyone famous in Eddie's Place, just tired technicians from the TV studio down the street, appreciating the good Italian food and fine bullshit.

We sat in the corner and Sandy, one of the waiters, who is round and short with tight pants that dig deep at his waist, making him look like a couple of sausage links, said, "What will it be? Osso bucco with polenta? It's the special. Or are you going to be vegetarian creeps like Sting, who is really getting on my nerves with his ordering habits and a lot more."

We nodded, yes, for the osso bucco.

"Tony Bennett's cousin Tommy Bennett ordered it before. He liked it so much he licked his plate. I was going to tell him that was an animal thing to do but I'm hard up for tips tonight."

"We'll tip you double tonight," David said. "We're very happy tonight."

We were. It was a perfect dinner. We ate in silence, drinking wine, staring at the twinkling lights strung all around. Otis Redding was on the jukebox. We talked a little about the plans. Making arrangements for Marie. Letting Tommy know. David's parents. They already had decided to "do" Central America next June, David said, and would visit. David groaned.

"It will be nice," I said.

"No, it won't."

"They're nice," I said. "I'll show them around."

David patted my knee as if to say, Good sport. But it wasn't that at all. I liked David's parents, Mitzi and Les. I liked them before I ever met them, just from the photographs. It all seemed so pleasant—a series of fluffy dogs, a wide Long Island lawn, two parents squinting in the Florida sun, holding tennis rackets in one hand, their son's thin wrist in the other.

Not that I was always convinced that David was their son. When I first met David I'd sometimes joke that he had created this past in his dark room, splicing himself to blond, smiling strangers. Then I met them. Well outfitted, cheerful people bouncing into theaters and restaurants, benefits and football games, they were nothing like David. It wasn't so much the physical difference—David's brown hair gets blond streaks in the summer and in profile he can be identified as his mother's son. It was the relentlessly sad cast of his eyes and mind—his appetite for lean, grim sorrow in the face of so much good cheer and expensive steak and stadium seats.

"You'll be bored to death."

I knew what he meant: even tans, even opinions. And I laughed. How well we knew each other. How well we fit—the other's past holding the other's dreams. My irregular past David thought substantial, superior; and David's normal past, which he thought boring, I revered as if it were some royal lineage.

I said, "I won't be bored one bit."

In truth, ever since I was a child and all the trouble started, I'd craved parents like the Kahns. The more regular and predictable, the more thrilling to me. Throughout childhood, I picked my best friends as much for their parents as for themselves. I favored conventional girls from conventional families, worshipping their sweater sets, their mother's baking and bridge, their father's accounting and merchandising and dentistry. The mothers in particular enchanted me, and I still tingle remembering them. Adele Schneider, for example, recording secretary of the local sisterhood, mother of Cindy, winner of the district spelling bee, and my best friend the dark year that started with Marie's return from Credemore and ended with Sam's disappearance. I still swoon when I picture Adele's perfect living room, the sparkling credenza, the porcelain shepherd boy and shepherd girl lamps smiling at each other across the gold brocade couch, Adele enthroned in a matching loveseat, me running to her side.

"How are you doing, Betsy?" Mrs. Schneider said, looking down at me as I kneeled beside her, her kindness preventing her from saying what she was really thinking, no doubt. *What* are you doing, Betsy?

I didn't know what I was doing. Just that seeing her on my way to Cindy's ruffled room, I had felt compelled to race to her side and sit at her feet. Looking up, seeking her gaze, I whispered, "I'm fine. How are *you* doing, Mrs. Schneider? What are *you* doing, Mr. Schneider?

"I'm writing out my pot roast recipe for a dear friend. *Pot roast royale.* My friend loves my pot roast."

"I love your pot roast, Mrs. Schneider," I said.

"Did you ever have my pot roast, Betsy?"

"I think so," I lied. But it didn't matter that I had never tasted it. I knew I would love it. I loved everything that women like Mrs. Schneider offered me. Chilled Mott's apple juice in small goblets with pearl-sized balls encircling the base, tuna salad, the palest and most wonderfully smooth tuna I would ever eat. (The tuna Marie made us eat those days was as brown as cat food and lumpy; it made you gag and in order to swallow, you had to hold your nose.)

"I'd like the recipe," I said, looking up at Mrs. Schneider.

"How nice that a young girl likes to cook. I admire that."

I didn't tell Mrs. Schneider that I didn't cook, that I planned to leave the recipe around for Marie, whose idea of a special supper was a can of Broadcast corned beef hash topped with a can of cream of mushroom soup and alternating dollops of mayonnaise and Cheez Whiz. That I hoped real cooking would distract my mother from her surreal fantasies: that we were being watched through the bricks and plaster. That the trees outside our window held tiny recorders able to catch thoughts and even dreams.

"My feeling about pot roast," Mrs. Schneider said, lowering her voice so that only I would hear her secret, "is that the onions make it or break it. Ten onions or more and you have yourself a *royale*. Skimp on the onions and you can no longer be sure you have a pot roast at all. You have a braised beef in my book."

I nodded. I would impress upon Marie the importance of onions. I wouldn't tell Marie who told me or how much I cared for her. That when I looked at Adele Schneider, at her thick ankles, her sturdy t-straps, her sensible double-knit suit, her blond hair, bleached and curled like a cabbage, I'd pray that I'd wake up one day with my mother gone, and an Adele type in the kitchen stacking pancakes.

"Really, I wouldn't mind," I told David across the table. "Your mother reminds me of Adele Schneider. I wouldn't mind at all." I felt excited. I'd be getting a new family at last. The kind I'd always craved.

"Who's Adele Schneider?"

"A lady from my past."

"I didn't know you knew such boring people. I'm disappointed," he laughed.

"Adele wasn't boring. She was the inventor of Pot Roast Royale."

"Tell me no more, please. I've known too many Adele Schneiders."

"I should learn to cook," I said.

"No!" he screamed."

"I always meant to learn to cook."

"Stop it. We do fine."

We each had two recipes down pat. I cooked ziti with red sauce, and fettuccine with white sauce. David cooked rice with beans or rice with chicken and peas. That gave us supper four nights a week and one night to eat out, with the weekends free for the streets, eating pizza and souvlaki and tacos, wherever our walking took us. It made us feel free. It made me feel young, very young, foraging for meals with Tommy at my side.

"Maybe I'll take up serious cooking," I said. "Maybe it's time to grow up."

"Maybe I'll kill you," David said, kissing my cheek.

"Those ladies had something," I said.

"They had nothing. That was the problem."

"They had their beautiful food."

"Face it. They were sad, fat ladies," he said.

"They weren't fat. They just made everyone else fat. Say you like them."

"I like them," David laughed. "I like Adele Schneider wherever she is," he laughed.

"Say you mean it."

"I mean it. . . . I love you, Adele," he called. "Really . . . I do."

I looked at David, at his eyes narrowed to laugh. I kissed his eyes, proud to be joining my life with his. I kissed his nose.

Then Sandy came by, setting down our check and a bottle of Sambucca. "What's all this public display of affection, and this happiness bit? Don't you know it's a lousy night?"

"Not for us," David said. "We're celebrating."

"What's there to celebrate these days? It's so shitty around here."

"We're leaving town."

"Lucky you," Sandy said. "I'll miss you two. I never chewed you two up for anyone."

"That's because we're nobodies," I said.

"Really, I'll miss you two, nobodies or not," Sandy said.

And he poured out three glasses and toasted *bon voyage*.

The TV studio down the street was throwing out a house—along with a front lawn and a stretch of picket fence. It was all made of thick cardboard, except for the lawn, which was made of that looped green cellophane they use in fruit stands. We stopped to admire the scene—a homey contrast to the rest of the garbage heaped high on West 68th Street. We leaned against the fence and looked up at the sky. It was a moonless night lit only by a few stars. But the white house before us shone bright against the dark sky, like a cottage in a story book.

"Let's practice," David said.

"Home sweet home," I said.

We opened the gate and tip-toed up the cardboard stones to the front door. For an instant it was easy to imagine that the door would open onto a room—a kitchen with a fireplace or a small living room with a bread oven in the wall.

"We're home," David said

"I wonder what's so funny," someone said.

We turned and saw a man coming toward us down the path with the slow and overly careful walk of a drunk or a psychotic. He wore rags, and rags on rags, I saw, layers of them with the wrong thing in the wrong place. On one leg was a dark green T shirt with the logo of a camp or school, on the other leg a striped ski scarf wrapped round and round. On his head was a pair of women's underpants, flopping onto his brow like bangs.

"Am I missing a joke? Tell me. I love jokes." He smiled.

"We were making believe we live here." I said.

"I hope not," he said. He lifted the underpants and rubbed his brow in worry. "This is my home. I found it last night. I slept on my front lawn last night. I love to watch my stars."

David and I looked at each other. We were thinking the same thought. What happens when they collect the garbage?

"Don't worry," the man said. "It's not such a small lawn. There's room for two more if you're desperate."

"We're OK," I said.

"You sure?"

"I think so," David said, quietly. "If not, we'll come back."

I loved him so much at that moment, correcting my certainty—not wanting to assert any superiority in having beds to sleep in, homes that would last beyond the next garbage pick-up.

"Can I visit *your* home?" the man said.

We said nothing.

"Oh wait," he said, reading our silence. "Forget it, I forgot I'm having company later. I'll have to decline."

We waved goodbye.

"It's so sad," I said as we made our way toward Broadway. "All the people trying to make a home from nothing."

I thought of the squatters I passed when I walked in Riverside Park, the Please Do Not Disturb sign they perched at their feet each night. I thought of Marie standing at the cottage door a few visits back, flinging the door open, shouting, I must ask you to leave my home at once. No FBI agents permitted in my home. I'd stared at the painted concrete block walls, the cement floor, the tiny casement windows, too high to see out of, and laughed. "Home." I thought of my father living out of cars and borrowed rooms. Tommy and me on the pullout beds of kind relatives, friends and strangers.

"One more month," David said.

"*You're* my home," I said.

And we sang the Billy Joel song—*Wherever we're together that's my home*—as we made our way up Broadway.

Bright and early the next morning, on the bulletin board in my building—between the notice of the exterminator's next visit and the fourteen-year-old girl on the eleventh floor who will "caregive" for human and canine "with equal respect" and the cards of window washers and piano tuners and the review of a "culinary comedy" at the 74th Street Repertory called *Bellyache* featuring Raul Feigenberg, who, the marginal red scrawl said, lived on the second floor and would sell you tickets at a discount after 11 p.m.—I managed to find space for a small index card announcing I was moving and getting rid of whatever I had, cheap.

That afternoon I got a call at my office.

"It's Yukio," the voice said. It was high-pitched and enthusiastic, like my haircutter's. "I'm too thrilled," it said.

"How's that?" I said.

"You moving and all."

I laughed. You don't like me, Yukio? I thought. You want me to go away, Yukio? But, of course, Yukio didn't know me not to like me, as far as I knew. And I didn't know Yukio.

"I *am* moving," I said.

"What you got?"

"A bed, a coffee table, a desk, a wing-back chair." I rattled off my possessions, the family stuff that was still upright, the few items I'd bought myself that might survive a few years with another owner.

"You got accessories in addition?"

"In addition I do," I said.

"Maybe I buy you in your entirety."

I laughed again. My entirety is leaving, my furniture is staying. "Be my guest," I said.

"I have no time to be guest. But I will look you over."

My furniture, I wanted to say again. You'll look over my furniture. I'm leaving.

"I meant feel free to come by and get what you need."

"I need it all. I live without any accessories in addition to certain basics. OK, I got a bed for sure but what about a table, slighting, a tea kettle, a toaster oven, an effective coffee maker. I live without all these things. I work so hard in movies I have no time."

"What do you do in movies?" I said.

"I'm movie star."

"I see."

I had never heard of a movie star named Yukio. The only famous Yukio I had ever heard of was Yukio Mishima whom I had once seen in a movie, killing himself, and whom I was supposed to interview in a student panel but couldn't because by then he'd killed himself for real. I wanted to say, I'm not sure my things will be nice enough for you. I know movie stars like to have nice things.

"Or that my professional objective. In meantime I'm in fashion angle. In new Jamie Leigh Curtis flick I do a lot in wardrobe."

I pictured Yukio, short and thin, crouched in the corner of a wardrobe, one of those old Woolworth's paper kinds with mock wood graining—the kind I had gotten Marie years ago for the corner of her cottage.

"Very sporty look basically but I added personal touch of class."

"That's nice," I said. "That you could do that." I really couldn't imagine Yukio doing anything. The picture of a small man wedged into a small closet stuck in my mind.

"You know accessories. Is important as basics—as I mention before. When they give me work as star I won't forget what I said. Neckties will still value."

"I have neckties for you, Yukio," I said. To the extent that I could understand Yukio, I knew that he was speaking metaphorically. But I felt a literal approach was the only way to move the conversation along. And besides, I remembered the clutter of ties the men in my family had left behind with all the other junk.

"I can't pay much," Yukio said.

"You can have them for nothing." I tried to remember Tommy's paisleys and stripes, knotted and tangled in the bottom of some drawer I had thrown them into years ago in a fit of resentment. You can have them all.

"No way. I believe in paying my way although I do like a striking bargain, too. For all of you."

I listed all the things I had that he might need. How good it felt to be rid of every old entanglement and encumbrance. How good it felt to be the one to leave, at last. All I needed was enough for the trip and a few months of settling in. And then I could rely on freelance work from New York editors I knew.

"Thanks. I'll come on down now if it's just the same to you."

"I'm not there. I'm here. At work," I said.

"All the same to me," Yukio said. "I'll wait for you. I'm 5D. Ring me."

Ring me. It reminded me of my childhood friendships—the tender if fleeting ones in this or that relative's apartment building, where we'd be stashed when our parents left. Ring me, call up to me, walk me.

"Around six," I said, feeling genuine warmth for Yukio.

"I can't wait," Yukio said.

I felt touched. I felt excited, too. That I could make Yukio's life cohere simply by letting mine go. But it was only the accessories I was letting go of, to use Yukio's language. The basics were staying or going with me. David. David and me.

I found myself about to peck a kiss into the phone, something I do only with David, my Aunt Elsie, and Margaret now and then. But I caught myself in time and simply said goodbye.

Goodbye, problems, I thought. My own, or rather the ones bequeathed to me by my family, soiled old ties and chairs and couches, soiled old memories. The ones lent me—Anna Lisa's worries, Sandy the waiter's search for amusing lies to distract him from pain in love, the man with the bloomers on his head and no home, Yukio's living without a toaster, a radio, a pot to boil water. I thought of Alan. Goodbye to Alan. The search for the most special of the special. Goodbye to it all. I'm going *home*.

Mitzi, mother of David, is a force—a hostess who brings her whole being to her projects, planning and re-planning every detail to ensure an event that seems to have made itself. And the next day, the day after Yukio came down to my apartment and said, "I love all of you fully," pointing to the wobbly tables and couch, the peeling recliner and battered pots and pans, "I love the post-modern mixtures throughout you," Mitzi called to ask if she should serve stand-up or sit-down. Either way it would be a buffet.

"It depends," I said. "Each has its virtue."

"You've got a point," Mitzi said.

I've always loved Mitzi for this—her absolute generosity with authority. Another woman of her background and domestic expertise would say, Depends? What the hell do you know? About terrines and souffles, mousses and cremes. Stand-up, sit-down. You of the cat food tuna?

"Depends on the kind of crowd," I said, encouraged by Mitzi, trying to warm to the topic.

Though I wasn't sure I could. It was early in the morning and I was still half asleep. And besides, I had little more to say. My basic rule for entertaining, of which I did almost none, was to switch over to paper plates and plastic cups as soon as I had more than two guests.

"You're absolutely right," Mitzi said. "It really does depend. On your crowd."

"I guess age matters," I said, trying to put some substance into my contribution to this morning talk. "For example, old people need to sit," I said.

It's strange. I was welcoming my new life, shedding my old life. But since the night I told David yes, old memories were flooding my mind like they hadn't in years. Now I saw my grandmother settled in her armchair, her perch at family parties, Tommy and me playing waiter and waitress, taking her order, bringing her platters, settling them on her ample lap strewn with the flowers of her cotton housedress, which we pretended was a tablecloth from France. I thought of my father's cousins, the whole overweight bunch of them, sitting around the folding table that Aunt Elsie had borrowed from a neighbor and set up in her living room after my grandma's funeral to hold the long buffet of deli platters. But the cousins pulled up the loveseat and Aunt Elsie's two Queen Anne chairs and sat hunched over the corned beef and pastrami like poker players absorbed in a hot game. Now and then they'd look up and send me or Tommy into the kitchen for a fresh stack of rye bread or some more pickles or cream soda. Being waiters for Grandma was one thing, but we decided this was too much, and escaped to Aunt Elsie's bedroom, telling everyone we were tired and sad.

In truth, although we loved Grandma Molly, we weren't feeling much sorrow that day. For we both believed that our father would sneak back to say goodbye to his mother, and so all through the funeral and the "funeral party," as we called it, we felt happy and expectant at the prospect of seeing Sam again. Mr. Brown and Mr. Gray, the two FBI agents who were on Sam's case at that time (we named them for the color of the suits they respectively wore) must have had the same thought. For they looked happy, too, sitting on the stairs leading up to the next landing, devouring the corned beef sandwiches I brought them, whistling between swallows.

I must confess that I was very fond of Brown and Gray. I was certain that they liked children, at least their own, which I imagined them each to have two of. And though their goal that day and other days was arresting my father, I reasoned that if Tommy and I were nice to them, they would be nice to us, and go easy on our father if they managed to nab him. The lowest of the low, Tommy insisted. THE TWO LEAST WANTED, Tommy called them, as our father's face stared out of MOST WANTED posters year after year.

That day, like other days, my brother ran a hostile parody of Brown and Gray for their viewing. While our agents chewed, he snapped their picture, as they had snapped ours and the funeral guests' earlier in the day. Tommy brought out a pad and took notes—as they had at the cemetery. For taking down names and license plates, my brother retaliated with his own observations, which he narrated aloud as wrote: *Chew with mouth open. Fart while eating. Wearing same old suits, one brown, one gray, both cheap and shiny showing large dandruff deposits.* He snapped a picture of me handing them food. He put down the camera and wrote: *Weak-willed girl collaborates with the enemy.* Then he lifted his arm and knocked the plate of potato salad that I was handing one of them, down to the tile floor.

"We're not the enemy," Brown said.

"Your father's the enemy," Gray said.

"My father will punch your face in for that," Tommy said, his own face twisting from rage and the effort to stop tears. "Daddy will kill them when he gets back," he said to me inside. Then feeling our father's rightful avenger, I guess, he punched me in the stomach, crying, "Take that, Judas girl."

"What did *I* do?" I cried, running through the crowd, around the cousin table to Aunt Elsie's bedroom, to dive on the bed.

"You thought like the enemy," my brother said, following me in.

"You *are* the enemy," our fat cousin Arthur, Aunt Elsie's son, said, entering the room and kicking us off the bed. "Both of you. The enemy of our great nation," he said, laughing hard, shaking his chins.

Fat people like to sit while they eat, I could tell Mitzi. And FBI agents, too. Especially if it's a funeral party. What more did I know of parties from my miserable past?

"I mean it will be just family," Mitzi said, "but even that's a lot. I mean there's Les's side, not to mention my side. And your side."

So it was for *us*. For David and me. I felt numb with dread. I had thought that Mitzi had consulted me not because I was the honored guest but only because it was too early for her to call one of her heavy-hitter hostess friends. I didn't realize that I'd be involved directly. Not that I didn't like parties, especially Mitzi's, which were always bright affairs with heaps of shrimp and crabmeat salad. And not that I wasn't touched by the gesture—a formal send-off from David's family. But why drag *my* family into it? I mean it was impossible to drag my family into it. I had no family and Mitzi knew that.

"No one on my side," I laughed.

"Oh, sweetie, maybe your aunt will fly up."

"Oh, maybe," I said, trying to sound agreeable, not wanting to dampen the cheerful, festive atmosphere that Mitzi was already trying to launch, calling me sweetie and all.

"I mean your Florida aunt might like to come up for a visit."

My Florida aunt. Like it was a bona fide category. Florida sunshine, Florida grapefruit, Florida aunt. In truth she was my *only* aunt though we hadn't seen each other in years, each of us, I guess, wanting to forget the long sad era we lived through together. Even the family of the gangster down the street from Aunt Elsie's old Queens apartment, convicted for laundering mob money in his live poultry market and for maiming rival gangsters ("poultry-style"—the *Daily News* said—which meant cutting off their hands and feet), had lived with more respect and cheer. Limousines picked up the gangster kids and took them away to the Jersey Shore and the Catskills. But after Boomie, my father's kid brother, died, and after Grandma, there were few people coming to our apartment, except for Brown and Gray. In the beginning there were sympathizers hanging around, but after a while there was just us—Tommy and me and Aunt Elsie and Cousin Arthur, who wanted us out of his life and his four-and-a-half room apartment.

Cousin Arthur was four years older than Tommy, and six years older than me. He wasn't really "mentally backward," as Aunt Elsie charged when she was angry, but obsessive and petty. Even at an early age, Cousin Arthur planned on a career if not in "legal communication," by which he meant being a court stenographer, then in "mortuarial science," by which he meant being an undertaker.

"I hear that's a stiff course," Tommy would joke, and Arthur, whom we never called Art or Artie but always the formal Arthur as if to keep a distance, would say, "You laugh now, but I'll have the last laugh, squirt, when I kill you and stuff you in the cheapest coffin known to man."

And he did somehow have the final say in lots of matters. Aunt Elsie would be out working at her secretary job, and Arthur would make up charts with which to torture us. Household Responsibility Chart. TV Watchers Chart. He'd always sign us up for "toilet and garbage patrol" on the former and sign up his own shows on the latter. Re-runs of Cold War era shows like *Dragnet* and *I Led Three Lives*, which Tommy and I would escape in Aunt Elsie's bedroom when we could. "Hey, don't you wanna watch your commie-loving father and his friends selling atomic secrets?" he'd call. "I have a feeling he'll leave home young," Aunt Elsie would say, full of hope. Finally, we went off to college; finally, our poor aunt moved to Miami, leaving Cousin Arthur alone in the Rego Park apartment.

Mitzi said, "I mean your Florida aunt might like a little break from her Florida routine, and a little crisp air."

What Mitzi meant to say, I think, was, Don't you have at least one relative in this world who can come to one of my parties? Make things nice and even and balanced. His side, her side. Poor Mitzi. Given what she knew of Marie, my father, Tommy, my Florida aunt was her only bet.

"I'll ask," I said.

Mitzi said I should get back to her with my guest list and any ideas for menu I had and we hung up.

I wished David hadn't left for work so early. My conversation with Mitzi, which had started off as light as one of her soufflés, had gone heavy and sad. An open declaration of the loss I was trying to forget.

Would I say goodbye even to Marie? Would I go out there again to say the things I'd never managed to say? That I forgave what she had done to me. And she, in time, should try to forgive me for all the betrayals and affronts, real and imagined, that she had stashed in the dark caves of her mind. Then kiss her hard and try to register her smell—to have it with me forever? Somewhere between lemon and pee. Register her last words: Good riddance, my dear. Toodle-oo, Samantha.

And then the phone rang. It was David.

"Don't feel bad you have no family. We'll have a party for your family, too," he laughed.

"Poison fudge and all," I laughed, feeling instantly better hearing his voice.

"I guess I mean your father."

"Party with the dead? Like the Mexicans?"

"Well, I guess I mean we go out there. See him. His grave."

It would help me to think about my life, David said. The past there. The future here. And that would help stop the flood of memories. Facing them head on would exorcise the worst. That sort of thing. It made sudden sense.

Suddenly I wanted to visit my father's grave. I'd never seen it. Since he'd died I'd never looked at his photograph or any of his letters, hiding them in the bottom of a trunk at the back of the closet, my logic being, I guess, that removing all mementos would remove all memories of losing him. Big surprise—it hadn't worked. Twenty years after my father's death, I'd still half believed he'd be back.

"You gotta face him," David said.

I needed a week to get ready, I said.

"Today," David said. He'd be over in an hour. And he hung up.

3: The Grave

TOMMY AND I were both away at college when we received identical letters from Aunt Elsie. She'd tried to call us, she wrote, but our dorm lines were always busy. So she was writing instead. *I am sorry to have to report that your father died. In his sleep, in the middle of the night, on my sofa. . . . He had come to visit—a very nice visit. . . . Didn't want to call you kids back home when it happened—you've been through so much. And you know me—I like to spare. I'm a sparer emotionally speaking.* The rest of the letter was about Aunt Elsie's feet. The doctor told her to keep off them. *Keep off my feet? I said. I told him, You know me, I'm an amateur social dancer and a mover-rounder by nature.*

Should I come home now? I had asked Aunt Elsie when I called her from the dorm lobby, the freshly opened letter still in my hands. I buried him, she said. There's nothing to do here. We'll just mourn him each in our individual way. You know me, Betsy, I'm not much of a mourner.

Evidently I wasn't either. For I just went up to my room, opened my geology text, studied for the midterm, stuffing my mind with thoughts of crustal plates and thermal plumes—so I wouldn't have to think about my father.

At the end of the semester, Tommy and I returned to our aunt's apartment—him from Berkeley, me from Ann Arbor—and cried in each other's arms. And that was it for mourning. We were used to his absence, and after the initial shock that his absence now was forever, I think we were both relieved to

50

be released from waiting and worrying. A couple of times that summer I asked Tommy if he thought we should go to the cemetery, and was happy when he said he didn't believe in "sentimental" rituals. A couple of times I asked Aunt Elsie what she thought was right, and she said she wasn't a "grave person" and, in her opinion, neither was I. And not since that summer did the thought cross my mind to visit my father's grave. But now David had convinced me that I should—that we should go together. I went into the bedroom to dress.

Checking myself in the mirror a few minutes later, I doubled up in laughter. I had put on a white blouse, a navy skirt, blue tights, ancient brown penny loafers. All in all, I looked ready for school assembly. And then I realized, of course, that I had dressed for my father. Aside from brief glimpses in dark parking lots and borrowed basement rooms, he hadn't seen me, for any extended time, since I was eleven, when my favorite outfit was official assembly dress and my favorite activities were official events—like marching the flag to the front of the auditorium as a member of the school color guard. That was the girl my father knew last, and, I've come to think, loved best. The photograph he carried in his wallet—and later, when he was on the lam, in the sole of his shoe—was of that girl. Which was not really surprising. Surrounded most of his life by bohemian leftists in their flamboyant internationalist get-ups—fringed Russian shawls and embroidered Mexican blouses, pebbly Irish tweeds and jaunty French berets—my father maintained an appetite for things American. His dress and his patriotism were simple and corny. And in my more cynical and bitter moments, I had wondered if it wasn't just his flag that he was showing off. Look at this snapshot! See what a good American I am! How dare you say I don't love my country! If he was so crazy about *me,* I'd think, why didn't he come back when he had the chance? If I was so damned adorable!

Looking in the mirror again that day, I evidently wanted to be more adorable than ever. My fortieth birthday looming, I fixed my Peter Pan collar, adjusted my tights and, twirling like

51

a schoolgirl, thought, Here I am again, Daddy, just the way you want me. Around and around I twirled, imagining my father could see me from his grave. Daddy, look, I thought, as if to win him back—before leaving him for good.

I guess you don't spend a childhood dodging trauma and in a moment of adult wisdom turn around and embrace it. And as soon as I got into the car my courage melted. My childhood had been a string of goodbyes. Goodbye to Marie as she went off to hospital wards and half-way "cottage communities." Goodbye to my father as he went off to jail, then hiding. Meetings with him, especially, were terrible teary events—the imminent separation hanging heavy in the air.

And here I was on my way to the biggest goodbye. Sitting beside David in the rented car, that afternoon, I felt like a fragile adolescent. And once we hit Queens, I started telling David it was a mistake. And he said rituals were important. "Important important," he said. David doesn't actually stammer but sometimes he repeats words or syllables when he's utterly certain about what has to be done, but doesn't want to overwhelm you with his conviction.

Not having the stamina to argue, I just started stalling. I decided we needed flowers. Then when I saw how nicely that ate up half an hour, I decided we should check the oil and antifreeze. In short, we halted and stalled, all at my instigation, and in the stops and starts I tried to get myself ready.

The route I chose took forever. "Let's try Queens Boulevard," I said to David. And he, sweet soul, said, "Good idea." I think when he saw me come out of the building in my hideous cleanteen get-up, he decided it was a day to accommodate. Queens Boulevard, as always, was thick with cars, buses, and monster trucks, and quickly we got ourselves stuck in a traffic jam—my unconscious plan.

Then more time got taken up with a fight with a traffic lady, who objected to our honking. She banged on David's window and said, "Now I want this to stop this second." It was I, in fact, who was honking, enjoying it immensely—honk, honk, honk—distracting myself from the task ahead. When the traffic lady yelled at us, David just smiled and said he was awfully sorry. He didn't know what had gotten into him.

I was very touched by this gallantry. It reminded me of Gatsby taking the rap for Daisy, and I found myself sniffling happily.

The traffic woman said, "I'm serious. Not another peep from you."

I said, "That's not a peep, that's the way I cry. My father died. We're on our way to his grave."

And David, who ordinarily has no patience with histrionics, said, "It's true, Officer."

"A likely story," the woman said. "Where's the body?"

"We're meeting it," he said. "We're late."

I didn't say, twenty years late—and you're making us still later, you ugly mutt, though that's what I felt like saying, studying the drab uniform and drab face, stippled with countless small moles, which she was pressing into our car. I said, "Very, very late."

"I'll let you off this time. Next time you won't get off so easy," she said.

"Thank you, Officer," David said again, swallowing a laugh. Then I felt the car lurch to the side and charge through a hole in the traffic towards some blinking lights. "Sorry again, Officer," David called out the window.

"What's your hurry?" I said as my shoulder bumped against the door. But I knew why he'd zoomed from the scene like a getaway driver. I was about to start honking again.

"Let's go home," I said. "This isn't helping me, it's making me crazy."

David said, "You'll be all right. Let's have some breakfast."

Inside a Flushing diner I covered my face with my hands. I was still feeling out of control. "Sorry," I squeaked. "Sorry, Officer," I laughed. Then I started apologizing in earnest. "I was nervous," I said. "Scared. This was a big mistake."

"Breathe deeply," he said. "This is one goodbye you can really manage. *You're* doing the leaving. And no one's getting hurt."

Then the food came. A platter of fried eggs and sausage and a platter of pancakes and bacon. Stacks of toast. Home fries. Coffee. Juice. Generally I love breakfast out, the special start it gives the day, the charge of energy and possibility. But that day, sitting before the array of dishes, I felt completely listless. I stared at it all, not sure where or how to begin. Then I saw that there was nothing for me to do. David was putting a plate together for me, like a banquet waiter. When I first met David, I thought his sharing of food strange. Want some? Want half? he would say, spooning whatever it was onto my plate. I'd never seen this before, except with Tommy, when we were young and sharing our meals and our lives. Though once we were grown my brother and I would give each other tastes only if begged, then retreat back to our own plates, ashamed, I think now, of the closeness we'd once known. And Cousin Arthur wouldn't ever give you so much as a lick.

I looked across at David. He was different from any man I had ever known. Another man, Alan, for example, would have been glaring at me or hollering, You almost got me arrested. You're crazy. Are you crazy or something? But David said nothing. David made peace. He called a meter maid "Officer." He buttered me a slice of toast and cut it into two triangles. No one but a short order cook had ever cut my bread for me. I looked at David's busy hands, half expecting them to trim off the crusts.

And then, I was flooded with tender family thoughts I'd buried for years. Uncle Boomie taking us to amusement parks and pinball arcades, letting us run free with pockets full of brass slugs. Spend it all, what's money for, he'd shout after us. Until he died. Marie too, waiting for my father to be released again and again, would indulge us, if she was home, in taxi rides the five or so blocks to our school. What fun, she'd say, as we'd bend into the Checker Cab and fold down our seats. Though we knew even then that fun was beside the point—the ride designed to save us from the taunts and stares of neighbors and shopkeepers. The same reason that allowed us to phone in lunches and suppers of cheeseburgers and club sandwiches and shakes and frappes. The same reason that told her to keep us locked in our apartment—so that stares and taunts, then later poisons and rays, could not hurt the children she loved more than life. And then I thought about my father's attempts at indulgence—bringing stuffed animals to many of our secret meetings, homely cheap pop-eyed things in garish colors, which I adored because they made me feel pampered and all-American, like the beloved daughter on some family TV series.

"David, this is too much," I said. "I'm drowning in memories. Let's just go home."

"Eat," David said.

I looked down at the plates that David had concocted for each of us. Some from his order, some from mine—the fried eggs running down and around a slope of pancakes, bacon and sausage poking out like shrubbery. The whole mess looked so beautiful, sogged and glistening with the yellow yolk and the gold syrup—like a bright autumn day.

I looked out the window. It *was* a bright autumn day.

"What a day," I said. And suddenly the dread was gone and my courage returned. It was a beautiful day for my goodbye. With the sun shining, out in the open. No dark rooms or dark cars. No I'm all right, Daddy, but when will I see you again? Don't worry, Daddy, I'm all right. But I'd feel better if I knew when I'd be seeing you again. We're going to see you again. Right, Daddy? All that was over. And seeing my father's grave would make it more over than ever.

David pulled out a pack of cigarettes from his pocket and lit up. "I'm really going to stop smoking," he said.

I said, "Oh, you will. . . . I know you will, yes, yes."

And we both laughed at my sputtering. But I felt serious, almost solemn. It felt as if some important ritual had taken place at our quiet breakfast, some mixing of spirit if not blood, making

David my new family.

David put out his cigarette, and I said, "Let's go."

It was like a small, quiet town. We passed through the gate and drove straight down "Main Street." We crossed an alphabet of streets like you have in small towns—Aster, Begonia, Cyclamen and Daffodil Lanes. At the corner of Main and Hyacinth we stopped at a large stone building.

"Town Hall," David laughed. "We may as well get hitched."

I said, "Kill two birds."

It had been decades since I'd been here to bury Uncle Boomie, the year after Grandma died. But I still remembered the gray building with its dreary stones, the kind used in massive turn-of-the-century mansions that end up housing the aged or feeble. Here, at Beth Israel, the stone building housed the office and the toilets.

I told David I'd be right back and headed up the wide steps. Last stop before the last stop, the driver at Boomie's funeral had said. How odd that I remembered that still. But it was so memorable, first, I guess, because Tommy had laughed and it was out of character for my theoretical and self-righteous adolescent brother to laugh at gross humor—unless it was his own. And second, because it *was* so gross—mocking our sacred purpose in being there, collapsing the most sacred activity into the most profane. But mostly I remembered, I think, because of the intensity of my old fear and suspicion, which came back now. Maybe they didn't stop most funeral parties here, I had thought. Probably most people on their way to burials have to go to the bathroom but probably they don't stop. That was what was most shocking and frightening about this whole "last stop" business. Was it a plot to degrade our family even more? Tempt us into the dark toilets as if what we were doing was done by your average mourner, and then photograph us? FAMILY OF COMMIE PAL DUMPS NEAR FAMILY GRAVE.

The ladies' room was just as I remembered it—dark and long

with a wall of 1960s smoky mirror. I looked in the mirror and remembered the last time I was here. I brushed my hair back into a pony tail, thinking that's probably how I wore it that day, for Uncle Boomie's funeral. Then I thought, of course—for it was my pony tail that Tommy used later to yank me from the grave!

In a way you could say that day had been a perfect funeral day from start to end—disastrous in every detail. First, there was the awful driver, Ira the Driver. He wore a button that said, *Ira the Driver—I drive you to the end of the world*. Buttons were just becoming popular then, Freedom Now, Ban the Bomb. And Tommy and I, seeing the button, elbowed each other, as if to say, Look, one of us. But then we read: "Ira the Driver."

Ira was a jerk—in every way, from his button to his boasts of the famous corpses he had driven. But that didn't stop Tommy from laughing loudly at everything Ira said, whistling at the cars that Ira pointed out, nodding in wild agreement as Ira announced which Yankees should stay on the team and which should "drop dead" by spring training. Clearly, Tommy missed Boomie, the last man in the family. And I tried to make believe his boy bonding with Ira didn't hurt, searching out my own bonding with one of our large lady cousins.

When Ira said we could use the facilities, I'd run in and hidden myself in a cubicle. When the cousins arrived I studied them through the door slit. One was named Rose and one was Dotty and one was Flo and one was Minny. But they were hard to tell apart—they all had short, dark hair, pale faces, red lips, black coverings meant to minimize their bulk. And often we'd say, Hi, Cousin Dotty, to Cousin Minny, who would say, Oh, actually I'm your cousin Minna, she's Dot.

Anyway, from my stall I stared out at them, as they preened, eager to distract myself from thinking about my dumb brother and his new best friend. I'd always thought the cousins huge and scary, but now they suddenly seemed funny and cute; they reminded me of the trained bears at the Moscow Circus my father once took us to, and I began to laugh.

"Oh, is that Betsy Rose?" one said.

"Are you all right, Betsy Rose?"

Betsy Rose. My father's politics accounted for both my and Tommy's names. Betsy Ross is the name my father selected for me, but my mother used the opportunity of his incarceration during my birth to change Ross to Rose on my birth certificate, having submitted her first born to Sam's "Thomas Paine Vogel" only to hear neighborhood wise guys rename him Thomas Paine-in-the-Ass Vogel. But for all intents and purposes, my name is simply Betsy, with my middle name pulled out like most people's for official uses. But to the cousins I have always been Betsy Rose. Maybe they'd come to visit me fresh from the hospital with my brand new names, and sitting around with Marie, eating whatever food she whipped up in response to their pleading eyes, decided it was all very strange and romantic—and southern. My mother's drawl, blond curls, easy laugh, her turkey hash, Whiz Pride soup, and ballerina walk added up to an exotic scene fit for a Betsy Rose to enter. I laughed again. Betsy Rose, Southern belle from the Northern Bronx.

I emerged from the stall, my face in my hands—to hide my laughter. One of the cousins rushed to me and said, "Don't cry. Your Uncle Boomie loved you very much. He wouldn't want you to cry."

Then hearing the words, Boomie and love, I began crying for real.

"Betsy Rose, if there's anything you want me for, just let me know. Maybe just to talk," she said. "About Boomie. Your dad. It must be hard. You probably feel like you live under a curse."

I shook my head, but, of course, it was the truth, which I'd never uttered even to myself. I was twelve and struggling to be cool, but I hugged her tight, and let her lead me out of the long, dark room into the light. All the way to the limousine I clung to her warm, meaty arm.

When I was in the Caddie, she said, "Call me. Visit me, Betsy Rose."

I'll call you, I'll visit, I wanted to say. I imagined a long afternoon, leading to an overnight, me lying on the cousin's mountainous breasts, talking then dozing then talking some more.

"Promise?" she said, and I nodded. I'd definitely call and visit if I only knew which one she was.

"What are you holding Minny-Dot's hand for?" Tommy said. "You going lezzy?"

I said, "Is she Minny or Dot?"

"Don't get so technical."

I turned to Aunt Elsie for help. Surely she could identify her own cousin, but she was sleeping, her head flung back on the pillow she'd made of Cousin Arthur's prayer book. And Cousin Arthur was useless. Out of the rabbi's sight, he'd stopped his phony *davvening* and was busy highlighting *Legal Terminology for the Transcriptional Professional*.

"What took you so long? I assumed you for deceased," he said, without looking up.

"A lot you'd care," I said. "She cares," I said, pointing to the cousin squeezing herself into a baby blue Impala.

Now, decades later, I tried to pee. My bladder was aching from all the coffee I had drunk talking on the phone with Mitzi, then with David in the diner. But I couldn't. I thought I heard someone come in and turn on the water, and I had the oddest thought that it was my father, turning on the tap to help me along. I remembered our long flight to Mexico, my seven-year-old body swollen, twisting and squirming in the tiny airplane toilet, Sam pressing the water button again and again. I can't, I'd said, and cried, which of course only made me need to pee more. What's wrong? Betsy, he said. I shook my head. We'd just endured a year of house investigations and tabloid catastrophes. In every way our family was *broke*. My parents couldn't find work. Barred from all union offices, my father tried to work as a carpenter, but no contractor would hire him, and when he tried to take on small, private carpentry jobs, the FBI told customers they had to cancel or face the consequences as an associate of an un–American felon. And a similar scenario—FBI agents telling parents to keep their kids away or else—had wrecked the dance studio my mother had started with her friend Rosie D'Amato. This was my first flight ever, and I thought the bathroom was a trick to destroy my family further. If I peed it would drip from the bottom of the plane, and they'd be able to follow us, and our plans for a new life in Mexico would be thwarted. And maybe beyond the elaborate paranoia, there was a simple reason, too, that made me squirm and cry and hold it in. Old simple spite. Pee for *you*? Why should I do a thing for *you*? You've ruined my life. I was thinking particularly about the day before, when I had brought a popular girl I'd worshipped all my stuffed animals as a goodbye present, and her mother came into the room and said they couldn't stay and neither could I. We were Red. They're just toys and I'm just a kid, I started to say, but she'd started counting, and by five we were to be gone, or else.

Sitting there now I thought again that I heard my father.

Betsy, Sss, Sss, Sss.

"Oh, shut up," I said now. "I'm so tired of you telling me what to do." I meant the later years when he was gone. Do this, do that. Don't do this, don't do that. Don't call collect, they'll trace it. Don't leave your name, they'll nab me. Do be brave, do be good, especially good.

"How good were *you*?" I said. "How goddamn good were you—running our life long distance?" It would be best if you kids didn't go to day camp this year or to too many large pub-lic events or to too many large public parks. "It's a wonder you permitted us to leave the house. To eat. To breathe. So just shut up."

Then I started laughing because I was so angry so many years later. Then I started crying because hadn't I just described Sam's life for years and years? Airless, viewless, full of deprivation and starvation. Living in stale motel rooms, movie theaters, and borrowed basements and cars, living on dry foods, beef jerky, saltines, cheese doodles—his favorite snacks becoming his staples, I imagined. Hardly living. Then dying.

Now at the mirror, I put on lipstick. Had Sam ever seen me in lipstick? Before he went away for good, I was too young to wear any, and after he went, even in my teen years, I never wore any lipstick to visit him. Again, paranoia, fear that my kisses would leave marks, noticeable marks? Or simple spite again? Look how pale I am—how sad and pale you've made me. Now, come on home!

I put on some lip gloss. Was there such a thing as lip gloss when my father was alive? I put on some blusher. Blusher had probably just come into style when Sam died. I put on some mascara. I'd kneel at my father's grave and say, Look, I'm all grown up. And then, I'd say goodbye. It's time to say goodbye, Daddy.

When I got back to the car, David was listening to Eric Clapton's song about seeing his son in heaven. It seemed fitting for the occasion—and I turned up the volume and then we took off.

At the last road, we turned and followed Zinnia all the way to the end of the cemetery, reaching a high cyclone fence bordered by leafless maples. I opened my window, poked my head out to listen. There was nothing to hear.

The day we buried Boomie you could hear the wild cries pushing through the fence. Another cemetery, I had thought, on the other side. For noisy big-shots, I'd thought. With Boomie gone, and Brown and Gray waiting in front of Aunt Elsie's building this time, our own small crowd was smaller by three from Grandma's burial. And we seemed small-time and meek as we sniffled and shuffled around the stones.

I wish we had a big crowd too, I whispered to Tommy. I bet they're rich over there.

Tommy said, You asshole, and snapped my arm with his *yam-ulke*. That's Belmont, the track.

You're lying, I said.

Yeah, like the *Unc* didn't take me there a hundred times. We bet loads. We had a ball. Most of the time we won tons.

It was intolerable. They had skipped out on me, my uncle and brother. Just like my father. Just like my mother. Who in the world could I trust now? I was all alone in the world.

Tommy said, You're too conservative. You gotta let loose, bet high. That's why we didn't take you. You gotta take risks at the track!

I would have if you took me, if you'd just given me a chance, I said. You could have taken me with you.

And the next thing I knew I was sitting on the edge of the grave, my feet dangling, like I was at a swimming pool. Then I had let myself down, onto the coffin. Why didn't you take me with you? Why didn't you take me with you? I called to my uncle.

Please, Betsy, oh, Betsy, I heard Aunt Elsie call.

Betsy Rose, your Uncle Boom loved you so. The dead can't take us with them! someone said. Come, Betsy Rose, come.

But I just sat there on my uncle's casket, looking at my own furious reflection on the glossy wood. I'd never leave. *Let loose. Take risks.* I'd show Tommy and Boomie too. I'd live in a hole in the ground and show them all.

Tommy was kneeling above me, calling my name. But I ignored him. We only came here once. You were on a class trip or we would of taken you for sure, he whispered down at me.

I looked up. Liar, I said.

Really, Bets. Your class was on some dumb trip.

Then why'd you say all those other things? About not wanting me. You were just kidding?

I was just being hyperbolic.

Really? I said, unsure of the word. But thinking it might mean that I could go on, that people still loved me enough to take me with them for a ride. Or would—if they were alive.

Really, you dummy, Tommy said.

I stood up and my brother bent down, and tugging on my arm and pony tail, he managed to lift me out.

Over the shouts of the cousins, Aunt Elsie, the rabbi, the spectators over the gate, I shouted to Tommy. Uncle Boomie liked us, didn't he? I meant, he liked me as much as he liked you, right?

Yeah, we're like his own kids.

Were, Cousin Arthur said.

David and I were out of the car, following a group of mourners down a path I thought I recognized as *ours*. It was a narrow path and in our bulky coats our progress between markers and stones was awkward and slow, for which I was glad. I held David's hand, readying myself. But this wasn't our lane, nor was the next one we took, nor the next after that. Everywhere I turned looked the same and there was no order to the numbers of the graves on the different streets. Surveying the patchwork quilt of stones, I felt desolate, like I was a kid lost at Coney Island, searching the sand for her family's blanket.

"This is hopeless," I said. "We'll never find them."

But then I turned and saw my grandma's grave. "Oh, there's Grandma," I said.

David read, MOLLY VOGEL. 1900-1963. OUR MA AND GRANDMA. And I began to laugh.

By the time our family was organized enough after Grandma's death to order a stone, Uncle Boomie had died and Aunt Elsie was so distraught and Cousin Arthur so preoccupied with his studies that Tommy and I were allowed to make all the decisions. A man called and said he was our family's tomb and grave provider, and we said, For Grandma, we'd like it simple, for that was Grandma, plain and simple. Tommy and I were on different extensions.

Just, Our Grandma, I said.

Our Ma, too, Tommy said. Don't forget Aunt Elsie and Daddy. She was their ma.

I should write, Don't forget Aunt Elsie and Daddy? the man said.

No, just, Our Ma and Grandma, Tommy said, and how long she lived.

I should write, How long she lived? the man said.

No, you're not listening, Tommy said.

I laughed. My brother's arrogance was inspiring.

We're good for the money, I said, trying to say something daring too. The sky's the limit.

Good, because your Uncle Boomie, may he rest in peace, didn't pay me for her. You'll have to be thinking about your Uncle Boomie soon too, he said.

We think of him a lot, Tommy said. He's our uncle.

Having had enough of us and our smart-ass orders, no doubt, the stone man hung up, saying he'd send us drawings. They came in the mail in a big brown envelope—our text topped with a Jewish star.

Even the non-political part of our family wasn't ever very religious, and Tommy and I crossed out the star, and on Boomie's drew in a small airplane, copying a piper cub from the library encyclopedia. For Uncle Boomie was a pilot during the war and his greatest moments, he'd always said, were up in the sky buzzing the Eiffel Tower. On Grandma's drawing we replaced the star with a triangle, representing the hamentashen she baked so well. I still remember our satisfaction as we drew in our changes, authorizing the revisions with our initials, which no one had asked for.

There she was now. Grandma with her hamentash. I kneeled before grandma and said to David, "I hardly remember my grandmother. Then suddenly she comes back. A lady on the bus will open her pocketbook and the smell—Evening in Paris, wintergreen mints, whatever—will do it. She's there."

David knelt beside me and said, "It works that way."

"I was mean to my grandmother," I said.

"All kids are mean."

My grandmother always kissed me with large wet kisses and I would always wipe them from my brow and lips, ashamed. I wanted dry, dignified "American" affection, not her noisy immigrant passion. When Grandma died, standing in the funeral home, I suddenly longed for a kiss from her. And as people made their way into the chapel, I lingered, and, lifting the lid and standing on tiptoes, I put my lips to hers. They were dry as sand, cold as winter.

Now I traced Grandma's names with my finger, her dates, the stark triangle on the dry, cold stone.

I said, "Grandma, forgive me."

And kneeling beside David, I imagined her saying, Don't make a mountain from a moleskin. Go on with your life, sweet girl. And though I knew rock and dirt and death separated us, I whispered, "Thank you, Grandma. I'll just see Daddy—and then I'll be off."

But then there was Boomie, right behind her. I touched the name, Bernard "Boomie" Vogel, the little plane, the cramped dates, 1925-1964. Not enough time to get any of your schemes working, I thought. Except maybe keeping us all alive.

Hadn't my uncle done that? First he'd saved Sam and then us? I tried to fit together the shards of those years. My father had unseated mob leaders in the mob-run carpenters union and lived. Was that partly Boomie's doing? I closed my eyes and saw my uncle racing down the street in pointy shoes, running frantic errands for local lowlifes. To save his brother's life? I do this for you wise guys, and you do that for me? I do everything you want, and you do nothing to my brother or his kids? Was that the story? I remembered calls in the middle of the night when we lived in Bensonhurst with Boomie and Grandma. Bernard, what kind of people call in the middle of the night? Is Sammy all right? Grandma would shout. Sam's all right, Mama, our uncle would say. And was that because our uncle was not?

"I'm sorry, Uncle Boomie," I said. For never appreciating you enough, I meant. For snickering at the pointy shoes, the cabana shirts, the greaser buddies. When for all I know that kept us going! "Can you forgive me, too, Uncle Boomie?" I called.

And through the stone, I imagined him saying: Come on, kid. In my book, there's zip to forgive. He was my big brother and he made me proud. You were my little kids . . . my whole world.

"Thank you," I said, to him, too. "I love you, too, Uncle Boomie."

Then I turned to find my father.

Up and down the Vogel rows I looked for him. I saw uncles and aunts and cousins. I saw Grandpa—Charlie Vogel—with a Jewish star and then tiny letters cramped at the bottom: Jewish Carpenter. He Fell That We May Rise.

And now I felt my father's presence. Who else but my father could have written those words! Years after his father's death, arranging for his new truth to be chiseled on his father's grave. "Dad," I said. "Is that your doing? You're too much, Dad." I remembered his old riffs about Jesus Christ the proto-socialist. Christ, the carpenter, the ur-working-class hero.

I was laughing, teary, pointing at grave after grave, looking for him. We passed great aunts and great uncles, cousins, searching up and down the rows. Beloved mother after beloved mother. Beloved father after beloved father. Bricklayers and bookbinders, cigar makers and tailors, lacemakers and homemakers. Long lives and short lives. I tried to remember the stories my father had told me.

"Daddy, Daddy," I called. I had so much to ask him. So much I wanted *him* to say. Or maybe it was very little: My life is over, honey. Go on with *your* life, honey. It's OK, honey, go.

Up and down the rows we walked, David and I. We walked and walked. Row after row.

After about half an hour, it was David who said it first: "I think he's not here."

I said, "Don't be ridiculous."

"We'll go to the office and ask."

"It can't be. He can't be gone."

A party of mourners arrived at our path. A woman with piercing navy eyes that matched her coat said, "I know it's hard. I lost Mother."

I said, "Did you find her?"

The poor woman gazed at me and tried again. "I know it's hard to accept. I haven't accepted it yet with Mother. But what's dead is dead."

"Dead is one thing," I said. "But this is ridiculous."

I don't remember the car ride back to Main Hall. I just remember the stone steps, studying the hopeless gray as I climbed to the office.

I said to the man at the desk, "My father, Samuel Vogel, is supposed to be at section 50, row I, in our family plot, but he's not there."

"Vogel?" he said, opening a file.

"Al, Abe, Anna, Arthur, Beatrice, Bernard, Bessie, Betty, Conrad, David, Donald, Doris, Douglas, Eli, Frank, Fred, Gerry, Gerta, Helen, Hilda, Ida, Irving, Irwin, Izzie, Jacob, Jenny, Leo, Lester, Lily, Melvin, Mervin, Moe, Molly, Natalie, Nathan, Norman, Paul, Pauline, Rose, another Rose, Seymour, and a Stuart are. That's it."

"Sam," I said. "Samuel."

"No Sam or Samuel. You sure it's not Seymour or Stuart?"

I shook my head. "Did you move him?"

"This is a complete file," he said. "It tells me he never was here even for a brief stay, shall we say. I mean, even if he moved, we'd still have him down here. But between you and me, they generally don't move from here."

I said, "Then where is he?"

"You got me."

I said, "Listen this is very serious. I want to know where my father is."

He said, "Look, if I knew where he was, don't you think I'd tell you."

I shrugged. "I guess so."

"You guess so! What do you take me for? Do you know the penalties for disposing of bodies in any irregular manner? Have you read the statutes?"

David said, "Take it easy. She's just upset. We're under the impression that her father's here."

"Well, he's not. Try Beth El. Beth Shalom. One of our sister institutions."

David said, "He's right. He's probably in a different cemetery. You'll have to call Aunt Elsie. Maybe she meant one of the other places nearby."

"Here are the numbers of our sister institutions. You can call over there and see," the man said. Suddenly friendly now that we were walking to the door.

"She said here. I'm sure I remember."

"Maybe you're forgetting," David said. "It was a long, long time ago."

On the ride back to Manhattan neither of us said much.

Now and then David said, "We'll get to the bottom of this soon. There's a logical explanation."

"Logical explanation, right," I said a couple of times.

"Something simple and obvious," David said.

"Something that's right in front of your nose," I said. "But you just can't see it. Even though it's so obvious. And logical."

"Like there was no room," David said. "So they had to use a sister institution, which we'll call."

"Right," I said. "Something like that for sure."

4: Questions and Answers

OH," AUNT ELSIE SAID, when we got back to the city and I called her.

"Oh, what?"

"Oh, that's strange."

"It is, Aunt Elsie. What happened? I don't understand."

"What happened. . . ," my aunt said. But then the line went dead.

I called her right back but got a busy signal.

"Maybe she had him cremated and she's embarrassed," David said.

"I wouldn't care."

"But she thinks you would," David said.

"I'll call her and explain that I don't care about these things."

"Good idea," David said.

But of course we were just grabbing at air. It could have been anything.

"It could be anything," I said. "Something terrible. Or scary."

"Like what?" David said.

And we both agreed that I was being melodramatic. Nothing was wrong. The only thing wrong was my aunt's phone. It was out of order, the operator said.

The next thing I knew, there were shouts coming from the living room. David-shouts, a rare phenomenon. Who was with him? I listened some more but heard no one else. I thought,

I've driven him nuts—me and my nutty family. He's talking to himself, screaming at no one. Then, from the interval between outbursts, I realized he was on the phone. Sweet, sweet David. While I was sleeping, my aunt's phone had been fixed, and he'd gotten through?

Aunt Elsie can be a little corny and repetitive, but even in my wildest moments of adolescence I rarely found a convincing excuse to yell at her. What could she be saying to anger him so? I thought of picking up the extension to hear but, out of cowardice, decided against it.

Then suddenly, David was tiptoeing into the bedroom.

"Hi," I said. "Everything OK?"

"I called all the sister institutions. He's not there. I called the front desk at Senior Seasons. They said your aunt had left. A bus had just picked up a group of residents for a trip to an elder hostel in Coral Gables. I told her we needed to talk to Elsie about a family matter and asked for the number. She said, 'The whole point of these elder hostels is to allow senior citizens to escape family matters,' or some garbage like that. I said it was urgent. She said, 'Only illness and death are urgent.' I said it involved a death. She started quizzing me who, when, where. . . . I said, 'Do you have a degree in journalism?' She went on and on about elder hostels. I called her a hostile elder. And she hung up on me. The long and short of it is that Elsie left and won't be back till next Saturday and that bitch won't tell us a thing."

"Saturday," I shouted, sitting up. "That's a week away. How could she do that to me?"

"The bus was there," he said. "She had to go. She'll call you when she gets there."

"You're sure?"

He stroked my head. " Just sleep, sweetheart."

Did I say, OK, Daddy? Or did I dream that?

I slept and woke, slept and woke, springing up from dreams to check if my aunt had called. It was only an hour, David said, then only four hours, then only a night, then only a day. Finally it was two days and my aunt still hadn't called.

I called my brother in Capetown, but his message machine said he'd be away at a conference for another week. I called Florida, pleading with the receptionist in my aunt's hotel, who now claimed that no one knew the name of the place that the group had gone to. I called senior agencies in Coral Gables, following all leads, but there was no Elsie Stark registered at any senior programs I could find. The third night I began to dream. I can't remember much of it except that Sam was there, lying in a coffin. I started talking to him. And though he was dead, it looked like he was listening because he kept blinking his eyes—like an accommodating stroke victim. Then I watched him struggle to lift his dead hand. He said, It doesn't move well when it's dead. He was dead but also alive.

Since my father died, I had managed not to dream of him, guided in sleep by the same logic that had me in my waking hours hide every photograph of him. One glimpse, sleeping or waking, I'd feared, would drown me in a pond of old ache. And waking from the dream now, I raced to the living room, turned on the television, tossed the cushions off the couch so it wouldn't be comfortable and conducive to sleep and dream, and there on the cushionless couch I sat, trying to shed the terror.

To stay awake I watched TV, which I rarely do—a special Asian porno show that had skinny girls who looked like Vietnamese boat people licking each other joylessly; a reality teen show called "Real Kids," where a real bulimic kid vomited and her best girlfriend cried about her mother's aerosol spray dependency; a prayer show, where the preacher and the people in his studio audience looked so satisfied and calmed by prayer, smiling with their big teeth and bright eyes, that I tried to pray, too. But I couldn't. I closed my eyes, and mumbled along with them. "I'm with you, I'm with you. I'm sending in my subscription to you for life-long membership. To you. To you." But hearing my voice bouncing around the empty room only made me feel more scared and confused. "Get up, get up," the preacher cried. And I got up—and shut off the TV.

I went into the kitchen looking for distracting activity. The cabinets were a mess, and I emptied them and put things together by categories, which would make it easier to give away or pack when the time came. Then I moved on to cleaning. I mopped and polished, until wiping off the Jubilee wax on the toaster oven, I thought I saw my father's nose, on my face. But then I quickly moved on to redoing the linen closet, which had no shiny surfaces in which to see things but lots of cluttered shelves that needed fixing.

At six that morning David appeared at the closet.

"Come on. You're going to work."

"Good idea," I said. I went to dress. "Funny. I forgot to go to work yesterday."

"That's because yesterday was Sunday, the day before was Saturday."

"Right."

"When did we go to the you-know-what?" I said.

"We went to your father's grave on Thursday," David said.

My father doesn't have a grave, I thought.

At the office I worked and worked to keep all thought at bay. I jammed more interviews into that one week than I usually scheduled in a month. One was with a famous, old actress who had given up speech in protest against child labor. Over lunch we passed notes back and forth on paper napkins. In one note she explained that she would begin speaking again when the President sent her a registered letter saying, NO MORE CHILD LABOR IN ANY U.S. OWNED CORPORATION. I have sent him a copy of the text I will accept. He need only sign, she said. I wrote back to her saying that this seemed unlikely. She wrote back: *Then I will maintain my silence of protest.*

It's not that I didn't agree with her thoughts on child labor—the horrible reality of hungry, sickly, overworked children, unprotected all around the globe. But suddenly I found myself going stiff with anger. I looked at her face, the fixedness of her jaw. I found myself wanting to pry her mouth open, to put my fingers into her mouth and pull out words. Talk to me, I wanted to shout. Just open your fucking mouth and talk to me.

I left that lunch early. *I'm sorry*, I wrote on my napkin. *I have a headache.* She wrote: *Goodbye. Avoid analgesics. Reckless advertising has created a national analgesic addiction.*

I walked down 57th Street bewildered. Was it just the sad subject that I resented when I was poised for a happy life? At Third Avenue I kicked a cab that was swerving around the corner and realized, of course, that the actress reminded me of my father. Righteous and pure and apart. She wouldn't talk. He wouldn't talk, he wouldn't sign. If he'd just done what they'd asked him to, he could have been with us. But he, like her, made a big show. All the way crosstown to the office, I babbled like a child. "You had to make a big deal." Betsy, you shock me, I imagined him saying. And you shock me! I thought. Not being buried where you're supposed to be. And no one's talking. All those fucking secrets all over again.

Back at the office, I plunged into work to escape thinking of him, talking with him. Then, the rest of the week, still with no news from my aunt, I kept up endless and thoughtless activity. When I could do no more of my own work, I did someone else's. I read Anna Lisa's letters and helped Margaret write answers. I advised the break-up of several live-in relationships, encouraged the maintenance of dozens more. *It seems to me*, I wrote to some, *that you can do no more. Tell your partner that you've had it. It might do the trick. Certainly you have nothing to lose.* I wrote to others, *It seems to me that you could be trying harder. Admit where you're wrong. It will encourage your partner to do likewise.*

Those letters have since tormented me. I'm not at all sure on what I based my opinion to give up or try, or indeed that I based them on anything. Margaret called me a genius as her desk became emptier and emptier. But certainly no intelligence or

73

judgment was involved. You pile A, you pile B. Only a treacherous rage for activity and order. They could have gotten similar results by going down the street and hiring the poor crack addict permanently installed in the pizzeria, tying and untying his shoe. When there was no more of Margaret's work, I helped Alan, sitting in with graphic designers, ad agency reps, distributors. I helped all around by answering the phone, taking messages and directing calls. In short, except for dusting and vacuuming, I intruded myself everywhere, till Alan told me to go home.

Home, those days, I washed what was washable, waxed what was waxable, sorted and resorted. I discarded old magazines in the garbage room at the end of the hall, discovered new ones in other people's piles.

"Let me call Horowitz," David said one night, finding me surrounded by a moat of magazines. "Horowitz."

"I don't need a doctor."

"You need something. Have you seen yourself lately?"

I didn't tell David that I had stopped looking in mirrors and other reflective surfaces since the night that thing happened with my father's nose.

I said I was just excited about leaving. Overexcited, by all the planning and preparations. It's not that I purposely kept the truth from David, about the dream, about my decision not to sleep, about yelling at my father on 57th Street. The truth was I had pushed all that from my mind as I charged ahead. I mean what was the point of all my busyness, if I had to stop and talk it over?

"You're driving yourself crazy, Betsy. I admit it's a strange situation. But your life has always been . . . strange."

"I can't take another piece of weirdness," I said. "Who knows what could be going on. People disappearing. Just like that. . . ."

"You sound like your mother, Bet. And you look like her, too."

While David slept my activity escalated. One night I took a

Vogue pattern I had bought on my way home and cut out the pieces for a dress for Mitzi's party. I moved the portable sewing machine, which my mother and Rosie D'Amato had bought to make costumes for kids' dance recitals, from the back of the closet into the bathroom—the only room besides the bedroom with a door and my only hope for not disturbing David with the buzz—and between three and six that morning I sewed the first dress I'd ever sewn.

At seven, when David awoke, I modeled it. It was a hooded caftan made of a couple of red silk saris that David had brought back from a work trip in Pakistan. I thought David would be pleased, but he shook his head.

"I'm a novice seamstress," I said.

"Please let me call Horowitz. This can't go on. You've got to take it easy."

"It's just that I've never gone away before," I said. "I'm not a big-shot traveler like you," I laughed. And then in the big mirror over the dresser I saw a pinched figure in a shapeless costume. David was right. I looked like mother—the clenched jaw, the nervous angles, the robe. And like my father, I thought—wizened, shrouded.

"I'm afraid," I said. If I took it easy I might sleep and if I slept I might dream again. But by now, my waking thoughts, the thoughts that clung to me—despite my constant spinning designed to throw them off—were getting as bad as any dream.

Brown and Gray had him dug up. I was cleaning the mock-copper canisters I would leave Yukio when I felt convinced of this. They'd been moved to the central office in Virginia and had my father's body moved to a Washington area cemetery to have him near them still, to pursue him in death as in life. My fatigue, each day, fueled crazier and crazier fantasies. He was dead but not in the ground. He was in a cage, beautiful and unchanged, his skin that rugged bronze of a bosc pear. I felt my lips press against the bars to kiss him like I used to. Then everything changed. His skin turned to tears—and I was no longer kissing him but drinking him. "Daddy," I cried out loud, "why can't you be like everyone else? Just plain dead, in the ground."

For days David continued to plead with me to see someone; for days I continued to ignore him. The Friday before the Saturday Aunt Elsie was coming back, I was too tired to keep busy, but too desperate to keep still. I looked through my phone book and tried to find someone I could call who might tell me something. Old family friends who had lived through those years with my parents. I hadn't talked to any of them in decades. Not that they were bad people, the Fines and the Levins and Rosie D'Amato and the rest. They were good people. And that had been the problem. They'd seemed *too* good. How are *you*? they'd always say, letting their eyes water up. Even if I was especially carefree that day, whizzing past them on my bike, they'd stop me and bother me with their questions until I started crying to get them off my back. Once the worst of the Fifties was over and they had some income and a little savings for vacations, they'd bring me back gifts, scarves from Greece and sandals from Guatemala, and, praising the handiwork, they'd get all teary again, for all the pain and exploitation in the world.

I wasn't happy, of course. But I was trying to get by, to be cheerful, if not happy, and to focus my questions on others, not myself. In high school, I found relief from my difficult family situation by joining magazine staffs and interviewing anyone I could, interesting and boring alike. So when the clan of family friends thinned out over time, I was glad. And when my father died, there soon seemed no reason to return the calls of the few loyal souls still around.

Sitting on the couch, studying their names, I felt soaked with shame. There was no doubt that Tommy and I had depended for years on the kindness of these people. Again and again, they'd come through with clothes and food and beds. The Simons in Mexico and then again in New York. The D'Amatos, who, though atheists, called us their godchildren to make us feel secure and loved. I remembered all that now—and my retreat from them—certain and extreme in the way that only a young jerk in the first obnoxious throes of the enterprise of self-realization can be. All in all, it seemed too much to approach any of them again.

I could call Horowitz. He alone of all of them was brutally honest if not totally pleasant. But we had always called him when Marie needed to be locked up and in truth in the shape I was in I was half afraid he'd want to lock *me* up. So instead I called Florida again, hoping that my aunt had returned early, but she was still gone. And then I did something I probably shouldn't have done—I called my mother.

In the thirty-something years that my mother had been on this ward and that half-way house, I'd had only a handful of phone conversations with her, if you can call them conversations, and they were all the same. I'd call and tell her I had to change plans and she'd tell me she was awfully busy anyway. I'd suggest a time and she'd say, At your own risk. I may be gone.

Now I said, "Marie, where is my father?"

I thought, let me speak directly and honestly. Maybe it will stun her into the same. A naive notion, which assumed that my mother was just a wise guy who needed a tough guy to set her straight.

"Your father, your father." It sounded as if she were straining to come up with an answer, and I wanted to cry hearing the old Marie in her voice, the Marie I hardly knew. Dutiful Marie who won the Virginia All-State History Award three consecutive years and skipped a grade for scoring highest in the county Historical Dates and Names Exam. Most of the time the Marie I knew was working hard to empty her mind of all names and dates. She made a point of not learning people's names, not knowing what month we were in. So that, in all honesty, she could tell police, FBI, House Committees asking again and again about people and events, "I just don't remember."

Now she said, "Oh, let's see, let's see. Oh, that's a rich one, the pot calling the kettle black."

I said, "I have to know. Where is my father?"

She said, "It's a wise man who knows his own father. You must be pretty dumb."

I said, "I'm not a man," and quickly regretted answering so literally, so stupidly. But I couldn't help myself—Marie always got me jumpy.

"Who are you anyway?" she said. "And what do you want? I thought you were a friend. Now I think you're showing your true colors."

I said, "Come on. It's me, Betsy."

"Listen, I got your number once and for all, sister. Here it is: FBI, 123. Open and shut case."

I said, "You know it's just me."

"Me, me, me. Listen, I puked up every last one of those chocolates you jammed down my throat. If I hadn't, I wouldn't be here today."

"Please try to think of what happened?"

She said, "Beware of freaks bearing gifts. In my opinion you're pretty freaky. And I'm not afraid to tell you. I no longer fear authority."

"Why would I hurt you?" I whispered. "I love you." I remembered one of her last children's dance recitals—before all the parents were scared away. Brown and Gray sitting front and center taking notes, my mother shaking as she guided us on and off the stage. "I love you so much."

"If this keeps up I'm going to have you arrested. There are higher up authorities than you. Port Authority and others."

"Mother, please, try to remember."

"Listen, Sister, even if I knew where my father sits, would I tell you?"

"*My* father," I said. "*Lies.*"

"Yeah, lies, lies, lies and more lies and personally I've had about enough. Operator, I'm ending this conversation, Operator," she said, as if she were talking into one of those old-fashioned phones from the Lassie show. "Operator, there's a maniac on the line and I'm ringing off."

78

I slammed down the receiver, as if it were her head. And then, feeling desperate, I did another thing I probably shouldn't have done.

When I said, Hello, Cousin Arthur recognized my voice immediately. "Good to hear from you, Kid," he said.

And though the voice on the other end was distinctly Arthur's—rough and raspy like Donald Duck's—I thought, This isn't Arthur. Cousin Arthur always made believe he didn't recognize me. Oh, it's you—I thought it was a friend of mine, he'd always say.

Now he was saying, "Long time no see, young lady. Long time no hear." And I was chuckling, in merry agreement.

"Cousin Arthur," I said, "Something came up. Could we meet?"

"Why not, young lady?" he said.

I said, "I'll wear a red rose."

"I never forget a face," Cousin Arthur said. "Especially of family members and loved ones."

I hung up the phone feeling the first sprig of hope in a week. Aunt Elsie might be at her hostel, but I still had family. Cousin Arthur might be a little stiff and silly but he was hardly the childhood ogre I remembered. Years had passed, we both had changed. Cousin Arthur would tell me all he knew. I felt so cheered that, stretching out on the bed, I closed my eyes for the first time I could remember in days and slept until it was time to go.

Dante's was a bar and restaurant across from the Queens County Courthouse, where Arthur worked. It was in a handsome, old four-story federal house on Courthouse Square. From where I sat I could see a long stretch of Manhattan skyline, from the Empire State Building up to the Triboro Bridge. I was grateful for the view. It allowed me to forget my surroundings, the lunching lawyers, court officers, defendants, the courthouse itself, which you could see from the wall of windows on the other side of the dining room. Despite all the years that had passed, despite my new mood of hope, I still had trouble with courthouses and what went with them.

The waiter said, "Are you Betsy Vogel?" and I said nothing. But my heart began to pound. I studied the waiter's face, the cleft that looked like a scar, the lidless eyes, the skin—an official-looking khaki—and waited for him to speak words that hadn't played in my mind in years: Follow me. We have come to get you too.

"Mr. Arthur Stark called and said he'll be here very soon. He was detained by an important case."

"Thanks," I said and looked down. My hands were white from holding on to the edge of the table. My heart was still racing, as if I were ten in the Federal Courthouse, not forty in a bar across the street from the County Court.

I ordered a martini to calm me. I thought again, Hurry up, Arthur. No more suspense. I guess I must have put my head down on the table and dozed, because the next thing I knew Cousin Arthur was tousling my hair and smiling down on me like I was on his Little League team.

"Rough case," he said. "Sorry."

I waved my hand as if to say, no problem. But also to wave away any attempt on Cousin Arthur's part to supply me with details of any court case. Partly to protect myself, from more remembering. Partly to protect Cousin Arthur, from lying. For he liked to lie when we were young, strut, play roles. Now he was playing lawyer instead of whatever it was he was in the court. He says he's big in the law business, Aunt Elsie would tell me on the phone. With lots of people under him. Always I'd think of Tommy and me squirming beneath him on the old Castro convertible, Arthur stretched on top of us, farting every chance he got. I'm not surprised I'd always tell Aunt Elsie. Big, with people under him. That was the Cousin Arthur I had known.

I doubt Aunt Elsie ever believed Arthur, but she never liked to hurt anyone. So she always played along with Arthur being a lawyer, and an eminent lawyer at that; and I always figured that was the least I could do for her, considering all that she'd done for us. And now, seeing Cousin Arthur looking sweet and harmless in his three-piece polyester suit, I thought, That's the least I can do for *you*, too. So be quiet, Cousin Arthur. Don't ruin it.

"Hi, there, Kid," he said.

Cheerfully I said, "Hi, there, Your Honor." I thought, let him be a judge. He looked touching, if not quite dignified, his neck red and straining in the tight collar, the purple spots where the razor had scraped.

"Impossible case," he said.

I touched my lips as if to say, no explanation needed. This was a new Cousin Arthur, amiable and kindly, and I would be a new Betsy. The old me would have quizzed him on the details of the case till he tripped himself up.

Thinking about it now, I wonder if it was really all mature benevolence on my part. Wasn't there a childish logic, too, guiding me—a scared, desperate logic? If I'm nice, he'll be nice. If I give him what he needs, he'll give me what I need.

"It's very nice here," I said.

Cousin Arthur said, "We like it. Most of us lunch here."

I smiled with understanding. We. Us. The big lawyers, big judges. I felt happy indulging him.

And Arthur said, "What is it, young lady? What can we do for you?" The greatest attorney in the world couldn't have been more clear and direct.

I said, "Where is my father?"

Cousin Arthur's eyes opened in shock, but then he slapped the table decisively. "Come now, he's dead."

"But where?"

Again he slapped the table. "In the ground, Betsy. You're making me say very silly things."

"I went to the cemetery. He isn't there."

Arthur nodded. "I see." He flung his arm over the back of the chair and said, "Oh, I see. Now *that's* a question." He kneaded his brow and closed his eyes, probing the question.

He opened his eyes and said, "But that's easy, too, Betsy. Think. An unmarked grave."

"Really, Arthur?" I said.

"Really, Kid, of course."

And then I thought, of course. It was the most logical explanation, and it had evaded both David and me. Hounded all those years, my father would have wanted privacy in the end.

I said, "You're brilliant, Arthur."

Arthur took off his pervert-style black-rimmed glasses, which only lately had come into vogue for normal people, and began chewing on the tip, like a law professor. "It was obvious," he said. "And now I remember that was the precise story. We should have told you sooner."

"I'm so grateful to you," I said. "I mean, I was all worried— that he was moved, or lost."

"Really, don't worry, Kid."

I said, "Thanks, Arthur."

Arthur said, "Let's order." And my mind dipped back to other meals across from Cousin Arthur, meals alone when Tommy was away at basketball practice or civil rights meetings and Aunt Elsie was out at Arthur Murray's or a mah-jongg game. Lonely meals. I should have tried harder. Cousin Arthur would have tried harder.

I said, "Oh, Arthur, I'm starving."

"Me, too," he said.

I giggled to suggest we were friendly and family. All around us people were eating lasagna and manicotti and clams, and I smiled, wanting it all, after a week of starvation. But when Arthur said provolone on white and a cherry coke, not wanting to separate us again, nor hurt nor provoke as I used to with insinuations of superiority, I said, "The same, please. Provolone on white. A cherry coke."

Truly, I didn't mind. When the sandwiches came, the cheese

had the bounce of a tennis ball and the bread the texture of a sneaker. But it felt so good to have the matter of my father settled, and then too the years of anger and spite with Cousin Arthur erased. I thought, Tommy and I must have been pretty unbearable coming back from Mexico, demanding our odd foods, whining to be taken to foreign films. You could hardly blame Cousin Arthur for fighting us with his advantages of age and weight.

"You're looking good, Kid," Cousin Arthur said. "Really regular."

I said, "Thank you." Again I was pleased with myself. Another time I would have pounced—Who are you with your cheap suit and your blotched neck to judge me? Besides Cousin Arthur did look sweet this way.

"Actually, I have to admit you always were a pretty regular person. I just never wanted to tell you."

"Thanks, Arthur."

I laughed. Not so much because this was Cousin Arthur's highest praise, but because it was so accurate. Regular—that really was me all those years. Regular, conventional landed me jobs like class *recorder*, in charge of writing down the names of those who spoke when the teacher left the room, and school *collector* in charge of gathering daily attendance reports and delivering them to the principal's office, where Tommy often sat, in detention. I laughed because, once again, Cousin Arthur had gotten things so right, surprising me.

"You were pretty regular, too," I said. It was close enough to what I meant. I meant we were a lot the same back then. Two squares, two duds. Had I known it earlier, I thought, my childhood might have been less lonely. When my brother spiraled away from me on theories and dreams, I could have chatted with Cousin Arthur about Oreos versus Hydrox, Good Humor versus Bungalow Bar, career choices in a changing world—his favorite topics.

Cousin Arthur said, "I don't mind if you call me Cousin Arthur, by the way. I notice sometimes you just say Arthur 'cause you know I used to get upset with the Cousin bit."

I nodded. We'd called him *Cousin* Arthur because the sound of it made us laugh, and also because it suggested that we'd never call him anything or even talk to him were he not inflicted on us by blood.

"So you're really surprised by your old cousin?"

"No, really, not at all, Cousin Arthur."

"I mean because I'm sort of brilliant now."

"You were always intelligent," I said. "In your way."

It must have been that qualifying "in your way," that did it. For the next thing I knew he was saying, "Look, it seemed the only explanation. I mean if I were your father, I would stipulate in my will an unmarked grave. So no one could defile me. Through defecation or other means."

I nodded absently. Then his words began to take on meaning—defile, defecation. What horror was he concocting? I looked across at him to see if I had heard him wrong. Had he meant deface? Desecrate?

"I mean more than one citizen would be tempted to express his outrage through defecation." He was nodding with self-satisfaction.

I said, "What? What the hell are you talking about?"

"That's what they said. I remember them talking about an unmarked grave 'cause he was afraid. That's exactly what they said. I'm not stupid. I'm not *sort of, kind of, maybe* just a little bit intelligent. I'm incredibly intelligent to brilliant, for your information. I was tested for my position and you wouldn't believe my score. I remember perfectly."

I stared, he chewed. To break the silence, I guess, he said, "How is your brother, by the way?"

"Good." If I talked as if nothing had happened, would he take back what he had said?

"When did you hear from your brother last?"

"Christmas." I told him the basics about Tommy. How he was

living in Capetown, working there, hopeful about the future there. How much I wanted to see my brother now, to have him next to me on my side of the table.

"Maybe I should write him to inform the additional family of the deceased of my findings."

Then the waiter set down the awful maroon sodas. Unmarked grave. Additional family of the deceased. It made no sense. He'd made the whole thing up. He was lying like he always did, posing, impersonating, trying to be important. And I had fallen for it. He was a mean dope—always had been, always would be.

"What do you really know?" I said. "Do you know anything?"

"Of course. I know plenty."

"Like what?"

"I know everything I was informed of when he died, your father."

"Who informed you?"

"Boomie and Ma."

"Boomie was dead."

"Maybe it was Ma and your African brother, actually. But I know the whole story. I remember it perfectly now."

"You made up everything. You don't know a damn thing."

He stared ahead, rubbed his chin as if in thought.

"You know what I know?" he said.

"What?"

"I know Africa is filled with crazy *shvartzas*."

I looked at the soda, at the bubbles rising to the top. I thought ten more bubbles will rise and this won't be happening.

"I know your family was always crazy for *shvartzas*."

I said, "Shut up, or you'll be sorry."

"Oh, yeah?"

I said, "One more piece of garbage from you and I'll slap your face. We'll slap your fat face."

"Who's *we*?" he said.

We? Who was we? I was speaking from years ago. Me and my

brother. I was speaking for both of us. To Arthur, to others. To lay off us.

I said nothing.

Arthur said, "This is getting interesting. What are you going to do, you and your all-powerful imaginary friend? Punch me in the puss or the gut to show me how much you love niggers? I guess you're still a violent commie-lover after all."

I counted to ten and then to twenty, but it didn't help. I stood up and held onto Arthur's collar, shaking him. For now, for all those years. For his offenses and those of all the other bullies we endured. Pushing our "un-American asses" off swings. Holding our "un-American heads" in the water fountain. To give us first-hand knowledge of Red Chinese torture tactics, which, they said, our father and his friends had invented.

"Hands off the merchandise," he said.

"Do you know a thing about my father? A goddamn thing?" I was punching his chest—for all the years of hurt—Your father's a killer, a faggot, a fink, a pink, a commie-loving stink.

"I know he refused to sign a simple piece of paper. I know he stood up for commies and *shvartzas*." He was whispering and staring straight ahead as if that would make him less noticeable to all the lawyers lunching at Dante's.

"What else, you worm?" I was pulling his hair.

"I know he's dead. Or deserves to be."

"Do you really know that?" Dead, I meant.

He shook his head.

"And the grave?"

"It's just my opinion. But I have a right to my opinion. This isn't a totalitarian state, you know. Though I know that's what you and your nigger-loving friends have always desired."

I slapped his face.

He whispered, "Now I'm going to have to take action. That's actionable. That's clear assault."

I shouted, "What exactly are you?"

He said, "If it weren't for you and your family I could have been anything. I probably could have been a highly paid paralegal and more."

I looked down at his face. It was a dark red. His mouth was wobbling.

"So what if I'm an assistant court recorder. Eventually I'll make court recorder and probably administrator. Anyway, I'm an American, which is more than I can say for you and members of your immediate family! Now get the hell out of here before we throw you out!"

Beyond the square were stretches of factories and a sky thick with smoke and smell and people racing toward the black scaffolding of the el train, as if from some imminent calamity. I felt enveloped again in that old time when cruelty and disaster threatened us from every corner. I thought of my mother, sneaking off to mass after one of Sam's arrests, the picture in the *Journal American* of Marie on the steps of St. Patrick's sticking out her tongue, her latest and most lasting nervous tick. The headline: RED PAL'S WIFE RUDE TO GOD. And closing my eyes, for the second time in days, the third time in my life, I tried to pray.

A logical explanation. Please, God, a logical explanation. I saw my cousin's miserable face. I imagined my father dead in a gutter, skin and bones beneath garbage and shit.

"No," I heard myself say. And the woman before me in the token booth line said, "No, what? I was here first. Don't you *no* me if you know what's good for you."

And I didn't explain but just waited, like she told me to, like I'd been doing all along.

5: Goodbyes

YUKIO RANG AND SAID
he felt a cold coming on, and since I would be "transferring"
him my kettle soon, why not now?

I said, "Oh, why not, Yukio." I needed distraction. It was two
days after my disastrous visit with Cousin Arthur—and still no
word from Aunt Elsie, though today was Saturday, the day she
was due back. Poor David had been trying his best to amuse me.
He'd spent the morning pulling clothes from my closet, first sort
of modeling them, then playing some mixed-up game, Stay and
Go or something. Stay meant go—to the Salvation Army—and
go meant stay with us, go to Guatemala.

All this because I had said I had nothing to wear to Mitzi's
party—which was that night—my feeble attempt to escape
from going, in the state I was in. And to prove I was wrong and
cheer me up, he was dragging dresses and skirts from the closet,
holding them against him, letting his pants drop, pointing his
toes, making me laugh. But then I started to worry again about
when my aunt would call and what she would say. I said, "It's
hopeless. Throw it all out." Which was when he started with the
Stay and Go, which, like his modeling, amused me, but which
by now, two hours later, was losing its charm. It now felt eerie
sorting clothes, dressing for a party, all premised on my saying
goodbye to my old life, when that life had suddenly risen up and
grabbed me by the throat.

David offered Yukio a Scotch, which Yukio accepted, admiring the polka-dotted glasses and the blue plastic ice-cube trays.

Yukio talked about his difficulties. Trying to improve people always and not getting recognition. Being taken for homosexual just because you're small and unsettled.

"When I get the pots and pans," Yukio said, "I'll take on weight. They'll be impressed and sorry."

Yukio walked around the living room and touched things, the pieces of his new life and respectability. Eager for the distraction of his enthusiasm, I stood beside him as he inspected. He said, Scandinavian wood, as he studied a plastic-handled cheese cutter, English brass for a gold-tone corkscrew, Irish crystal for some pressed-glass carafe that California wine came in—and I nodded, not to lie but to calm us both as we looked over the apartment of junk and near junk, whose shabbiness Yukio seemed not to notice.

Yukio said, "It is so very cheerful here. Maybe I just move here when you leave me."

Out of a reflex toward niceness, I was about to say, Oh, Yukio, I won't leave you. But I saw he was smiling widely. There was, of course, nothing that he wanted more than for me to leave.

"Maybe," I said, half hurt.

Then, because it was three o'clock and I'd been waiting for my aunt's call since seven and needed fresh distraction, we talked about the pros and cons of a new lease for Yukio in my apartment and that led to a discussion of New York real estate versus Tokyo and Hollywood, two other places where Yukio had lived, still more marginally. In Tokyo, it seemed, Yukio lived one full month in a garage where his friend, a jazz singer, was working as a parker, moving from car to car each night.

"I've slept in some beauties," Yukio said, "Bentleys and more. But it's still not a home, no matter."

So we toasted Yukio, his better times. "To Yukio," David said. "His success and prosperity. His new home."

"And to you," Yukio said. "A speedy trip. And safe and sound."

Then the phone rang and I knew it was Aunt Elsie.

I said, "Hello, Aunt Elsie."

And Aunt Elsie said, "Hi there, darling."

I saw David walk Yukio to the door with the kettle and I blew Yukio a goodbye kiss. I was light-headed. Half from relief that my wait was over—my aunt had finally called. Half from dread of what I might hear.

I stalled. I said, "Tell me, what exactly is an elder hostel?"

She said, "You don't want to know. A horror. They plan your every move. Now it's hear about the history of the piano, now it's do your woodworking, now it's eat your grass sandwich, special for your elder insides. It's not for me. You know me—I'm a self-starter."

True, I thought—and it's been so long since I've had a chance to chat with my self-starter aunt. For that's what she was—a starter if not a finisher. I thought of all the projects that she'd begun and dropped. Electronic mah-jongg, which she planned one day to patent. I thought of Cousin Arthur's bar mitzvah, which never happened. How she was still looking for the "right hall" when Arthur was fifteen. But maybe that was just to look full of good intentions and conventions, to cover her dread at having a bar mitzvah and no one showing up except for all the old FBI agents, the VFW, the American Legion, who'd kick us, spit at us. For years, Tommy and I, following our aunt from one Jewish Center to the next, wondered what would happen if the right hall was ever found. Cousin Arthur, a Hebrew school drop-out, would have nothing to say. Surely the whole event would only humiliate our family more. I hate the paneling, we would say. Ugly wallpaper. Or, the guy's a thief, and Aunt Elsie would agree. He can keep this smorgasbord, he can keep his whole damn affair.

Get to the point, I thought again. Why had she hung up on me? Run off to the hostel? Where was my father? But afraid, I started thinking of anything else that I could manage. How no one in our family had bar mitzvahs. How no one was religious. How as young children during the Fifties, Tommy and I would identify possible friends by asking kids if they "believed in God," using our question as a political gauge. When someone would say, If there were a God would he allow racial discrimination? or something along those lines, we'd know we had found a new buddy.

Now Aunt Elsie said, "At night I snuck off to the game room behind the cafeteria. Pac Man and some computer shoot-'em-up games, which are not my cup of tea. Nothing beats plain pinball. But still it beat the planned activities I was stuck in during daytime hours."

And then before I faced whatever truth Aunt Elsie had in store for me, I escaped into one last round of rumination, thinking about how on the surface my aunt seemed so different from my father and Boomie. How as a girl, then a young woman, and now an old woman, she was fated to behave, to preserve decorum and conventions. Or at least to try. In truth, she was congenitally as wild, I think, as her brothers. And as she proceeded through her "normal" life, her nature oozed out at the sides, ruining her earnest efforts and what she took for her dreams. She learned mah-jongg to fit in with the neighborhood ladies but then couldn't resist developing her plan for the electronic version. I thought of all her mixed-up preparations for mah-jongg games in the apartment. Bustling about anxiously to get everything right, she would get everything wrong. Conventions would be maintained but the wrong ones, and so instead of serving the little tidbits served at the other ladies' houses—cashews, peanut clusters, halvah—she would lay out a buffet of stuffed derma, pickled herring, sweet and sour meatballs, a Bar Mitzvah of treats, which the ladies, laughing into their cocktail napkins, would drip on the baby blue carpeting, which belonged in the bedroom anyway. And then, of course, there was her attempt to create the All-American boy, which backfired as well, leaving Cousin Arthur. I thought, had Aunt Elsie been born a boy, what would she have become? A *professional* ballroom dancer? A game inventor?

My aunt said, "They had bingo, which I loathe. Some awful Balkan folk dancing, though I'd brought plenty of gorgeous ballroom tapes. . . ."

I allowed myself one more thought of Aunt Elsie, tiptoeing into the apartment from Roseland, one grand defiant dawn, just in time for breakfast, her guilty happy smile. Then I cleared my throat to plunge in.

She said, "Your throat is dry. Those New York radiators. . . ."

I said, "My throat is very dry."

Aunt Elsie said, "Those New York apartments. They overheat. . . . Anyway, it was a boring, boring week. But you know me, I don't make trouble."

Then I started. "*I* don't want to make trouble," I heard myself say. "But why'd you run out on me? Aunt Elsie I went to see my father. But he wasn't there. What's going on?"

Then there was a crashing sound. Then more silence. Then Aunt Elsie again, "I dropped the phone. I hate these portables. I find they slip." Then she cleared her throat. "Not there?" Then all I heard was her heavy breathing, then coughing and then some crying that sounded like gagging. Then she said, "I know. But I never meant for you to know."

I said, "Know what?"

"Oh, Betsy, do I have the strength to remember?"

I said, "Where is his grave?"

"Where is his grave?" she said. "Is it easy for me to say?"

I had questions to ask Aunt Elsie; but now she was turning it all around and asking me the questions. A stalling tactic, of course, which I recognized immediately. I'd been doing it for years—asking other people questions, disclosing nothing myself.

I said, "Just say where."

"Is it ever so simple, Betsy?"

I said, "Why'd you say he was there?"

"I wanted to protect you. Isn't that me—a protector?"

I thought, I don't know you. I don't know a thing any more.

92

I felt like a big blank infant, knowing only some unnamed ache inside me, knowing only that there was so much I didn't know.

"From what?" I finally said. "I don't care if you cremated him. I don't care about any of that. I just can't take secrets any more."

And Aunt Elsie said, "I'm old, Betsy. Forgive me. Won't you forgive me?"

"Of course," I said. "Just tell me the truth. Where's his grave?"

"Don't hate me. There are some things that are hard to get into. Betsyla, I'm getting old. I got to look out for my health. Don't I?"

"Yes, sweetheart," I said. "But just stay calm and tell me. If I can't ask you for the truth, who can I ask?"

It was a rhetorical question, but she answered it, the only one she answered. "Doreena, ask Doreena. She knows. Don't you think Doreena can help?" And then the line went dead.

I called right back but the same receptionist said she'd just left for the Miami Symphony Senior Citizen Series and wouldn't be back until late. And I couldn't call Doreena—because I didn't know who she was.

It was hard to concentrate on Mitzi's party. Aunt Elsie could be petty but never cruel. Why then had she done what she did? I'm a protector, I heard her say. Was that really it?

Mitzi took our coats and Les led us from the study back into the living room and said, "I love the view in the rain. The 59th Street Bridge is so evocative."

"It *is* lovely," I said. And of course it was. Stretching before us, covered with rain and fog, it looked like a Chinese landscape painting, close yet far, cool yet intimate. But still I couldn't get my aunt from my mind. Queensboro Bridge, she would say, not 59th Street. I thought, on one side, it's called one thing, on the other side another. On one side we say *protection*. On the other we say . . . *deception*? You hid the truth from us. You hid *him* from us.

93

David took my arms and pushed me forward, which, I guess, was becoming David's function more and more—pushing me forward against my backward drift. After the talk with Aunt Elsie, when I started talking about finding the woman named Doreena whom I didn't know, or didn't remember, David had said, Your aunt will call back and explain it all—what happened back then. But it's just that, you know—*back then*. It's not your present life.

I'd said, What if it were your *back then*, David?

"No difference, you or me. Move on."

Now he was moving me on into a crowd of relatives—aunts, uncles, and cousins. And face to face with them, I closed my eyes and willed myself to do it, to move on, to forget my own family, at least for now—Aunt Elsie, my father, Doreena, whoever she was, kin or kith, friend or foe.

David's family. There was something unreal about them all, the cause of which I couldn't quite say. The smiles, the bodies in their orderly lines like chorus dancers, something else as well that made the party seem staged or dreamt. Then the introductions began, the pecks on the cheek, and a sort of friendly chaos started up, dispelling the odd composure.

"Uncle Hal," someone said. "Aunt Shirley." "Uncle Bill, Cousin Lila and the boys." I repeated the names, returned the kisses, tried to link names to faces. And suddenly it worked. My family—thoughts about my aunt, my father—fell away and I felt here with *this* family, spinning about in their swirl. One would say, "I hear you're a local girl, Betsy," or "I hear you're in magazine work." And I would say, "Oh, yes, and you, Uncle Ross, and you, Aunt Helene?"

Cousin Jay had made half a million dollars his first year in general dentistry. Cousin Jay had a wide, white smile like Les, and then looking across the living room and dining room I saw that it was a family of wide smiles. I thought, at least a half of the half million must have come from family business, even with a family discount, that's how straight and bright the teeth in the room were.

There was Uncle Aron, who had a ladies sportswear business and whose philosophy, he said, was that women should accept their hips. "They're mine," he said, gesturing to the women in the room, their bottoms draped in beige crepe. "The A-line is the best friend of women." And when I agreed, he invited me up to the showroom. "35th and Seventh." Any day I wanted.

Aunt Sookie, his wife, said, "You'd better hurry up, Tootsie, because Sook-Ar Sportswear is going bankrupt the first of next month."

I looked down in embarrassment but Uncle Aron said, "Don't feel bad for us, we've stashed away a lot."

There was Aunt Dee-Dee, who had two orthopedists for sons and a daughter married to another top man in ob-gyn, who had between them two tudors and one ranch but in very good taste, two beach houses and two ski houses, again very classic—no phony chalet shlock. Three girls and three boys, all progressing wonderfully both academically and athletically.

Cousin Erik patted the couch and we sat down. "I'm a psychiatrist," he said. Then he told us about his third marriage, or rather his third divorce, how he should have seen it coming when his first two wives became best buddies. Because one night they called his third wife and told her that he threw terrible tantrums and broke valuable items, which he had with the first two but hadn't with the third. But then when he heard about the call, he threw his first tantrum with her—he was so outraged by the gang-up—and then she ended up on their side.

"At first I was depressed—no eaty, no speaky. I'm an analyst but I almost took Prozac, I was so low. Now I'm glad that everything happened. I never was myself with the third."

I said something like, That's too bad.

And Cousin Erik said, "Are you on the couch?"

I said, "No? I'm not?" I felt a stab of alarm. Was I that mixed up? Was I slipping off the couch without knowing it? But then I realized what he meant by "on the couch" and I said, "No, no. I've never had time or money for that."

And he said, "Let me know if you want to try. I like to get family members rolling."

David and I said, "Thanks." Erik said, "Be yourself." And I walked across the room and sat down next to Les on the corner of the sectional.

Les asked, how did I like everyone, and I said everyone seemed so nice, although I really wasn't sure about what I thought. He said he had seen me talking to Uncle Aron and Aunt Suki so maybe I'd already heard. LeMitz would be going out of business just as Sook-Ar would, the menswear side of the family business.

"The times," I said. I felt, Tell me no more. I felt leaden with all the details and confessions, which was odd in a sense, because that's precisely what I was looking for from my own family. The truth finally out.

"No, it's me. I'm not a businessman. I look like one but I'm not. It's OK though. I'll be happier now. We'll visit you kids. We'll go to Florida. You'll visit us when you get back from Central America."

I nodded and Les said, "Really, I'm excited about the true me emerging. The true me is a vegetable."

Maybe it was the wine or the build-up of exhaustion—Les suddenly didn't look like Les. His face began to ripple and darken—a julienned beet vegetable, I thought. I shook my head to dispel the crazy vision.

"By the way, call me Dad," he said.

I nodded again. I was staring at Les's face to see if he was himself again. But his face seemed to be narrowing now, his brow deepening, his skin bronzing. Suddenly he looked like my father. Dad, I thought. Could it be you?

I must have said, "Dad," out loud. For Les said, "I'm glad you feel comfortable, Cookie. Think of us as your family now. You know, Cookie, I'm a dreamer too, like I hear from Davie your dad was. In my fashion . . . in my fashion fashion," he laughed. "I mean, it wasn't good enough to build an award-winning ladies sportswear concern. I had to establish a menswear side, too. Give men the same fashion opportunities. You know, a Man of La Mancha syndrome. I overextend."

He pointed to the men in the room. "They're mine. We brought in the black blazer. It's dressier than the blue blazer and I'm proud of the look. . . . But extending into menswear cost me the business."

Uncle Arnie came over to the couch and said, "I hear business is lousy. I'd give you the shirt off my back, except *you* gave it to *me*, Les."

Les laughed and fingered Arnie's black twill, like a lover. I thought had Aron and Les not dressed every member of the family in their own outfits, the businesses might still be thriving. But no one seemed to care. It all seemed inconsequential, like the talk and events in dreams. I'm dying. Have you eaten your french fries? We're bankrupt. Heard any new jokes?

And then I realized the source of the dreaminess I had felt when I'd arrived. They were all dressed in the same clothing, the women in Aron's beige, the men in Les's black twill. The only two colors for family members, except for David and me. In my red caftan, I suddenly felt like a clown.

I laughed out loud. On the one hand it was very funny—this family, held together with their countless confidences, stitched together in their common costume. And then I felt like crying. On the other hand it was very touching. In our family they dressed you only when you died.

I looked at the bridge again—the tangled lines, the misty blur. What was the truth about anyone? About this family, about *my* family? This person, that person. Were my father here beside me now, what would he tell me? 220 hitters, he'd probably say. Something like that. I closed my eyes and saw him, heard him, his repertoire of judgments about everyone else: What you basically have here are 220 hitters.

Until I grew up and went to baseball games on dates, I never knew what that meant though I'd retained the phrase in my

own arsenal for years. 220 hitters. Nothing much. Or all–right-
niks. Which meant all wrong, no good. What does it all stand
for? my father would say were he there in Mitzi's rooms, gesturing to the pale couches, the perfect outfits.

They stand for nothing, my father used to say, the times he
lived with us, out of jail, out on bail. He'd be pointing out a
smartly dressed family, perhaps an insurance broker and his wife
and daughters on their way to synagogue in white suits and
white hats. As a child I learned to nod because I wanted things
smooth and nice the times he was with us, but inside I never
understood the failings of such people. Nor, I think, did Marie,
who, when she was with us, would point out the intricacies of
style, what was smart, what was smashing, what was snazzy. All
of which Sam reversed with a word or two. Lightweights, dead-
beats, 220 hitters. Zip.

Standing in Mitzi and Les's living room, I thought about all
those people my father had made me reject. Stephanie Eastman,
the most popular girl in my first and second grade class. I looked
at Cousin Lila, her careful curls, her tailored jacket and was
reminded of Stephanie—announcing one afternoon with the
largesse of royalty that she was planning to come to my house
to play that afternoon. My heart raced, when she said, I'll visit
you today, and I pressed her frail body tight against me, feeling
the barrel buttons of her car coat dig into my chest. She was an
imperious little thing, decked out in ringlets and crinolines, but
she did nothing wrong, as far as I could tell, when she came to
our apartment. She ate her Mallomars and drank her milk and
placed her glass in the sink. She asked Sam what he did profes-
sionally. Her father was by profession an orthodonist, by avocation a stamp collector. Sam said he was by vocation an organizer
and convict, by avocation a mystic, seeing worlds that didn't
exist. Forget that one, he said later. She stands for nothing, that
one. I should do him a favor and write her off. And it was only
in secret that I met with Stephanie, and only occasionally, when
she'd announce that her afternoon was free suddenly and she'd

be willing to do homework with me at the back of the library, where she wouldn't be seen with me.

My afternoons were busy anyway with Sam's friends, or rather my friends, the ones Sam had chosen for me. Alexis Cato, the daughter of a superintendent up the street, the only black child in the neighborhood. Or Cora O'Brien, who wore thick glasses and painted murals of wild horses on her bedroom walls. The kid's got character, my father would say. Or Leslie Doray, a terrible stutterer who sang operatic arias flawlessly. (Sam eventually broke the stutter by training Leslie to sing her sentences, then to use a rather unobtrusive tune for everyday conversation.) Brenda Silver, an expert on aborigines, who had cerebral palsy and a genius I.Q. My chosen friends—the neighborhood rejects.

Cora's father was an engineer on the old Third Avenue el train, which ran near our house, and it was Sam's habit, when he was home, to line us up afternoons on a bench in the park just below the tracks, to wave at Al O'Brien. Cheer the man on, he would say, borrowing Al's brogue. We all would wave, and Brenda would raise her steel brace in salute. To the man who headed the grievance committee of the Transit Workers Union local, and his train, which serviced working-class neighborhood after working-class neighborhood from Yorkville to the North-East Bronx. Al's an unsung hero, my father would say. A hero of the common man. And I would nod because Cora was there, but also because I was afraid of Sam's disappointment if I spoke the truth—told him that I found Stephanie's orthodontist father more appealing than Al O'Brien, who smelled of sweat and track dust, and that I secretly wished Dr. Eastman would wire my whole mouth with steel so I'd look rich.

Stephanie's family's crime was that they were petit bourgeois. As children, when Sam was around, we heard it many times a day. This one's a selfish bourgeois. That one's a petit bourgeois nonentity. Bourgeois, petit bourgeois—to my father, we came to understand, it meant they cared not a speck for the "common man," but to us bourgeois seemed a potent obscenity. And after Sam was on TV one time and some kid pinned Tommy in the schoolyard and said, Your father's a commie fuck, Tommy spit in his face and said, Your mother's a whore. Your father's a bourgeois, if you want to know the truth. What's that? the kid said. Someone who sucks assholes for a living, you ignoramus, my brother cried.

In truth if no one was looking, I loved the freaky friends my father had picked for me. We constructed stage sets for operas and plays we'd written, performing them along the beach at Pelham Bay. But when Stephanie and the other girls saw me crossing the movie lobby with the group on Saturday afternoons, I'd separate from my best friends, and hang out at the candy counter, in case the cool girls wanted to talk to me. They had a claim on me that the people who loved me never did, and for years I lied to my father, saying I detested the popular kids, meanwhile meeting them in secret and feeding them different lies that put me in a better light. Like Sam was just our stepfather, whom our mother had promised to divorce as soon as our real father, a POW in Korea, was released from Communist prison.

David squeezed me from behind and said, "Hi, Mopey. You'll be all right, all right. I can tell you're moping about the past. So they didn't dress all the same in your family and confide whether they were happy with their number 1 and number 2 this morning. Who cares? I like you anyway."

Then Mitzi appeared with a tray of champagne and said, "Let's toast the kids. Short and simple. Be happy."

And then the room echoed with all the clinks and her words. Be happy, be happy. It really looked like a Broadway production, the final number. Be happy, Be happy, Be happy, in black and beige, and the lights off the bridge and the sparkling glass. And again I couldn't stop laughing. It was so corny. Then, like before, I felt myself on the other side: It was also so simple and direct. In my family no one would ever say, Be happy. You'd have to hear what Marx and Weber said about happiness, and Eugene Debs and Mother Jones. The whole point being, of course, that there was no such thing as being happy. As long as there was exploitation in the world, personal happiness was a myth, a bourgeois myth. A flimsy dream built on the backs of . . . people who never even got up to bat.

Now I looked at all the aunts and uncles and cousins with their good will and best wishes: Aron and Sookie and Erik and Hal and Shirley and Bill and Arnie and Lila and the boys. And I thought, if I said, I'm coming down to meet you, to see your fall collection, let's say, you'd be there—35th and Seventh. I thought of all the street corners I had stood on for secret meetings with Sam. I remembered one Christmas Eve waiting for him outside a Macy's in Queens, the busy street finally growing hushed, and then just Tommy and me and the Salvation Army Santa Claus left on the corner. Daddy? I said to the Santa—the times he met us after he went underground, our father had appeared in disguise. Daddy, is that you? I said. But Santa Claus said, Sorry kids, taking off his hat and wig and beard from a face I'd never seen before, putting on an old fedora. I remembered Tommy patting my back as I cried. He couldn't help it, Bet. If he didn't come, it's 'cause it wasn't safe. He would have come if he could have. You know that. Sha, sha, sha.

I looked at them lined up there, my father's enemies, smiling at me with their big friendly mouths. Small-time, Betsy, I heard my father say. Not the big-time enemy. But not to be trusted nonetheless. With the future of the world.

They were gathering around the bar, signing something.

"We didn't know what you could use, so it's just a little *gelt* in this hysterical card which yours truly selected and our signatures with little personal touches attached," Aunt Lila called.

"Yeah, like hurry up and get married and get pregnant," Uncle Bill said, pointing to his message.

It was a giant card, as big as a tabloid, in the shape of a little house. *Congratulations,* it said on the outside. On the inside: *On shacking up.*

Les called, "I'm going to sign this Dad if you don't mind."

"Never mind Sylvia Pines or Syl. You're family, so it's Sookie or Sook, from now on, Toots," Aunt Sookie said. And she took the pen from Les and scrawled, "Good luck in Guatemala and after."

I imagined Tommy laughing, calling, You're such an asshole. My father snickering, Look what you've come to, Betsy.

They're so nice, I thought. These all-rightnicks, 220 hitters. "So sweet," I said, as each one showed me their signature and message.

I began to laugh. I don't care what you think! I was talking to my father. Were he here, he'd say, So they sign a shmaltzy card. They're the kind of people who would sign anything just to get on with the party.

You bet, I laughed to myself. Birthday cards and bon voyage cards. Occasions which you were never around for. Because you wouldn't sign. Which started all the trouble. What's a little signature? I remember Aunt Elsie saying. And a few names? Just tell them the ones they know already.

But he wouldn't. "He had to make a stink."

"Who made a stink?" David whispered.

"You know who," I said.

David took my arm, led me through the foyer into the study. "Maybe it's been too much for you."

"Where is he?" I said.

"He's dead, Bet."

"How do you know that?"

"No one told you otherwise."

"No one told me anything but lies."

Early the next morning when I opened the front door to get the *New York Times*, a telegram was sitting on the doormat. Who sends telegrams in the last decade of the twentieth century? But before I could finish asking the question, I knew the answer.

Suzyla. It's not what you think. Let's talk. Aunt Elsie.

Aunt Elsie, I wanted to say. I can't begin to think of what to think. So just tell me. And I dialed my aunt's number but again there was no answer.

It was only seven in the morning, but Elsie was an early riser. She just wasn't picking up. The telegram was for effect—to look like she was keeping in touch.

I called my brother, but got his machine again. "What do you know, Tommy, that I don't know?" I said.

At eight when David woke, I said, "How can I go without knowing?"

"If you don't find out the story by the time we're ready to go, you'll find out when we're gone. They have phones outside of the USA."

"She won't pick up. And Tommy's not calling me back. There's some big secret no one will tell me. But I've got to know the truth now."

"Bet, this is crazy. How do you see this little movie of yours playing out? You meet your little old aunt on a dark corner with lots of fog and flickering lights and you beat the truth from her?"

I laughed. I knew it sounded crazy. The TRUTH. Now. What do you know that I don't know?

"Next you're going to tell me, 'Goodbye, my love.'"

"Try to understand, David. It's the only thing that makes sense for me . . . ," I heard myself say.

"What the hell are you talking about?"

"I can't go, David. I love you but I can't go. Not now." I hadn't known I was going to say it, but the words popped out. "I can't go."

"Betsy, you're writing a script for a very bad movie. People don't talk like this in real life. Look, Betsy, it's me. Remember me? As in you and me?"

I felt his breath, smelled his morning smell—spicy like mustard.

"Of course I remember." I began to cry. "I can't help myself, David. Look at me, I'm not myself."

"Why do I think this is not just you staying here for an extra few weeks, seeing some people, making some calls. Why do I think this is a big, big deal?"

He wrapped himself in the sheet, looking battered and bandaged. "I can't believe this is happening."

"David, I don't know where he is. Or *if* he is. That's a big deal."

"Why is it a big deal? He's gone from your life. And has been for decades. In time you'll know why. Give it time."

And I nodded, like I had when all this began. Go away. Happily ever after. New life. Then and now, what David said made sense. And no sense, too.

"What are you afraid of, Betsy?"

I shook my head. "I don't know. I'm afraid of things I don't know. . . ."

"Betsy, you know *me*. Our life together. "

I kept nodding but I couldn't stop crying.

David said, "Don't cry, Bet. Just think. Why do you have to do this? I'm trying to understand. I'm trying really hard. Remember me? I 'm the guy that tries really hard . . . really hard."

But I went on crying and so did he as we repeated phrases, like drunks.

"Soon, soon," I said again and again.

And he said over and over, "How do you know? Maybe you'll never come back."

"Believe me. I promise. It's only for a while. I'll meet you there. Soon."

"How do you know that? That it will be soon?"

"I know. It won't be long. We'll be together. Believe me."

Old words I hadn't heard in decades. *It won't be long. We'll be together. Believe me.* Over and over I said the same thing, repeating words I hadn't heard in decades. The words *he'd* said. When he left and never came back.

Outside it was a drab December Monday. David said he'd go

back to his studio until he left, leave for Mexico City from there. It would be easier that way. We'd avoid goodbyes.

"Not a goodbye—just a delay," I said. But I could hear in my voice how far away I already was.

While David packed, I walked along the river to 110th Street and back, and when I got back to the apartment, he wasn't there. His things were gone; his keys were on the kitchen counter as if he were a thoughtful weekend guest. A two-word note was on the refrigerator door: *Love David*. A simple goodbye, of course, with a comma forgotten. But for a moment it seemed a command, a reminder to love him, as if I could ever forget.

6: Visit to the Doctor

I KNEW HIS NUMBER by heart and dialed it quickly. But when he picked up after only one ring, I was totally unprepared. I heard the old voice, which I hadn't heard in decades, and my throat began to fill with tears and my voice began to fade.

"It's Betsy," was all I managed, sounding like Brando's Don Corleone.

Like it hadn't been fifteen years, but only days that had passed since we'd last spoken, he said, "Betsy, Betsy. You OK, Betsy? Something wrong physically?"

Then, still weeping, I said that I needed to see him. That I needed to know the truth. I was going to find my father. Dead or alive. Nothing was going to stop me.

And he said, "You sound like him—'nothing's going to stop me.' A big shot. And look what happened, Betsy."

"What happened, Dr. Horowitz?"

"Come on over, darling. You'll calm down. We'll sit down, we'll talk. Like two rational human beings, we'll discuss the entire situation."

Leo Horowitz's waiting room was changed, which should have been no surprise. The last time I was here, I was seventeen. I remember the day well for I was intending, after my yearly exam, to ask to be fitted for a diaphragm. I had practiced what to say: I need protection. But then I lost courage and said nothing.

I always lost courage with Dr. Horowitz. I feared bothering

him with my problems—enlarged tonsils, itchy legs in the winter, breasts that I thought were growing at different rates. My fertility. For Horowitz, we were told, was a hero. Our hero, my father would announce when Horowitz would appear. And then my father would blush and look generally humbled. Because my father's occasional awe was usually saved for a member of the working class, the likes of Al O'Brien, I'd search his face for little twists of irony. But there were none—just the bright flush of pure reverence.

As for Horowitz, there was nothing in his face, his clothes, his walk that made you think *hero*. He had the sway back and dome belly of a blundering toddler, pigeon toes and a shapeless face that reminded one of Bisquick. He had none of the polish of conventional great men, a president or senator, let's say, or the confident oddity of ugly great men like Schweitzer or Einstein or Stephen Jay Gould. Yet a hero he was. A great hero. He had saved my father's life. And so, bourgeois or not, you honored him. You did not bother him with passing aches and pains, with self-indulgent notions of deformity.

It was sudden, Horowitz's rise to heroism. A dermatologist whose older brothers had died—one while doctoring members of the International Brigade in the Spanish Civil War, and one in a Nazi ambush in Tunis—Leo Horowitz, due to age, temperament and an inconsolable grieving mother, missed out on wartime heroics. He gave his mind and hands to patients in an East Side hospital and office; but his heart remained with his dead brothers and their causes. Then one morning in 1952, riding the subway to his practice on East 64th Street, Horowitz read an article in the *New York Times* and, by the time he looked up, both his and my father's fates had been altered. The article was about a union leader who had refused to sign a loyalty oath, and then was jailed for contempt of Congress. The article quoted the union leader as saying that prison doctors had failed to keep his heart from beating twice as fast as it should; and private doctors were afraid to come to the jail to treat him, fearing guilt by association, political harassment and damage to their livelihood. According to the *Times*, the unionist's wife, Marie, had said: "Unless he's treated he'll be dead by May1 or Labor Day at the latest. I mean, we're all dying of fear in the U.S. of A. But I'm just so surprised to see doctors, who have been trained to face frightening things from livers to entrails, scared."

Horowitz passed his stop that day, and kept riding south. At the City Hall subway station, he called his secretary and told her to cancel his appointments, and then he walked five blocks east and entered the Tombs. After three hours of talking to wardens and judges across the street at the Federal Courthouse, he was allowed to see my father and then, later in the day, to return and feed him digitalis and diuretics.

And that was that. My father's heart settled down, and Horowitz became a hero—a hero to the second power. A hero's hero. Both men agreed that Horowitz had been saved by the act as well. After Harold and Ernest, he felt his life amounted to zip, my father would say of Horowitz. We jazzed him up. We jazzed you up, Leo. And Horowitz would nod. I lived on the surface before I met this character, he'd say. In his book, *Beneath the Skin of Capitalism*, Horowitz wrote: *I lost my livelihood and my old life on that subway ride but I feel I gained in the long run. Isn't it worth anything to find certainty and justice? What else is there to live for?*

Certainly for Horowitz, after the day in the Tombs there was nothing else. His old practice fell away. And his new friends— lefty activists in labor, civil rights, peace—became his patients, and what they couldn't give him in money, they gave him in spirit. And he gave them his new confidence and vigor, slapping their arms and backs—You're all right, you'll live—sending them back to the struggle with renewed belief in their own strength.

Today I looked around the waiting room, thinking about the last time I was here, seeking protection. Just as I was now, in a sense. Back then, I must have looked particularly disheartened, sitting on the examination table with my sprawling hormonal discontent. For Horowitz, instead of slapping my thigh and saying, You're all right, you'll live, had said: You're all right? Your period's regular? You need help? I could help. I was as usual too scared to bother him with my petty needs, though this one had seemed more pressing than the others. And I was scared, too, I think, of his sudden fall from certainty into anxiety. So I said, I'm fine, and gathered up my clothes and hurried from his office. Still I remember feeling relief that Horowitz would help, which I took to mean give me an abortion if I needed one. And pride—Horowitz would break the law for *me*. I, too, would inspire his greatness. I remember riding the subway home in a state of odd delight. It was all fantastical—I wasn't sleeping with men yet. I had wanted a diaphragm more for my relationship with women than with men. Everyone was getting fitted and more than anything, of course, I wanted to be like everyone. But, then, years later, it wasn't Horowitz that I turned to. By then Horowitz had started his no-pay mobile clinics in Newark and Trenton, so I left my fate to a small doctor with hairy hands in a back street in Miami. A tiny scheming man, not a great hero, but with lots of time for the likes of me.

Now it was years later, and Esther, Horowitz's redheaded wife, was no longer sitting at the desk by the door. Instead there was a woman whose hair and clothes and eyes were all the same pale bronze. She said, "The doctor is expecting you, Ms. Vogel."

I thought of Esther: Betsy, come here so I can see you. Like a Picasso. A classic period Picasso. I have never been remotely classically beautiful, and Esther's comments always told me more about her than about me. Her blind enthusiasm. But that was true of all of my father's gang in those days.

Now the receptionist said, "Take a seat. He'll only be a minute."

I sat down on a backless black bench against the wall, under a poster from a museum I had never heard of, and picked up a magazine. *People Magazine*. In the Fifties and Sixties, it was *National Geographic*, a coded message, to me, in those days: I care. I'm with them—the black and yellow and unclothed and unfed.

Now *People*, which said, in a sense, just the opposite: *These* are my people, Mick and Cher and Keanu. I put down the magazine featuring an article on Tom Cruise's gym workout. Not so much because I was morally offended—what after all was *Big Apple* but a romp through chic-dom, and a less spirited romp at that. And not so much because I generally tried not to read *People*, so as not to be tempted to plagiarize, a temptation when you're writing about people written about already and then some, and you really don't care. No—I put down the magazine because again I was scared. This was OK for me, but it wasn't OK for Horowitz. I was afraid Horowitz himself would be hopelessly changed. In a minute he would emerge from his office in Italian slacks, an open neck, gold chains. Hi there, he would say. So what do you think? They're getting divorced? They're seeing each other exclusively? Their abs are getting somewhere?

But I needed the old Horowitz now—certain and reassuring. Heroic Horowitz. The man who saved my father. Once again I needed him to determine my father's fate, to make some pronouncement—living or dead, here or there. I was turning forty, but sitting in Dr. Horowitz's waiting room, I might have been ten. My life was slipping from me just as it had before. Only this time I was letting it go, letting David go, the only certainty I had ever really known. Forty and giving up what I was sure was my last chance for love and home, to find someone I wasn't even sure existed any more.

I leaned against the wall, waiting for my father's old friend to appear, and my stomach registered the same fear I'd felt waiting on the bench in Foley Square to hear my father's fate at the last trial. I felt the same old churning. What was I waiting to hear now? Living or dead? But something more. Loyal, disloyal? To *me*? Was that it now?

Then Horowitz was standing before me. So much was the same. The plaid flannel shirt under his white coat, the knit tie, the brown corduroy slacks—the uniform of the intellectual left-winger back then, but in Horowitz always marked by an added vigor, the plaid big and bold like a hunter's, the corduroy wide and thick. But so much was different. The coloring was all wrong. The shirt was faded and limp as if it had been tossing in a hot clothes dryer for the past twenty years. And Horowitz was all gray—his moustache, his beard, both of which were new, his skin, whatever of it you could see, the hair on his head. I felt alarmed. The old Horowitz was bald, the new Horowitz had hair—a wig, a patchwork quilt of gray fuzz, like stitched-together mouse skins.

And he was shy, this Horowitz, which he'd never been, and I was shy back, when I didn't want to be anymore, when I wanted bold candor and clarity at last. "Betsy," he said, and I said, "Dr. Horowitz." He said, "After all these years, you can call me Leo, Betsy, Betsy." I said, "Leo, Leo." Then he said, "This is Kim." And I shook the receptionist's hand.

I thought, Well, I'm glad Esther's not here. She'd hated paperwork and I was glad they could finally afford to hire someone. I thought of Horowitz's financial hardships over the years, my family's contribution toward them. For after that first visit to the Tombs, Horowitz continued to treat my father—in Lewisburg and Leavenworth, Attica and Sing Sing. And the press continued to cover it, with headlines like, SKIN DOCTOR GRAFTS NEW LIFE ON RED ALLY, and that sort of thing, leaving Horowitz almost as penniless as us.

"Anything more you need done?" Kim said. Again I searched Horowitz's face for the old Horowitz. I closed my eyes and tried to imagine what he would say. Not a thing, dear. Go home, dear. That was Horowitz's style. Commanding and certain, but suffused with the fluid humanism that marked my father's whole crowd. Especially with employees, whose subordinate position they would attempt to overturn with phrases bestowing respect. Señorita Martinez, my father called the girl who mopped up at the hotel off the Avenida Reforma, though she was no more than fourteen years old, hardly five feet, eighty pounds at most, and called Flaquita (Little Skinny One) by everyone else. Mrs.

Hughes, he called the woman who came to help when Marie went away the first time. Mrs. McGovern, the one after Mrs. Hughes disappeared. Good day, Mrs. Hughes, Goodnight Mrs. McGovern, insisting all the time that they call him Sam, that they let him lend them money which he had borrowed in the first place to feed us, insist that they leave early to avoid the press of other domestics working for exploitative, thoughtless people. But Horowitz said nothing. He simply beckoned me into the office, leaving Kim to apply a coat of nail polish.

The office, too, was changed, yet unchanged. There was the same big, old desk, which always seemed too large to have ever come through a door. The oxblood leather chairs. But there were flimsy chrome standing lamps arching precariously from the corners, and posters of flowers replacing the Moses Soyer prints of weary modern dancers.

Through the doors, the examination room looked much the same. I remembered years of embarrassment, enduring Horowitz's hands palpating my bare belly, or smacking my backside after a shot, or his head bent over my chest, ignoring my young breasts, catching the rhythm of my racing heart. Then seeing him the next week at a civil liberties fundraiser, both of us saying hello as if he had never seen me naked on the table. A good crowd, he'd say. We'll do all right. And I'd nod and hope he'd forget me for the rest of the evening, forget to call on me to help with the after-dinner collection. It was bad enough being there, but having to walk back and forth before the crowd, gathering the envelopes, Sam's forlorn child, was unbearable. Especially with Horowitz watching.

And here he was again, watching me. "How many years?" he said. "And to what do I owe the honor of this visit? What is this about finding your father?"

"I went out to Beth Israel," I said. "I know he's not there."

Horowitz said nothing.

"What do *you* know?" I said.

"More than I want to know."

"Did you see him dead?"

He shook his head. "We had lost touch."

"Until he died," I said, "we kept up as best as we could. We met up with him in different cities. He called. Didn't he ever call you?"

"Up to a point."

"Up to what point?"

"1966 . . . or '67 . . . I think. But just let it go, Betsy."

"Let what go?"

"It's not easy to explain Sam to anyone. Listen, Betsy, he went too far. He's your father and it's not pleasant to perform a post-mortem before family, but he went too damn far. Even for us, and we were hardly your John Q. Public, you understand."

I said, "What did he do?" I was clutching the chair's arms, afraid to hear.

Horowitz said, "Why are you dwelling on the past, Betsy?"

"Because I thought one thing and it's not true. He's not where I was told he was. So anything could be true. He could even be alive. . . ."

"Look here," he said. "I'm going to show you something," and he beckoned me to a wall of gray file cabinets that were shedding a coat of white spray paint. He riffled through the files, clipped something to the screen on the wall.

"Look," he said. "That's Sam." It was an x-ray, blinking and winking like an old friend in an old home movie. "Sam's heart," he said. "Three times the size of a normal heart, thirty years ago. He's dead. Add to the picture the cigarettes. Add to that some booze, I'd imagine. We're talking a 50 percent chance of mortality even with normal factors for that age group. With this heart, the cigarettes, the rest, we're talking 98 percent. He's dead."

"Are you sure?"

"He's dead, don't worry."

It was like the old Horowitz was back but flipped upside down. You're all right, don't worry. You'll live, don't worry. But now everything was reversed. Don't worry, he's dead. Is this what he tells his patients now? I thought. Does he slap their backs and say, It's all right, don't worry. The end is near.

"Are you really sure?"

I was staring at him, him at me. Then he looked down. "I don't know," he whispered. "I guess he could have lasted. If he took his medicine. But I don't know if he took his medicine. I was no longer looking after him. Betsy, I've made myself not think about him for such a long time."

"You cared for him for such a long time."

"He should have come back to us."

"Maybe he couldn't."

The gray film was flickering, darkening. Horowitz was biting his lip, straining for composure.

I said, "Such a big heart. That's what everyone always said. A 'bleeding heart' For all the workers in the local. Their families. Every injustice that caught his attention." Then I started laughing, a tinny laugh. I said, "Can that do it—triple your heart size—huffing and puffing for every last asshole on earth?"

Horowitz said, "He got carried away in the end. I mean maybe I'm entirely ridiculous. I wear a wig. But I know who I am. I mean, here I am for anyone to see, anyone who wants to. I'm not much anymore, but there it is."

I took his hand and he said, "Horrible rings," nodding to his fingers. "She bought them, Kim. She's hopelessly limited but it's so wonderfully obvious. She takes me to shopping malls in New Jersey after work. We shop, we eat in the food court. I hold her hand with these ugly paws. I do believe that Esther understands. Besides I'm fairly depressing to have around these days. It's distracting, this new life—totally meaningless and totally distracting."

I stroked his hand.

"It's all very ugly. I understand it must all seem very ugly to you. Ugly, pointless. If Sam had ever gotten to this point, he would have had the courage to check out. When it got this ridiculous." He laughed.

"That's the difference between me and Sam. I latched onto big ideas, but I knew if it got hopeless to let go. So I'm pathetic but not dangerous. But he held on to his ideas and blew them up bigger and bigger, like some giant balloon. You know that your father was never a member of the Communist Party. He was too much of an individualist, couldn't function with their kind of discipline and authority. He was a premature anti-Stalinist with the first rumblings of the Stalin trials. But he respected a lot of American communists and socialists who had done so much to build the unions, the civil rights movement, and so on. He knew that most of them were obsessed with a better America like he was. Yeah, a lot of people admired Russia, but I didn't know one soul who was interested in a violent revolution. When the Taft-Hartley required all union officials to sign loyalty oaths, Sam not only refused to declare that he wasn't then nor had ever been, but even thought about joining the Party openly. In defiance. Everyone is scared and quitting, and he's joining. He never did but you get the idea. No small gestures for Sammy. And then it got even worse. His ideas finally carried him far away like some flying monster."

I felt totally confused, my mind too weary for his similes. I needed clear, simple phrases. He's here, he's not here. "What happened?" I said. "Tell me very simply. What he did. Where he is."

"I don't know the details."

"Tell me what you know."

"He went over the edge. They say he did things."

"What things?"

"Destroyed things."

"Oh, who says? Really, what things?"

But Horowitz just sat there, shrugging.

"And you believe it?"

He shrugged again. He didn't come back even when times changed and he could have. After a while everyone who disappeared came back. I don't mean just the CP leaders who went underground to escape the Smith Act. Thousands of people on the Left, or friends and family of people on the Left, lost their jobs and disappeared into other cities, or Canada, or Mexico or Europe for new lives. But lots came back. That is the ones who hadn't killed themselves or died early deaths." He laughed a miserable laugh that sounded like a gargle. "That loyalty oath was repealed. The Smith Act was overturned. HUAC went out of business. It was a different world. He could have gotten a deal."

The climate changed. I laughed. That's what he told us when he left. I'll be back when the climate changes. He left in the winter and I always thought my father would return in the warm weather—when the trees budded, he'd be there. That first spring, I played hooky most days, waiting for him, until Boomie explained about political climate.

"Look, Betsy. They said that's what he did and I believed them. It's not as if he called and told me another story. And there are other stories, too. . . ."

"Like what?"

Horowitz looked away. "I don't believe those other stories, Betsy. I refuse to believe them. But whatever it was, it was ages ago. Betsy, let it go."

"Maybe he's in jail somewhere. Maybe he's living on the street." I thought of the bum in the cardboard house. Yukio in the Bentleys. "Maybe he needs us."

"He was beyond needing anyone, I think. Or at least knowing that he needed anyone. Bummy, in his own way, was more together in the end. A small-time hood, but he took care of you kids."

"Not Bummy, Boomie," I said.

"Your uncle played it small, but he played it straight. Your father had to play it big all the time. So who was the hero, really? The bum or the big-time idealist? You have to wonder."

I said, "Boomie wasn't a bum."

"I know, I know," he said. "I'm just excited."

116

"Anyway, you were the hero to Sam."

"Yes, because I saved *him*. So *he* could save the *world*. Don't you see, I was just the service mechanic. Sam was the big guy and we all knew it. In the height of the late 40s Red Scare he won the presidency of the local. Then from jail, he kept fighting. To repeal Taft Hartley. To keep the union in the AFL, which was tossing out all 'disloyal' unions like rotten eggs. To repeal the anti-communist laws, which had silenced labor. All commendable in my book. But then he went too far. I believe that. The other stuff I don't believe. . . ."

I said, "What other stuff? Who else can I talk to?"

"Your aunt has her theories, I'm sure. You could talk to her. But if I were you I'd give up."

I shook my head. "I can't. I'm not sure why, but I can't." Tossing in uncertainty all those years. And just when I thought I had a grip on my own life, uncertainty again? "I'm sure of only one thing right now—I can't give this up."

"Betsy. It will only break your heart."

"Why? What do you know?"

He shrugged again. The certain Dr. Horowitz shrugged again.

I said, "Who's Doreena?"

"The girlfriend. Wasn't that her name?"

"I don't know. I didn't know there was a girlfriend."

"You really don't know much. Well, you're really better off."

"He left us for a girlfriend?" He's alive and living with this Doreena? I thought. Or he's dead, he died in her arms? My chest was aching like it hadn't in decades, with miserable, shameful, self-pitying thoughts. Daddy, I thought, why don't you love us? Why do you pay more attention to everyone else? The carpenters. Their families with their disgusting sick kids. The people in Just America who call and sit around all the time eating our food even though we're poor. And now *her*? Your girlfriend with her ugly name.

Leo shook his head. "A girlfriend. I wish it were that simple."

He stood up and walked over to the screen. "Big hearted,

weak hearted. It's all mixed up. It's hard to say, he was this, he was that. But it's all over, anyway. When I was around him, I felt so sure of everything. But it wasn't just the politics. It was feeling personally powerful. Like I made a difference in this fucked-up world. Now the few times I'm sure of anything, I'm too tired to do anything. A genocide here, a famine there. Like my mother used to say to Harold and Ernest, 'What's it to you?' That's my mentality now. I pay no attention. When I was with your father, every injustice was a personal crisis.

I really may find him," I said.

Horowitz shrugged. "I doubt it, honey. But if you do, would you do me a favor? Would you give me a call? Because I miss that rascal more than I can say."

Yukio came to take his things and I said, "Just take my whole apartment." I wouldn't be back. I put some clothes and papers and books in storage, and left him the rest.

Alan left a message, "Get your *tush* in or you're fired." I left a message back: "I'm fired. Thank you." I meant it.

Then I called Aunt Elsie and told her I was on my way. To talk.

7: Florida Aunt

FOURTEEN HOURS of gagging on the smell of recycled toilet and writhing from the need to pee. I was thirteen and Tommy was fifteen and we were taking the Greyhound bus to see our father. Thanksgiving in Cleveland. A rich uncle was flying us out, I told my school friends. Every rocky mile, as my stomach flipped and my bladder dropped, I'd try to imagine how he'd look. Knowing we'd be leaving soon, being with him was fraught with pain; but finding him was pure joy—that moment in the depot when we'd discover his old eyes and smile, in yet another new disguise. A man with red hair and a red beard, a bald man with black glasses, a hobo in a cap. Our father's familiar features in strange people in strange cities.

We'd always take buses to meet up with our father, and so it felt fitting now to start my search on the Greyhound heading for Miami. The minute we pulled out of Port Authority, I felt his presence. The people's transportation, he'd say when we met him in this or that bus station. Now, I studied the people across the aisle and recalled my father's coaching in reading the signs of oppression. A woman whose crimson hands folded on her bible said domestic worker and praying to make ends meet; a man whose dusty boots spread before him said tired and construction; a mother whose home-made sandwiches for her kids and paperback book in a recycled wrapping paper cover for herself said, We get by—but just.

Awake and asleep, as a child, I'd dream of sweater sets, sparkling orthodonture, and other "bourgeois" affects, to lift me from poverty and shame. But when my father would talk about a new world for all people, his eyes turning from gray-green to emerald as he spoke, I couldn't help but warm to his vision. In my father's new world, there would be no more swollen ankles, calloused hands, worried brows, worn pants and coats—all those marks of suffering that my time with him on streets and trains and buses had imprinted on my brain. When Uncle Boomie tucked us in at night, promising us the beach and amusement parks really soon, and Aunt Elsie tiptoed from our room claiming a new fox trot or lindy record would be ours the next time we went to Fordham Road, I'd think, ungratefully, But our father promises a whole new world when he gets back. Then I'd fall off to warm, fuzzy dreams of a fairer world, in which angora and cashmere, full bellies and peace awaited *everyone*. And when we traveled on buses beside the people, to meet our father, Tommy and I would tell ourselves that we were part of a special brigade—enduring the fumes of human secretions and excretions, to meet the man who would one day produce the brand new world.

The last few times we saw him, our father would say that he'd like, one day, to organize in bus stations. For more bathrooms? I said once, with full sincerity. For national elections probably, he said. Or large social justice campaigns. There was less fear on buses and in depots, he'd noticed. More openness. People won't be afraid to take my leaflets, he said. Or bring them home: They can say they *found* them on a bus. Maybe he could live in a depot. Had my father lost his mind somewhere along the way? For the first time now, I found myself wondering, remembering his later schemes. His napkin campaigns. Wrapping tips for the diner waitress in little napkins on which he'd written messages: *Peace is good,* war *is bad.* Or, *War kills so let's kill war for good. Everyone should have a job to call their own. Civil liberties—we own them by law.* My father, who'd always spoken eloquently, reduced to small desperate messages headed for the garbage can. Had he wandered off to madness? Had he and my mother, in the later years, exchanged secret messages on moonbeams? Had I lost my mind too, riding in a bus, sloshing in old memories and new terrors? Imagining him there at the end of the ride. My father with red hair. No hair. Whitened skin. Tanned skin. No skin. Just bones.

I had stretched out on my seat, but in Philadelphia, he came on and said, "I'd like to sit here if you please."

He's from another country, I thought. His is a bolder idiom. He doesn't mean to be rude.

"If you don't mind, would you move your legs?" he said.

I wanted to tell him there were many other seats. But he knew that—and that I was thinking that. For he said, "I want company. Is that a crime?"

He sat down beside me, and then there was no possibility of musing or quiet. For his voice was booming in my ear.

"Business or pleasure? Coming home or leaving?"

My eyes closed, I said, "Leaving. Family business."

His name was Victor, he said, and he was going home. He traveled often. "I wish that I could be a more stay-put person. At least once a week I'm leaving Miami. I am your modern-day nomad, I guess."

I sat up, rubbed my eyes. Sleep was impossible. I thought, I wish you were a more stay-quiet person, too. But then I thought, Take a look. See what a nomad looks like these days. If my aunt didn't come up with answers, that would be me.

Gold chains, row after row of them, sat on his hairy chest, which peeked out from the open neck of a black silk shirt. He could sell a chain and fly to Miami and back, I thought.

"You're headed for Miami? And you live . . . where?"

I shrugged.

"I can give you tips on Miami and bus travel in general if you plan to bypass aviation as a rule."

I shrugged. "I'm not sure of my plans."

"Well just in case . . . here's how it goes. In Miami, I stay at the Algiers, which gives me a special rate. I could tell them you're my friend. Then as for when I'm moving around, for that I have several advices. Advice 1: Take dramamine for nausea from the rocky ride and bathroom and to sleep. Advice 2: Wash and Dry for bodily clean up. If you spit out and rinse well, you can even use towelettes for teeth. Advice 3: Postcards. You should take them with you so people in upcoming spots could expect you. Also, they are pleasant to write while bussing. Advice 4: Reading could make you vomit so stop it if you feel funny or you could get very dirty, smelly, as well as ashamed. Advice 5: You should make friends. This makes you unlonely. And it also uses up time. If you want I can write my tips down if you have paper which I forgot. Advice 6: Bring pens and paper." He laughed.

I said I thought I'd remember. And then because I thought he might be nuts, I smiled to show good will, then closed my eyes to signal sleep and no more talk. He was scaring me.

All the way to Baltimore, while I pretended to sleep, falling off for real now and then, he sang in Spanish. Children's songs. Love laments. Military marches. In Washington, when we stopped to eat, he told me he was feeling lonely and asked if we could be table partners in addition to bus partners.

I said I was very tired and couldn't talk.

He said, "That's me. Too tired." And he sat down at my table. "I scarcely sleep any more. I'm so busy. I am talking to every group in every city. Looking for her. There goes sleep."

He said if we ate, we'd both have more pep for the trip.

We ate vending machine sandwiches and coffee at a crumb-covered table.

"Tip 7," he said, "is that you should pack some nuts, fruits, juice packs. The food is inadequate in the bus stops. Use the toilets but not the food."

"Thank you," I said. "I hope I won't be traveling for long."

"I know, it's very stressful. The only place I know true relaxation is in the dining room in the Algiers. Under their gauze umbrellas, if I rest my head on the table, I can actually snooze. There in the Tamarind Room it's as if what happened to her and them never happened. But I won't burden you with the details. They're unspeakable actually. . . ."

I nodded, saying nothing. He said, "Now your turn. . . . You spoke of your family's business. What kind of business is it? Retail, wholesale? I want to know all about my new friend."

Was he nuts? Was he dangerous? "I meant family matters," I whispered, afraid not to answer him.

"Then we have that, too, between us, partner," he said. "Because my work is for my family's business, too. To fix up everything that happened. To find her and fix the family business once and for all."

"Who's her?"

"My sister. I'm looking for her. She went here from my country, Cuba, on a plane as a little child. She was a Peter Pan."

"Peter Pan . . . was a little boy in a book . . . and movie. . . ."

"Ha ha and I don't know that. They called them Peter Pan after the boy and the other childrens in his group. The Catholic Church organized Peter Pan Children with the Americans. Fourteen thousand childrens and her came here because they said Fidel was going to take the childrens from their mamas and papas and put them in communist child camps. So we sent Marta. My parents were to come the next month. I was living with my grandma who I wouldn't leave. Meantime the Bay of Pigs and no one could go. Meanwhile there weren't those camps. But we saw that too late. Mama and Papa came five years later when they could get out. Some Peter Pans were with families, some in orphanages, but the padres didn't keep track good. Later I came. My parents died and I look and look."

"How long have you been looking?"

"Full-time only ten years. Before that part-time for six."

And then I must have turned white. For he said, "Don't be afraid. I won't leave you alone."

Would I end up like him? Month after month, year after year?

Babbling to strangers? I felt weak. Back on the bus, I stretched out on a seat and hoped he would get the hint and sit far away. But he climbed into the seat behind me.

"Call me if you need me. I doubt I'll snooze."

In the middle of the night, in North Carolina, he said he was a sad man. "On the bus I often remember how it was with Marta. For example, right now in my mind is when I rode her on my back all the way to the lighthouse up the coast from Varadero. I could still feel her little froggy legs, and then later her face with the water drippings like pearls. I have no one to share with. Except on the bus when I find another person who I could tell could be a partner. Now your turn, if you please."

I told him I didn't feel well and needed to be up front, and found a seat near the driver. The truth was I *didn't* feel well. Bus nausea—and fresh fear. Was he totally mad? Would I ever get away from him?

The driver was a jolly black woman named Michelle Hawkes according to the ID pinned to her full chest. Michelle had a row of photos, entitled ALL ELEVEN GRANDS taped to the dashboard.

"I think something may be wrong," I said. I motioned towards the back.

"Victor?" she said, "Is he chewing your ear off? That's just his way with a new friend. He gets lonely. That's Victor. He's been riding with me a long time."

Outside of Charleston, he came to check on me. "We do that. We look after each other, like family."

And Michelle said, "That's true."

When we stopped in Savannah for breakfast, I found a phone booth. I tried David's parents to see if they'd heard from him but there was no answer. I tried Tommy, but got his machine again. I have my family, I thought. I have a real partner. They're just not answering.

"Nobody there?" Victor said, appearing outside the booth.

Back on the bus, he said, "You still look afraid. I wish I could convince you to depend on me." Then he said, "Talk about afraid. Once in my country I had so much fear for my family's business that I fainted and cracked my head after soiling my pants."

In Miami, he handed me his card and asked me for my Miami number. I escaped to the bathroom and then, when the coast was clear, ran for a taxi.

The bay appeared suddenly, all around. Then, over the causeway, the endless stretch of ocean emerged, aqua and silver and as still as sleep. I hadn't slept for more than a few minutes in twenty-four hours, but I felt wide awake. I couldn't shake Victor's lunatic energy. Or memories I didn't know I had.

This ocean, ages ago, with Tommy and Boomie. Staying at the Fontainbleau, floating all day on plastic tubes, paddling in now and then for snacks. Boomie in his cabana suit is busy with business, whispering secrets to other men in cabana suits, or playing pinochle and poker at the table in a maze of bamboo and palm. That's my niece in the pink latex halter. That's my nephew in the flamingo patterned swimsuit that matches mine. Their father's away on a big business trip and they get bored with the nannies I hire. So I keep them with me. No bother at all.

And Cuba, too, on the same trip. I remember that now. The old Cuba. Feathered dancers at the show, Aunty Conchita, Boomie's dancer girlfriend for the week, the chandeliered casino where Tommy and I sat on Conchita's lap, getting tipsy on the dregs of her mojitos. Boomie loosing all his money, then Conchita. We left in the middle of the night, slinking along the Malecon, playing Boomie's favorite game, Who can find a car with keys in the ignition first. Tommy won with a red and white Chevy coupe, which we drove to the airport, hiding in a men's room stall with Uncle Boomie till our plane was called.

Then Miami again, this time in a rooming house five blocks from the ocean, with a crazy community kitchen with three stoves and five refrigerators, but we had no money and nothing to cook. The lady boarders, their stockings coiled at their ankles like pet snakes, followed us around with offerings of chicken legs, seeded rolls, farmer cheese. We gotta rest our stomachs, our uncle made us say. I remembered how, hungry and ashamed, in the middle of the night, with no money for the bill, we snuck away again, Boomie explaining to us that his tuxedo and portable radio left on the aluminum settee might very well be considered payment in full.

He had come here in a boat in the middle of a scirocco. The cab driver told me his story, as we drove past gay bars, deco splendor, old people on city benches at the edge of the beach. I thought of my aunt, who would be old now. I hadn't seen her in five years, and I was scared. Maybe she just couldn't remember what I was asking her about Sam. Maybe she'll have forgotten more by the time I got to her. I imagined her shaking her head and telling me, It's not working so good. You want to know about your father who is my brother? Do I know him well? Give me a hint. His initials and occupation.

His cousin set out on the next boat but drowned, the driver said. "*Mon dieu*, what fate for that guy."

Then we were at 68th and Collins, Senior Seasons, the United Labor Retirement Apartment Complex, where my aunt had arranged to live her golden years. And again I felt my father's presence. I gave the driver thirty dollars for an eighteen dollar fare, insisting he keep the change. It won't buy those poor souls back, but we got to stick together, I heard my father say. How did *you* die, Daddy? I thought. By water, or fire? Or are you alive? Buried alive in some miserable life?

Charlotte was the first person I saw in the lobby.

"I'm Charlotte, the receptionist. I spoke to you a few weeks back and I want to apologize for what must have been a frustrating exchange. It's just our disclosure of information policy. Anyway, you must be Betsy. Aunt Elsie is waiting for you at the pool complex. She's a doll. We all love her."

I followed the signs out to the pool. The old people were waving, and I waved back—to a row at the right of the pool near the towels, to the row at the left near the metal picnic tables.

I searched for my aunt's green eyes, pug nose, bright buck teeth in the line-up of white hair and bronze skin, but the glaring sun erased all details.

Then I heard, "Wake up, El." And the chorus rose, surrounding one of its members.

And then as she stood, I saw Aunt Elsie, in a pink mumu and red ankle-strap jellies, running towards me, excited as if she had just heard her name called from a quiz show audience.

"You know me when it comes to excitement. I get overexcited easily and knocked out."

The chorus cried, "She was excited, overexcited."

And we hugged and both cried a little, and some of the ladies cried, too, and a few clapped.

"My room," she said, when we got upstairs. "Room and a half really." She gestured to the dining alcove. "Room and two halves actually," she laughed, gesturing to the sleeping area.

"Two rooms," I laughed.

"Or a room and two nooks," she laughed.

"You like?" My aunt gestured to the white couch, a white mock wicker coffee table, a matching dining table and chairs. "Everything came together. It's hard to get anything but white here—furniture, shoes. But I got a good buy and I'm hardly home to get it dirty."

"I like," I laughed, studying the room. "Remember when we bought the Castro convertible?"

"I've seen worse," my aunt said, forgiving then and now my awful choice—mock Chippendale in a Black Watch plaid. "Remember the dinette set?"

We'd ordered it from a mail order catalogue. Maple Early American. Cousin Arthur lost the instructions for assembly, and

Tom and I, working with no directions, lost heart in the middle of our attempt to put it together. We banished it to the basement storage room, where the super, taking pity, worked on it on his days off, without success. When guests looked with sorrow on her battered table and chairs, we'd tell them about the custom set we were having built by a local craftsman.

"Custom crafted takes a long time," my aunt laughed now.

"A lifetime," I said, patting her leather hand.

My aunt had said she didn't remember. But the whole room was an altar to memory. White picture frames coordinated with the furniture—fifty frames a quick scan of the room told me. Frame after frame, photo after photo, and in the corners and sides of the frames, smaller pictures were wedged in, like facets of a temple mosaic. On a 1930s studio portrait of Grandma with a palace backdrop, there was a picture of Arthur in a Giants suit sitting on her lap. And on a picture of Boomie in his plane, a photo of Tommy and me was settled on the wing. I found our grandparents at their wedding, and angled into the frame with them is the family they eventually would issue—teenage Elsie in a long striped bathing suit, Boomie in a convertible, Tom aged two or so, and me, probably a year, in a carriage, poking each other's eyes and crying.

"I like everyone together," Elsie said. "The family keeps me company. Even when you're not around . . . or gone."

"I see. We're all here," I said. But then I saw that it wasn't true. My father was nowhere to be seen.

"There are no pictures of my dad," I said. "How come, Aunt Elsie?"

"No pictures of your dad? How come?" Aunt Elsie echoed.

"Yes, why?" I said.

"He's dead."

I pointed at Grandma and Grandpa, Uncle Boomie, Arthur's father, Uncle Joe, who I'd never known. "*They're* dead," I said. "But you have *them* here."

"I mean he's totally dead."

"And them? They're *totally* dead, Aunt Elsie!"

"But I have a bridge to them. At our elder hostel we read a book that made the very interesting point that between the land of the living and the land of the dead there is a bridge of love. I guess I knew all that unconsciously, you know. No love, no bridge. No love, then really dead. Not like the others. Even if his body isn't dead, he's dead"

"He isn't dead?"

"I didn't say that. I'm just talking about the bridge of love. For me the family is all. But not for him. For him it was always the Family of Man. But I still loved my brother. Maybe even more because I had so much respect for his activities for others. But it's all gone, all my love. On account of what he did."

"What did he do?"

She shook her head.

"Why won't anyone tell me anything?"

"To protect you."

"From what?"

"I'm not a destroyer. I'm not going to tell."

"But you're a liar," I said. "'Died on my sofa. . . . Buried him. . . . Mourn each in our own way. . . .'" I repeated her words.

"A nothing fib. Compared to what was going on."

"What was going on? You haven't told me a thing."

"You don't really want to know. Do you really want to know?"

And when I nodded, she went into the walk-in closet. To cry, I thought, but she returned with old papers bound in yarn.

"Here," she said.

Here were the photographs missing from the wall. My father in uniform in Naples, Vesuvius erupting behind him. With my mother on the steps of City Hall, glued together in an extravagant post-War kiss. At Coney Island, reading on a blanket, with Tommy and me on his shoulders slurping frozen custard. In Washington, on a stage with Eleanor Roosevelt. On a construction site, handing out picket signs: No Safety, No Work. A *New York Times* article about Sam refusing to sign the loyalty statement. The *New York Times* article about Leo. The *Journal American* article about my mother at St. Patrick's. Photos outside Foley Square, two in prison garb and shackles, two in suits out on bail. I'd seen it all ages ago. But then a headline I'd never seen before. Half of a headline. FUGITIVE RED FRIEND SIGHTED. . . .

Everything except the piece of headline and the words *San Francisco Chronicle* was crossed out with black marker. And part of a date. 1970. The year he died.

"What's underneath you don't want to know. So it's crossed out."

"Aunt Elsie, this is ridiculous. Nothing can be worse than what I'm imagining.".

"What are you imagining? I'll tell you if you're hot. . . . Please, Betsy, don't make me say the words."

"Say them, for Christ's sake!"

"Don't shout," she said. And she started crying. "Later, maybe later, Betsyla, sweetheart."

In the morning, Aunt Elsie announced that she'd slept on it. She wouldn't ever be ready to tell me. It would break her heart to be the one to tell me. But she wouldn't get in my way to find out. She walked me to her local library on Arthur Godfrey Road, and told the librarian who supplied her with her mysteries that I was her niece the journalist, and here to do a story. The University of Miami Library was part of a consortium of media archives, and the best place to do research in U.S. newspapers, the librarian said. After elaborate directions, Aunt Elsie hugged me tight. "You're sure, Betsy?" she tried one more time.

At the bus kiosk, I stopped for coffee to fuel the day's mission, remembering that day just a couple of weeks before, with David in the diner in Queens. All my life, I'd prepared for the next catastrophe. But would this be the worst one yet? Maybe Elsie and Leo were right and I was better off not knowing. Then, I felt his breath on my neck, then his words in my ear:

"You thought I abandoned you but I've been following you. I knew you'd be in need of a friend to carry you on."

Then seeing my alarm, he said, "I'm not dangerous. It's just that we're both on missions. Doing our researches. Fate throws at the same directions."

"Where are you going?" I said.

"The University Library. The Public Library is always a possibility. But I prefer the University—where there are more newspapers and records. You, too, are on your way to the University library on the MB 132? I know it must seem strange. Me, again. And I'm strange to begin with, with my talking habit. But the family's business will not be resolved one, two, three. You may ask how I could tell you could be my partner from the start. It was your nails. Don't take me wrong but they're yukky. They told me you're searching for something and not taking proper care. Your coat after lunch was buttoned wrong and your panty hose were wrinkled. You have a lot on your mind. After a while at this life you can tell your own kind. You'll see. Long and short, you need me."

I shook my head. "I just need to find a newspaper," I said. "And then I'll be done."

"In one day," he laughed. "Not if your problem is anything like my problem. What is your problem, in specific, if I may ask?"

"My father."

"Vindication?"

I shook my head.

"Restitution?"

"I want to find him."

"Oh, straightforward location. . . . Just like with Marta," he squealed. "Where was he last seen? East coast, west coast?"

"I don't know. He may be dead," I whispered.

"That's a sad one. Like mine with Marta."

"Probably dead, " I said.

"No say that," he cried.

By now we were on the bus going south. He'd nestled in beside me and I pretended to sleep, and soon did for real.

Then he was calling, "Rise and shine," nudging me as the bus entered a drive with overarching eucalyptus trees—a long, shimmering tunnel of light.

"We're here," Victor said. "Onward."

The reference room was built in the round, and with its plexiglass dome, center island and chrome and birch seats, it looked less like a library and more like a modern theater. And it was noisy like a theater, when the lights first dim and everyone gets out their last cough, crumples their last piece of paper, bites their last mint, the whole place rustling like brush fire.

"Noisy," Victor said, as if reading my mind. "That's because there are so many Cubans. We're noisy. Are your people noisy?"

"I guess so," I said.

"Don't tell me you're Cubana?"

I shook my head, "Jewish, Scotch-Irish."

"Cuban, Cuban," he said. "And before that Spanish, Spanish. But look how we have our noise and journeys in common."

A librarian raised his finger to his lips and Victor whispered, "Sorry, sorry. . . . Right, we're so sorry?" he laughed, and beckoned me, like we were twins on a jaunt, to the stairway, then to the microfilm section underground.

Here giant machines, old and gray and bulky, were lined up like a robot army. And not for the first time since I'd begun my crazy search did I feel caught in a horror movie. I put in a request for reels of the 1970 *San Francisco Chronicle* and wondered what terrors the article would reveal. That my father had transformed into a monster?

When the boxes with my film arrived, I just sat, afraid to begin. Victor was already seated at a microfilm reader, busily turning knobs and levers like a manic kid at an arcade; but seeing me sitting there, he called out, "Sitting gets us nowhere. I'm here, *mi hermana*. Here I am for when you get afraid."

"I'm not afraid," I lied. And to get him to keep quiet, I shoved in the film and turned on the light. I cranked through roll after roll, searching for my father, glad when I couldn't find him on each new page. Page after page of Nixon. Page after page of the Senate—debating how many U.S. advisors were in different parts of Southeast Asia. The middle of a war, but my eyes were drawn to cheerful nostalgia. Men's hair was still a neat hedge around their heads, women's hair was still flipping at the bottom in little upbeat gestures of agreement. A 4 1/2 room apartment in the Mission district rented for $237—a fifth of what I paid for a smaller apartment. I. Magnin was selling mink coats for $800, seal capes for $1000. Women's boots. . . . Then, Earth Day in April. Then May 4, 1970: Four unarmed students killed at Kent State. And then, just when I thought I'd never find him, he appeared.

November 4, 1970. He was wearing glasses and had a mustache, probably a disguise, but I made out the cleft in his chin, his light eyes, even before I saw the headline: FUGITIVE RED FRIEND SIGHTED AT BOMBED ARMY CENTER. Then the story.

A San Francisco recruitment center. . . . A Sunday morning. . . . Two men thought to have entered through a basement storeroom. . . . A small homemade device. . . . An unidentified gas filled the entire office with foul-smelling smoke believed to be a toxic gas. Exact identity of gas not determined, but sarin and mustard not ruled out. The center has been sealed off and will be closed indefinitely. Two men caught on camera fleeing the building. One identified as Samuel Vogel, a former officer of Local 666 of the Federation of American Woodworkers and renowned communist ally, whom the FBI has been pursuing for fleeing on bail. A second man was identified as Terence Lutman, a night manager of Foundations, a San Francisco bookstore known to be a hangout for anti-war and leftist circles.

Poison Gas. Sarin. Mustard. How could that be? Terror is the tactic of desperation and insures only isolation and reaction. . . . My father's rhetoric zoomed around my mind. They like to blame us for such things. Blame! I thought. They saw you. They showed your photo. He must have known there'd be cameras in a government facility. Had he wanted to be seen? Why would he want to be seen? It made no sense. It was senseless. I felt senseless. I could hardly feel Victor's hand on my shoulder, or hear his voice calling, "Are you done? Me, I'm done."

I studied the face of the "second man." A beard and black glasses. The beard didn't go with the glasses but I couldn't say why. The glasses looked familiar but I couldn't say where I'd seen them before.

I made a photocopy. Then I spent another half hour searching indexes for more articles. But came up empty.

Outside, Victor said, "You look like you saw a ghost. Soon you'll not react so much."

"I saw his photograph. And another man's who somehow looks familiar."

"That's good. I never found Marta's picture. But I will one day. Especially now. With you at my side."

I shook my head. "Victor, I think I'm done." I meant with Miami. Maybe my whole search. I wasn't sure what I knew except that it was too awful. A device. Smoke. Poison.

"Don't give up, *mija*," he said. "Our search has just begun. Yesterday I neglected to point out in my advices the importance of fun amid all this," Victor said. "When despair strikes especially."

And I felt too weak to do anything but let Victor lead me.

The rest of the day was a blur. Victor raced us to a bus, which took us to a place called Monkey World. Every few minutes bells rang. Every few minutes a voice on a loudspeaker announced which habitat would be presenting next and which lane to rush down in order to assure seating.

Path A to the Chimp Show: A naughty chimp rides his bike and doesn't want to stop to eat his dinner. The trainer scolds him, he repents, eats his dinner standing on his head, repents, smokes the trainer's cigar, repents, pours a basin of sudsy water intended for washing his paws on his trainer's head, repents, does the macarena instead of taking his nap. Next path and the Spider Monkey Show: Three spider monkeys make donkey ears behind their trainer's head when she wants to teach them their school lesson; they pelt her with peanuts when she threatens extra homework, and tie her hands behind her back when she says she means business.

And then it was over for this show too.

"I told you this was just what you would need to break your sorrow. Ready for more of our cousins?"

"I've seen enough," I said. The relentless rebellion of monkeys brought me back to my father. Poison gas! My father's world was meetings and rallies, picket lines and negotiations. Jails and pleas. But there was no escaping the fact that he was there in the building. I saw his face.

Down a winding path, we found a bench. Victor said, "This is nice, right? I remember sitting beneath the cherry trees with my uncle just before she left. There was machine gun fire in the hill beyond the orchard, and the trees shook so hard we wore a coat of white petals. Marta shook, too, in my arms, and I told her we'd always be together. I'd always protect her. I remember."

"Don't," I said. "Don't remember."

"It brings my Marta to me."

"Let's just sit." Pink blossoms cascaded all around, their fresh fruity scent filling my lungs.

"Sit and forget?"

"Yes, or at least try." Deeply I breathed in the blossoms' scent, as if to purge myself of him. His crazy smile in the photo, the smoke behind him.

"I'll try. I can't say I'll be so good. But I'll try. It's true—it's important to try here and there in our life for some peace."

Then Victor was snoring beside me. I closed my eyes and tried to see nothing. But the blank screen of my mind kept streaking with images. His face. What was the source of the smile on his face? Relief? Pride? A little of both?

Then something was coming towards us, scurrying and screeching. Monkeys escaped? What would they throw on *my* head? Dirty water? Monkey dung? My hands covered my head and I began to whimper. But it was just a crowd of visitors running toward the next show, their cameras flying, their mouths chattering, their arms swinging.

Victor rubbed his eyes awake. "There you go again, being fearful," he said. "You need to work on knowing who is your friend and who is your enemy if you want to make a head away in your search."

It was going on a hundred degrees, but I had begun to shiver.

"Let us rest," he said, and gestured behind the trees. He took my arm and I followed down a hill to a small copse of palms at the far edge of a glen. When I lay down on the grass, he took off his shirt and laid it over my chest and arms. But I couldn't stop shaking. He began to rub my arms and then my chest, my belly and then my legs.

"Please, cover me," I said.

"This is all I have." He gestured to his shirt on my chest.

I pulled him down on top of me and asked him not to move. I was shaking with cold and fear and had the feeling I'd break like an icicle if I wasn't warmed.

"Better?" he said. The memory of the articles and photographs, the cries of the monkeys and the people seeping through the trees, the thought of smoke and poison—I pressed him to me like a giant doll or stuffed animal—and it was better.

I don't remember falling asleep, just waking with a start. "It's Brown," I said. "Under the beard and glasses."

Victor, who'd been sleeping on top of me, woke up too. "What's that?"

"The other man in the photograph. That's Brown."

I recalled the face, the lashless eyes, the button nose and apple cheeks I once longed to caress. It was all there, with the beard. "Brown . . . or maybe Gray."

"Congratulations," Victor said. "You're making much progress in a single day. See how I help you along!"

We stood and walked to the front of the park and found our bus. As we made our way up the coast highway, sky and water sparkling with the late afternoon light, I tried to clarify my *discovery*. Brown, Gray. It made no sense that my father was with one of *them*. Had his golden tongue convinced *our* agent to come over to his side? But the father I knew would never do what the article said.

"I'm all mixed up," I said.

"I understand. Love takes time. Especially in the age of AIDS. We'll go home and hug hard again, and you'll feel more better."

I put my fingers on my temples to help me think. Home. Where was home? Where was David?

"If you will live with me at the Hotel Algiers it will be easier. We will search together every day."

I shook my head. "Victor," I said. "I'm sorry. I have a home .. . another life."

"Ha ha ha," he laughed furiously. "That's a funny one. Don't lie in my face and I won't lie in yours, my love."

Was he once sane? Had his "search" deranged him? Or was *he* an FBI agent posing as a lunatic? Following me as I looked for my father. Had Brown or Gray or some other agent sent Victor to me?

"Are you some sort of police?" I whispered. "FBI?"

"Take that back," he cried.

"You don't know my father? Brown? Anyone?"

"Take all of that back. Don't break my heart more than it's been broke. I'm just your friend."

All the way up to Miami Beach, I said I was sorry.

Victor said, "What are best friends for if not to have a lover's quarrel and then make up right away?"

"El's at the pool," Charlotte said, and I walked through the lobby to find her.

The sun was setting, but late afternoon rays shot silver streaks on the water. I saw my aunt at the side of the pool, reading, her toes playing in the water.

"Did you enjoy the library, tootsie?" And before I could answer, she said, "Want to go swimming?"

And from the end of the pool, down near the game room, other ladies called, "Sure, take a swim. Why not?"

"Here." Aunt Elsie handed me a bathing suit. "I brought one down for you in case you came back. Early, I mean. And this. . . ." She handed me a shower cap—puffy plastic with pink butterflies. "Regulations," she said, waving her hands in contempt.

Then I was in the water, then underwater, wanting to wash off every speck of the day. Victor's body. Sam's face, Brown. Gray. To remember only David. And Brighton Beach waves on his back, then giggling on the sand as the sun set, passing a bottle of Stoly.

The oohs and ahs of my aunt and her chorus of friends trailed me underwater.

"Lovely form," someone called, as I moved back and forth across the aqua pool.

"A regular Esther Williams."

"It's such a pleasure to see someone make use of the water."

"My sister was in the World's Fair Aquacade of 1939. Your niece reminds me of Flossie."

I twirled, I dove, I flipped in the empty pool. I looked up at all of them, and for one long minute, I thought: Stay. Under these adoring eyes, with these adorable admirers. Thirty-nine with dimple thighs, yet admired like a teenager. I thought, Stay. Don't go on with it. How many more Victors would I run into, leading me down strange, scary paths away from my life? How many more shocking facts would I have to encounter?

"How long will the girl be with you?" someone said.

My aunt said, "She has an enormous business meeting coming up. So we'll see."

Was she covering for me? In case I left quickly? Or did she want me gone, to be done with me and my questions?

When it was just us alone, Elsie didn't want to talk. I could tell from her mouth, the way it drooped, as if it would quiver and send her whole face and body into spasms of sobs if it was asked to speak. And now I understood why. Why she had hung up the phone. Asked questions so I would ask no more. I, too, wanted silence, as if saying nothing, we could make it all go away.

We rode the elevator in silence. Silently we changed clothes, toweled hair. Silently we set the table, squeezed pot cheese, cucumbers, borscht, sour cream onto the small table. Silently we chewed, swallowed. I patted her wrist tentatively as if keeping time to a jazz song. Her hands were folded tightly together like the hands of a good schoolgirl. Look, how good I am, they seemed to say. I don't deserve to be called on any more. I shouldn't have to answer any more.

"I'm sorry, Aunt Elsie," I finally said. "Can we talk?"

"So you had a nice day?" she tried.

I shook my head. "I'd like to forget it all, too."

My aunt beamed up at me. "Oh, couldn't we, honey?"

I shook my head.

"You can't? For a while I couldn't either, I guess. But it was so long ago. You forget."

"Who's the other man? Isn't it one of those agents that used to hang around us?"

She waved her hand. "What an imagination you have."

"I know him."

"Lots of people look like lots of people."

"Isn't he Brown? Or Gray? One of them?"

Again she waved her arm. Let it go. Let it be. Go on with your crazy ideas.

"You know who it is?" I said.

"I only know what you know now. The article. And Doreena Jones. Her I know. Knew."

"Where is she? Don't you know?"

More head shaking. "Can't I stop you, Betsy? I really want to stop you."

I shook my head.

"You're going to get hurt. There's been enough hurt."

"I just want to know. I mean I don't really want to know. I'm so scared. But I can't stop."

"Your grandma. Maybe she knows something."

"Aunt Elsie," I said. "Stop." I meant stop your living is dead, dead is living. "Grandma's been dead for ages."

"I mean the other one. The one from the other side."

"Grandma Alice?"

I hadn't thought of her in decades, my mother's mother, the grandmother from the other side. The bad grandmother, we used to call her.

"She's still alive? Where does she live? Still in Virginia?"

"No, I heard she moved to Florida. Somewhere inland."

She might as well have said, "To where the right-wing low-lifes live." You could hear the contempt. "A town called Do Nothing." She was laughing. "No. . . . Carefree, that's it, Carefree, Florida. She's been there for years. Probably still is. They don't die easily, that type. They're too busy snooping . . . and telling everyone's business. . . ."

"I'll call her." But I felt frozen. Grandma Alice. "I'll call her later."

Aunt Elsie held my hand. "Don't rush, darling. Maybe you'll change your mind. About this whole business. It was all years ago. I swear, some days I can hardly remember."

The hotel up the street had a flashing sign for the Buccaneer Room—an all night coffee shop and I walked up the street, sat down at a booth in the long, empty room and ate a stale cruller and a cup of burnt coffee. On my napkin, around the face of the winking pirate, I tried to compute the time in Capetown. It was four a.m. here; it was eleven a.m. there. If my brother was back, he might still be home.

I found the pay phone in the back. It took a few minutes for the call to go through—the operator finding codes, checking

my credit card, getting a clear line. Finally the phone was ringing and I found myself thinking, Hang up. My heart was pound-
ing—with terror—of what Tommy would say. Of what I would
say to him. Then Tommy was on the line.

I said, "It's me."

"Where are you? You sound far away."

"Florida with Aunt Elsie."

"Is everything OK?" he said, alarmed.

"She's OK," I said.

"Just a vacation?"

I said, "No. Not a vacation. I came to talk to Aunt Elsie. To
find out about him."

"What? I can't hear you."

"Do you know, Tommy?"

"Bets, what's going on? I can't hear you, Bets."

I guess I was screaming, shouting over the static, for the waitress and counterboy were peeking around the corner, smiling
nervous smiles.

Tommy said, "This is crazy. What the hell's going on?"

"Have you known all along? And just not told me? Do you
know something, Tommy, something I don't know? About him
. . . and not told me? Why don't you trust me, Tommy?"

"Know what?" The static had stopped and he wasn't shouting
anymore; he was whispering. I could hear fear fluttering in his
voice. He knew nothing.

"That he didn't die?"

My brother said, "That he didn't die?" Repeating my words
as if to help him grasp the idea. And again, "He didn't die? Who
didn't die?"

"Daddy. Not when we thought he did."

"Not when we thought he did?" he said. "But later?"

"I don't know."

"What do you mean you don't know?" His voice was low
again, weak.

"Tommy," I said, "are you all right?"

"I'm all right. What the fuck's the matter with you?" He'd raised his voice again.

"Why are you mad at *me*?"

"I'm not mad. I'm all right. Just shut the fuck up."

I knew he meant, Tell me no more. Take it all back. But I was tired and scared and I started to cry.

"Just shut up," he said. "Stop pushing yourself into the middle of everything. You're always fucking jumping in the grave."

I said, "I only did that once."

"You're always doing it. It drives me crazy. You always do it."

"That's not fair . . . we haven't seen each other for five years. How could I be driving you crazy?"

There was a long silence. Tommy said, "I'm sorry, Bets."

Then I was sobbing. From sorrow—that my brother and I were fighting? From relief—-that here was my brother, on the other side of the world, feeling every shock of desperation I was?

"OK, what have you found out?" he said. "Besides that he didn't die when Aunt Fibster said he did?"

"Why don't you meet me? I'll tell you when you meet me."

"Meet you?"

"Tommy, I'm looking for him."

"Looking for him?" my brother said. "You really think he's still alive?"

"I don't know." I told him about the recruitment center. The homemade "device." The smoke. Thought to be poison. Sarin and mustard not ruled out.

"'Thought to be poison.' What's that supposed to mean? 'Not ruled out?'" And then, "And you believe that garbage?"

I said, "I don't know what I believe. And you know what? There was a man with him who looked just like Brown or Gray."

"So? There are lots of ugly men with dandruff shoulders and black pervert glasses. He had a new friend. What are you spinning here, my sister the creative journalist?"

142

"Tom, they said his name was Terence Lutman and he managed a lefty bookstore. But he looked like . . . FBI. . . ."

"And you're the big expert. Stop weaving theories out of nothing."

"Does the name Terence Lutman mean anything to you?"

"No."

"Does the name Doreena Jones mean anything?"

"No."

"Do you know that Grandma Alice is still alive? I'm going to try to talk to her."

Tommy said, "This is too crazy. She's still around. And you're going to talk to the fucking bitch."

"I'll call you after I talk to her and see what she knows. We'll make plans. Together. OK?"

"We'll see," my brother said. "Depends . . . I'm in the middle of a huge campaign. I don't have time for this."

He sounded like *him*. On the move to change the world! But I could hear dread deadening my brother's voice. "I know it's scary. But not if we do it together."

"I'm not scared. Just busy. And ideologically opposed to dwelling on the past. When the future needs me. . . ."

"Tommy, please, we'll be together," I said.

"I told you I wasn't afraid," my brother whined.

"OK, OK, sha, sha, sweetheart," I said.

And Tommy started bawling. "I thought all this shit was over. Dead and buried for-fucking-ever."

8: Grandma Alice

IT WAS TOO EARLY to call her. I walked along the beach and then at 72nd Street I walked across the causeway. In the City of Miami I walked into a park and sat on a bench until I saw enough people moving around to declare it morning.

At a phone booth at the edge of the park I called information for Carefree, Florida, an Alice Dawes, and was given the number for an A. Dawes. I shook as I dialed.

"It's Betsy," I said, when a tinny voice answered.

"Betsy?"

"Marie's girl."

"Oh, the girl. How's Marie?"

"OK. She's OK."

"How are you?"

"OK."

"And the boy, how's he?"

"Tommy's fine."

Then we both were silent. "Anything special?"

"I thought I'd come visit. I'm in Miami."

"With the sister?"

"I'm with my Aunt Elsie. I thought I'd come visit."

"You'll find me changed."

I hoped she was right.

Jean Villard, the Haitian cabbie had given me his card, and when I called him he said he was on his way to visit an uncle on the west coast of Florida. For a hundred dollars he would take me to Carefree and then get me on his way back. I was glad for the escape from buses, bus stations, Victor, and other scary faces mirroring my future. But it was a sad four hours. No ocean, no shimmering palms, no glistening slopes down to bays and waterways. Jean told me about the drowned cousin's family, his own daughter and wife still back home. Every few miles on the endless blacktop, we passed a cluster of shacks with flapping wash and rotting cars. "Like my country," Jean said, his eyes that nostalgic mix of sadness and longing.

Then a billboard with a picture of a lagoon and flamingos. WELCOME TO CAREFREE, FLA. FAMOUS FOR ITS LAGOON LIFE. Some life: trailer park after trailer park, rows of aluminum "homes" on cinder blocks with card tables and wobbly tripod barbecues, and white haired, white-shoed people sitting still in the rippling heat.

Flamingo Village, the community in which Alice said she lived, was the sixth park we came upon. I looked around from trailer to trailer wondering which would be hers. The mock stucco Mediterranean? The mock Tudor? The battered silver Airstream? The trailer covered in plastic logs sporting plastic window boxes with plastic flowers looking like the witch's cottage in "Hansel and Gretel"? That was probably hers, I thought. Then I heard a wheezy laugh, and then there she was, having snuck up on me from behind, silently guiding her wheelchair.

"This way," she said, and I walked beside her to a trailer with a little porch and plastic pillars. Very Old South, I thought, bitterly.

The steps were steep, and I reached out my arms for her to lean on me, but she stood up on her own and ran inside.

"The chair's just for now and then," she said. "For getting around in the heat. I was left it by a friend. You don't look like *her* at all," she said. She was looking at me hard with those icy aqua eyes.

I nodded. She meant Marie, of course.

"It's been about thirty years," she said. "I don't think I saw you since your family moved to Mexico."

Moved to Mexico. It sounded so genteel. So normal—since you moved into the new house, added the new wing.

It was in fact *after* Mexico. I was eleven. Marie had been away for two years. Sam after a full year at home had been arrested, and then, out on bail, had disappeared. The spring after the winter he left, I spent Easter vacation with Grandma Alice. Courtesy of Tommy. For the week before in the back of a closet, my brother had found a bag of letters addressed to me from our governor, mayor, junior and senior senators, and congressman. One from each of them offering some variation on, Thank you for bringing my attention to the matter. Thank you for taking an interest in government. Tell, tell what you wrote, Tommy had commanded, twisting my arms behind my back. Till I broke, and told. I'd only asked for help, I said. Help! Tommy shouted. You traitor! They'll send over make-believe social workers to plant secret cameras. Not that kind of help, I explained. I just told them that Daddy didn't mean to cause trouble to America, I said. That he was sorry and wanted to be cooperative. My brother got me in a headlock. Sorry, he shouted, taking me down to the floor. He's not sorry, he said. Except to have a daughter like you, who gave the government the idea that he was about to break. I bet that's why they arrested him again. To get him to give up. Cooperate. Sign. Give names. It's all your fault.

When spring vacation came, my brother stopped denouncing me only to banish me. He used his news route money to buy me a bus ticket to Lynchburg, where Grandma Alice was living then. Aunt Elsie said it very nice of Tommy to provide me with the opportunity to travel. But I knew that for my brother, the trip to Grandma Alice was a statement. You are a traitor, like her. And also of course a *sentence*. A week with her.

It was a week of torment. I'd do grand-daughterly things, like find drawers to explore, and she'd slap my hands. I'd ask if we could bake, and she'd give me a quarter for a Devil Dog. At night, I'd ask her to tuck me in. And with her standing over the bed, I'd cry, My father, my brother, I missed them so. I wanted her to stroke my brow, rock me till I couldn't think. But she'd only laugh. You can't miss them. Your father is a commie dupe and your brother is following in his footsteps. I miss my mother, I'd try. And she'd ask me not to speak of her ever again. She'd brought shame on the family. Am I OK, Grandma? I earnestly asked the last night. Had I ruined everything? I meant, as Tommy had said. You seem nice enough, she considered. But I don't really know you. The next day, after only three days, she told me it was time to go. The neighbors were talking.

Now it was some thirty years later. "Nice to see you," she said.

The inside of the trailer was surprisingly bright. The back windows were wide casements which faced onto a puddly lagoon—with a real bird poking at the edge, a spindly heron with his head in the tall reeds. Through the windows the water shimmered and the room itself dazzled, like a small chapel carved of ice. Then I realized it wasn't just the water shining in that gave the room its glow, but the room itself—all the shimmering things lined up on every shelf, on top of every table.

"It's all been left me by friends."

I nodded. Had she ever had friends? That Easter, she'd kept me hidden in the house. I'd never seen anyone, not even a neighbor.

"Around here when they die, they generally just leave it and you can go and take what you want. If you're fast you can get a lot of good things."

I looked around at the "good things." Toasters, rotisseries, electric percolators, electric frying pans, crock pots. Glass vases, cups and saucers with floral patterns on little stands, thermos jars.

"They come in handy. If one breaks you got another. . . . How's the boy?" she asked.

"Tommy's in Africa now."

"Like *him*. Poking his nose where it doesn't belong. Not happy with what life offers us." She opened her arms, gestured to her full room.

"And who are you like?" she said.

"I'm not sure."

"You know I really think it's Josephine that you favor."

I forced a smile, trying to recall who Josephine was. One of her sisters, no doubt. It had always been like this—Josephine or Kitty or Louise or whoever. We never mattered, me and Tommy, and even Marie. It was crazy that it hurt me still after all these years, remembering the brutal clannishness which excluded even her daughter and her family from the circle of affection.

The other family, the important family, was made up of her three sisters, Richmond "girls" who followed her to the coal town of Chester when she married my grandfather, whose miner's salary miraculously supported them all. Marie married Sam because he was nothing like her family—he loved *everyone*, her included, a nice switch. She was buoyed up by the generous impulse, which gave her a fair share, if not always a big slice. I looked at Alice's downcast mouth, which time had reduced to a slash. Did I still hate her for what she'd done back then?

"Josephine . . . come on, you know her, my second youngest sister. A very sensible girl. She died during the war."

"I never met her then. I was born years after the war. 1952."

"Oh, right. . . . But I see a resemblance. She wanted to become a teacher. Are you a teacher?"

"I'm an editor and writer, actually."

"What sort of editor and writer?"

A damn good one, I wanted to say, trying to remember if that was so.

"A popular magazine," I said.

"Popular as in pinko?"

I shook my head. How ridiculous—after all these years I still wanted to please her, to reassure her I wasn't like them. How pathetic, I felt. And furious.

"Good girl," she said. "Not that I care anymore. Not that I cared all that much back then. Though it was a little depressing when the neighbors stuck the newspapers under my nose and those nosy men came poking around."

"Poor you," I said.

"I'm glad you understand," she said, deaf to my sarcasm. "They never understood. You're more like me and my side. Understanding of human nature."

I laughed.

"Your mother and *he* made a big deal. I got scared and got a little noisy, it's true, and I said some things that weren't nice. I wasn't always friendly."

Noisy, nice, friendly. The woman had a kindergartner's code of conduct.

"Later on I did some things that maybe weren't thoughtful. I talked to some men who came to see me. All I said is that I never liked the likes of him. I only said what I believed about America going Red. And about him being un-American for not signing that he wasn't one of them. I told them I was very different. I wasn't for all that integration the commies were always pushing on us in the South. And how I was for private property, of course." Again she gestured to her storeroom of goods. "But I meant no harm. Of course *she* made a big fuss. She could be such a fusspot."

A crackpot in the later years for sure. But before that my mother was a free floating spirit with no mind for small details, petty accounting, little grievances.

"And you took money?"

"Just a little. I was in trouble with my bills. Those men gave me some cash. But only a couple of times."

"Do you know how much you hurt her?" I saw my mother rocking herself on the hospital bed, calling, Mama, Mama, oh, Mama. While, I, all of ten, held her to my breast.

"I was scared. They said they'd tell all the neighbors. They said my sisters would lose their jobs. What would you have done in my shoes?"

I looked down at her shoes, the enlarged pinkies poking through rips in the white leather. Miserable feet, miserable shoes. I felt a wave of nausea.

"I sent her a three orchid corsage for her birthday once and wrote on the card: Sorry. But she sent it back—made the florist return it to me, scrawled all over the note for everyone who cared to see. File it under L. Lies, lice, loathe, she wrote and a bunch of other awful L words. My sisters said, Cut her off, talking that way to her mother and all. But I still tried. After I moved down here, I sent you and the boy a crate of oranges once and once some coconut patties, but they came back too. Someone paid for the return shipping just to make a stupid point. In my book that's extra mean and unnecessary. It was so embarrassing. Everyone around here seeing oranges delivered to *me*. No one here gets oranges delivered to them. I had to say there'd been a mix up with parcel post.

"I've been here for twenty years. For half of them I tried to apologize. Your mother returned my letters. 'I know no one by that name,' she'd write by my name."

"She probably didn't any more."

She touched her head. "You know she thought people were following her?" She rolled her eyes.

"They were." FBI. Police. Two by two, trailing us from this house to that house. This country to that. "She just couldn't tell who was who," I said. "Which people around her were friends and which . . . were not."

"I was friendly. That was the whole point of my orchid and oranges."

"Oranges. She needed you. We needed you. Where were you?"

I looked at Alice, the avalanche of skin around her eyes and mouth. I tried to imagine needing her. Tried to remember the ice in her voice when she said, The neighbors are talking. You'd better get packing.

"You're shouting, Betsy. You were never one to shout."

I tried to imagine our lives had Alice been different. Christmas vacations with our grandma in Virginia, then Florida. Coming back with gorgeous tans. Giving kids something to talk about. Besides Sam, and Marie, and all the shame and dread of all those years.

"Look, I said I was sorry to her. Now I'm going to say it to you. Sorry."

"For what exactly? I'd like you to answer that. What are you sorry for?"

"For that whole business."

She smiled and I saw Marie's smile, wide and winning, and I felt my heart flutter.

"She had nobody," I said. I remembered one time, when she was taken off to jail with him for obstructing his arrest—for shouting and kicking when they came to get him. When she came back the next week, I answered her in monosyllables. For her behavior had embarrassed me before the NYC policemen who'd wrestled her in the living room, and before Brown and Gray, who'd watched and scribbled from their usual perch in the outer hallway. You're in cahoots with the law, she said finally. I figured it out. The next day she decided to have herself locked up again, choosing the hospital over any more jail—or me. You're not on my side, she had said, as she left.

Alice said, "Point accepted: I should have helped out more."

Helped out. The expression suggested dropping off macaroni casseroles now and then.

"But it's nice that you're trying to make peace, visiting and all. That is why you're here? Not on account of anything that happened . . . to anyone . . . to my daughter?"

"Nothing happened to her. But he's not buried where I'd been told he was buried. That's why I'm here. To see if you know anything. . . . I'm looking for him."

"Oh, that's a good one. Looking for him," she laughed.

I wanted to cover my ears or run out the door to get away from her icy laughter. "I'll be quick. I came only to find out what you know."

"What *I* know? You stare at me like I'm a moron and you want to know what *I* know. Morons know nothing, my dear. You know that."

"You know nothing about him?" I said.

"A friend to communists if not exactly one himself. Enemy of the Commonwealth of Virginia with his promotion of integration, inter-marriage, and so on. Everything I've said."

"Dead or alive?" I said.

"Oh, dead. You know you really are a little strange, like her. I swear."

"Why are you so sure he's dead?"

"That's an easy one. I'll show you."

I followed her out the back onto the gravel and sat down on one of the hot, wobbly bridge chairs.

"Sit," she said. "Wait."

Like my aunt, she went inside to dig up whatever of him she could find. What terrible remains would *she* lay before me?

"Here," I heard my grandmother say. I opened my eyes.

No pictures, or newspaper clippings. But a pile of pale blue carbon paper, pressed together like petals of an old corsage.

"You want proof. Here's proof." Her voice sounded shrill, victorious. "See for yourself," she said.

To Alice Dawes. A hundred dollars. From D. Jones.

"What's *this*?"

"A receipt from the money order, silly," she said. "He left me an allowance. Like a little trust fund for my old age. If he were alive, he would have needed the money or sent it himself."

"This means nothing. Maybe D. Jones just sent it for him." I thought of David and me, each in charge of different jobs and felt a lump form in my throat. "Maybe D. Jones just pays the bills."

She shrugged. "And sometimes, this Jones person bothers to

152

put in a little note." She handed me a piece of lined looseleaf paper with a scrawl: *Sam wanted me to send this to you. D. Jones.* "See,
not Sam *wants*. But *wanted*. In my book that's dead. Besides, if he
were alive he'd send me a big boring letter each time, telling me
what to do with the pittance. Include the names of all the poor
slobs I had to share it with."

"How long has this been coming?"

She shrugged. "Maybe twenty years or so. But not every
month. Just now and then. Look I'm sorry I showed you. I knew
you'd get the wrong idea. I just did it to give you proof. "

"It proves nothing," I said. But I wasn't sure if it did or not.
"Why would he give *you* money?" Why not me? I guess I
meant. It's true I got by and so did Tom. But twenty years ago
we were hard-up kids. And Marie still had so little. And Tom and
I needed *something* all these years. An envelope. A note.

"I guess he told that person how I needed money. His type
believes in that. Giving according to need. It makes sense."

"Maybe my father had it sent to you because he was afraid to
write to us. And you were probably supposed to pass it on to my
mother. Because you were her mother. . . ."

"I learned my lesson with the corsage. She just would've returned it. But OK. From now on I will. If any more money orders come, I'll split it fifty-fifty. I've been meaning to put some
aside for all of you anyway. And a little for my old age."

I looked at her, the folded skin, the hair gone white, then yellow again. What age did she think she was—if not old?

"Do you know who D. Jones is?"

"Nope."

"Do you care?"

She shrugged.

"I think she was a woman he was with after Mommy."

"Marie was already in the booby hatch. Right? *D.* I didn't
think man or woman or anything. I just figured it was one of his
communistic friends. Giving things away."

I started to laugh. The crazy irony of it. My grandmother

despising him and everything he stood for, but claiming her fair share of his pie. And him giving it to her.

Then she was laughing. "I guess it is a little weird. You think I'm awful. Sometimes I guess I am. But not always. Sometimes I'm a lot of fun." Her spotted hand was on my arm. A leopard's paw, ready to claw. But she patted me—a few little taps. An old lady's hand taps. Tentative with shame—for the old skin touching you. "You can stay, you know," she said.

I laughed. How gracious. It was getting late—where else did she think I'd go? The Carefree Hilton?

"For a while. For as long as you want."

"Thanks," I said. "But I can't."

"I guess it's not such a good idea. Young people have to live their lives."

I had to laugh hard not to cry. I was hardly young—and I was throwing away what life I had. How much I missed my life, David. How crazy it felt losing him, finding her. How much it still hurt, those icy blue eyes. Those icy blue papers. Not a word to us all those years.

Maybe he was dead, maybe he wasn't. Maybe he'd intended the money to go to us and Marie. Or maybe he hadn't. Maybe it was an extravagant, ironic gesture. Like saying, Here I am, another Jewish Carpenter. Loving those who hate me. Would I ever know? My brother said he'd meet me. Maybe he'd change his mind. Maybe I should change my mind too. Give up my crazy chase.

I thought of Victor. Suddenly, I wanted to ask him things. Did you ever want to just give up? Forget it all? Because it's all too ugly.

I slept outside on an air mattress that Alice said had been left her by a friend who'd recently died in her sleep.

"I do think you're like me," she said, laying a sheet on me and patting my hand. "I think in my shoes you'd have done what I did. Which doesn't make us bad. I think we're basically nice. It's not like we don't say we're sorry. But they never forgive us."

It took me forever to get to sleep. When I finally did I

dreamed I was in a coffin beside my grandmother. Our shoes poked out of the wood. Our toes poked out of our shoes. We had different feet but we shared our shoes.

I woke, in the dark, shaking. Tommy had been right to send me to her. She was right—I was like her. *My father doesn't mean to make all this trouble for America. He's really very sorry and wants to be more American.* I remembered that note I sent to God knows how many public officials. Had my brother told my mother? Is that why she called me an FBI agent and went away for good? Had Tommy passed on the news to my father? Is that why he never came back? Because I was just too awful?

In the morning I woke to her face above mine.

"I made breakfast," she said. Through the window I could see an electric percolator going, a steaming waffle iron, an electric griddle with bacon sizzling, eggs frying. I tried not to think of my last big breakfast—of David. David and me eating eggs and pancakes on the expressway out to Beth Israel. It was a month ago, but it felt like a lifetime.

We ate outside. In the grass at the side of the lagoon the heron poked, awkward and uncertain. Where to now? How to proceed? I thought.

"Where do the letters come from?" I said. "What city?"

"Let's think. San Francisco. That's the postmark. Not that she thinks to put her address in case I need something."

I asked if I could use her phone to call Jean, who said he needed only an hour.

Later Alice wheeled my bags to the driveway in a wheelchair, adding to the pile a valise that wasn't mine. "For you and your brother. Share it."

I unzipped it. A toaster, an electric frying pan, an iron and a percolator, a couple of vases and teacups.

"One of those vases is good," she said. "One of those is crystal. Fancy pantsy, the lady who left it. Maybe you could give that one to *her*."

She handed me a twenty dollar bill. "And fill it with some flowers. Maybe she'll start feeling better if she hears I'm not so bad. I'm not so bad, right?"

She said she'd tell a neighbor to call me when she died. "You can have it all, then," she said. "You can sell the trailer. It's worth a few bucks. And there'll be some of his money left."

I looked at her face, pale and bony, imagining her dead.

And then Jean arrived. She poked her head into the taxi. And for the first and last time, I kissed her.

"You're not so bad," I said. For she wanted me to say it. And I needed to practice forgiveness. Of whom, I wasn't sure.

9: Rosie

Union square, December 9th, Tommy said when I finally reached him from a phone booth at a gas station where we stopped for gas. I should hold on tight. He had a meeting in Toronto but he'd come to San Francisco first. We'd do this together.

"You know who might know something?" he said. "Rosie and Arn." He said as long as I was bussing it out west, maybe I could stop to see them. If anyone knew anything it would be Rosie. And if Rosie knew anything, she'd tell. "We were like her kids," Tommy said, and his words gave me courage for one more stop.

Jean said he would drive me to Jacksonville, where I could get a bus to Santa Fe. On the ride north Jean and I talked about the landscape, buildings, what they had in Miami and Tampa versus Port au Prince and New York. Our homes. Used-to-be homes. With used-to-be friends and family. Jean said he could use the appliances but not the glass or china. His life was plain. He would be selling his quarter share in the taxi soon and take his test. He'd been a doctor in Haiti and hoped to be a nurse's aide within three years.

"Next time we meet it will perhaps be in a hospital," he said. He smiled and I tried to.

Unless you love degradation, danger and dirt, there is nothing to do in the Jacksonville bus terminal but sit in one spot. I sat on my portion of a molded plastic line of seating and reflected on whether, with the right detergent, the surface could ever get clean. I doubted it. The yellow plastic seemed to have permanently absorbed the dank dark air.

Two transvestites sat to my right. Their faces were blue with suppressed stubble, their fingers thick with rings, their feet spilling over the edges and sides of their high-heeled sandals like softened brie. They were talking about someone named Lacey Frilly Starlight. Two drunks, a man and a woman, huddled to my left, every few minutes waking from drunken snores to grab at each other, in affection or hostility it was impossible to say.

They called out my bus and I walked slowly towards my gate. I passed a woman with three kids draped on various parts of her—lap, knee, breast. I left Alice's things on my seat and wondered if she'd take them. Or the transvestites? Or the drunks? I thought of my father as I imagined Alice's hoarded property gone to strangers, felt an old fire flame in my chest. See, Daddy? I'm doing what you want me to.

In the bus, I felt dizzy and nauseated. I'm not so bad. I'm not so bad. Her words echoed in my head as I fell off to sleep. I woke up in Little Rock, tried Rosie but there was no message machine. I tried her again with no success the next morning when we stopped in Oklahoma City. And then I fell back into a deep sleep, in which I remained till we pulled into Santa Fe.

Rosie D'Amato was my mother's friend. The two of them had been young dancers together when half of the young women imports in New York were modern dancers and half of those were political activists. My mother and Rosie though had been ballet dancers and were bonded by their belief that their legs and will were stronger than those of any old modern dancer. They both grew up in the South in brutal Jim Crow years, finding in civil rights and dance the tickets to a new, if arduous, life. They met at a New York ballet class where another Southerner, hearing their drawls, confided her feelings about "uppity New York niggers." Their joint response became family lore, with each of them taking turns acting out their rejoinder. From then on they were a pair, taking ballet classes together, organizing performances of young ballet dancers from all around the globe, raising funds for low-cost dance studios in Harlem and Yonkers, and founding their own "New Steps" studio together on Fordham Road in the Bronx. When one was sick the other would cover her classes. And when sick became more frequent than not for Marie, Rosie continued to teach for my mother, insisting we take the money. And when they lost the studio, they ran around town side by side, scraping together whatever they could from Broadway chorus lines and garment center modeling gigs.

Rosie and her husband Arnie, a machinist, had no kids. Though we lived with Grandma and Boomie and then Aunt Elsie as our immediate family crumbled, until we went off to college we often spent weekends with "Aunty" Rosie and "Uncle" Arn. Arnie had asthma and when he got too sick to work, in the mid-Sixties, they moved to Santa Fe, where the air was better and living, before the town got discovered, was easy and cheap. Here Rosie set up "Maria's Kids"— children's ballet workshop, named, I'd always assumed, after Maria Tallchief, the American Indian prima ballerina—and here she taught kids from both the towns and nearby reservations. That was the last we heard. We graduated college, became "adults" and lost touch.

I was nervous to be appearing out of nowhere. But Tommy's words, "like her kids," echoed in my mind. And making my way down the side street from the bus station to the plaza, images of Rosie buoyed me up. Her beautiful black eyes, which would instantly forgive my silence. Days at the beach, Rosie walking with my mother, arm in arm like they were performing a *pas de deux*, me wedged in between, trying to mimic their grace.

Now it would be perfect again. I would spend the night with Rosie, of course, like in the old days. And we'd talk and talk into the morning. She'd tell me everything she knew. And maybe what she told me would allow me to go home. I remembered the kinds of things she used to say to make things all right as I lay as a child in her silky arms. Your mother loves you, she's just sick right now, soon she'll feel better. But you have *us*. And with her words in my head and her hand on my brow, I'd fall off to sleep, waking the next morning ready to brave Cousin Arthur and the schoolyard bullies.

I bought Rosie roses—her favorite white roses—from a vendor in the plaza. And then, remembering a Mexican bracelet she'd bought me, which I'd never thanked her for, I bought her a Hopi bangle with a serpent crest, imagining it encircling her slender wrist. It was late in the afternoon in the middle of winter, and Santa Fe was cold and growing dark, but the last rays of sun reflected off the snowy hills bathing the whole plaza in white light. The Indian vendors displaying dazzling silver and painted pots, the lumenaria dotting the plaza with amber, the guitars and horns blaring from a Mariachi band—all seemed a celebration choreographed by Rosie to welcome me *home*. And with my gifts in my arms, I strode across the plaza, down North Guadalupe beyond Paseo de Peralta, to Rosie's house at the northeast edge of town.

It was a small adobe with a large, glass extension. A small front lawn was filled with sculptures of children bowing, flipping, twirling, reaching. Maria's Children: Ballet for Flexible Bodies and Minds, the sign said. It was a wooden sign, painted pale coral with turquoise letters, and it reminded me of my mother, the blue-green scarf she wound on her head for class, perfect against her peachy skin. Before I could compose myself, white lights switched on and a bell went off—sounding like the old temple gongs that she and Marie loved to use in class.

"Can I help you?" she asked, stepping out onto the porch. Her face was much the same but pleated with wrinkles. Her eyes were unchanged, even in the twilight glistening bright like black olives. "We're closed. But can I help you?"

"It's me," I said. "Betsy."

She said nothing.

"Marie's girl," I tried. "Marie and Sam's girl."

In a second, she'd understand, I thought, and open her arms and I'd run into her embrace. I walked up the path now, extending my flowers.

But she extended her arms only to settle them on the porch pillars, blocking my entrance. "What do you want, Betsy?"

"I'm so sorry I've been out of touch. You know how it is. . . ."

"No, I don't, Betsy." I was standing now before the porch steps and she was staring down at me, like I'd come to rob her. "I only know that I haven't seen you in twenty years. That your family is no longer in my life. And I'd like to keep it that way."

I felt faint, and needed to sit, but I knew I wasn't welcome on Rosie's steps. So I just worked on taking in air to remain upright.

Finally I managed to say, "Why, Rosie? Please, Rosie . . . can't you . . . forgive me?"

Rosie forgave the whole world! The parents who pulled their kids from her school, the superintendent who let the FBI into her apartment to set up the wiretap. They were manipulated—that was her refrain. The undeveloped are easily manipulated.

"Please forgive me," I said again.

"It's nothing personal, Betsy. Nothing you did. And I love your mother still. I named this place for her. Marie's Children."

"I thought it was Maria," I said. "For Tallchief."

"No, it's Marie. For *my* Marie. She was beautiful, generous and very fragile. And she broke. I think of her every day. But I try never to think of him."

"But it's *me*," I said. "We liked you so much. . . . We loved you. Me and Tommy." I waited for her words: We loved *you* so much. . . .

"Really, Betsy, just leave."

"Why?" I moaned.

But she'd already turned her back to go inside.

It was still light enough to make out the children on the lawn and with my bags and flowers I wandered out to them. The sculptor had done them well—the chubby ones had dimples and darling folds at the back of their necks; and the thin ones had jutting knees and ankles, nervous hands and toes. I felt four, not forty, as I sat down in Rosie's yard, half believing she'd soon come out to lift me from the cold ground and lead me to her warm bed. I knew it was a child's wild fantasy in a wounded middle-aged mind, but I was too sad and scared to think another thought. And too tired to move, I just sat there with Marie's Children till it started to snow.

On the bus to San Francisco, only my brother's voice saying, the 9th at Union Square, the two of us together, gave me the will to go on. My heart felt broken, my brain battered. What had my father done to make Rosie hate him—and, in turn, us? To make our best friends our enemies? How do you go on when your best friends hate you?

At our first meal stop, the beef was gray, the hamburgers black, the hotdogs olive-green. I bought six bags of peanuts and three Mounds bars to keep me for the next twenty-four hours. But as soon as I put a peanut in my mouth, I started to gag, and then like a drunk I staggered along the street, retching and vomiting. I found a bathroom but the stench was impossible. I found a lot filled with junk and puked some more and peed on an ancient big-wheel.

Back on the bus I wanted to change my clothes, and I asked the driver for my bag. It was impossible, he said, to retrieve baggage mid-trip. What was the problem?

"My medication," I lied.

He said, "Oh, in that case," and opened up the bins, standing over me, watching, as I thumbed through my things for a bottle of aspirin, pulling out a change of clothes as if an afterthought.

He looked at me impatiently and I was sure he smelled the puke. I missed Michelle, the friendly driver from my last long ride. I even missed Victor, his encouraging tips.

The next day I had no appetite at all, and I guess I was dehydrated—for I no longer needed to leave the bus when the others left, to find bathrooms or lots. Now and then, I dry heaved into a brown bag I found under my seat.

The woman across the aisle, I noticed, was laughing a lot. I sat and watched how she threw her head back and opened her mouth just before she laughed, like she was getting ready to get her throat cultured. She was happy, she said. She was happy about her decision, getting out from under her sister's thumb, leaving the beauty parlor. She talked to the woman in front of me, saying that the truth was that she was never cut out to be a beautician. The only reason she'd gone in for it was because she came from a long line of beauticians and felt pressured into it. She was tired of being stuck with washing and manicures while her bossy sister did all the fancy cuts and perms and got the big tips and genuine appreciation. Executive secretary was more her speed anyway, since she liked to dress and never felt truly herself in uniforms. She was going to start a new life in California, learn office skills and show them all. Call her sister from some fancy office and say, Guess what's become of you-know-who?

The woman on my side said, "Get really good with the computer. Secretaries are going out of style."

I'm not sure how long they were talking, how long I was listening, thinking, What is *your* life, *your* future? But I must have been staring for a long time with my mouth wide open. For the one next to me was saying, "Are you all right?" And the other one was saying, "She doesn't look quite right." I remember a fleeting thought about how everyone was starting a new life while I was going after some old life, a passing thought about who was more forlorn, then hearing them saying, "You all right? She all right?" Then feeling cold sweats, hot sweats, then their hands on my head.

"Febrile," one of them said. "I'm good at telling. My brother's a nurse."

The other said, "For sure."

And then all the passengers, a dozen or so people, and the driver, too, were standing over me, nodding in agreement, saying that I was hot as a stove. Someone produced a thermometer. My temperature was 103. "That's high fever for an adult," someone said. "That's fiercely febrile." They agreed that everyone would eat fast at the next stop, get us into San Francisco before schedule. They produced fruit and drink, debated solids and liquids. I drank only water but then stopped because it made me retch, and when we pulled into downtown San Francisco in the middle of the night, I wobbled across the terminal like a drunk. The ex-beautician offered to stay with me, but I said I'd be OK. She gave me the thermometer and I gave her a hundred dollars to help set herself up. I said I didn't need it—I'd be seeing my father soon. She tried to refuse but I ran away. Up the street was the Hilton, where I checked in. By then my temperature was 104.

10: Dreams

I DREW THE THICK DRAPES and crawled under the covers with my clothes on. And there I slept and woke and slept and woke, sliding back again and again into the same dream.

A figure in a hooded robe and mask says, I'm here to testify. Then punish. What did I do? I cry over and over.

#1. You were seen at Public School 32 The Bronx besides a Mrs. Grady. When she said everyone must stand up and be counted in the battle against communistic evil, you were seen saying, I agree, I agree. Count me, count me. You were seen jumping in the air.

#2. On several occasions you were seen in the hallway of a Queens apartment building talking with a Mr. Brown and Mr. Gray. When asked to tell about your father for his own and the national good, you did. You told the names of the books he read. The names of his friends. Leo and Esther. Arn and Rosie.

#3. You put in an application to join the Puff Balls Girls Club and were told to appear in a sweater set fully prepared to disclose a secret. They went around the room telling secrets about their bodies and boyfriends; when your chance came, the rule changed. They prepared a statement with your secret. You cried but then you said it. *My father is a traitor.* When they then said, OK, now sign it, you were seen signing.

There's a #4 and #5, a #6 and #7. I've told more secrets, made-up and otherwise. I've signed lots of letters and affidavits. With #7, the "testimony" ends. Those are your 7 Deadly Sins, the hooded figure says. And now for the sentencing.

Solitary confinement. Exile. Death. Which shall it be?

Then I am shouting, calling for my mother and father and brother to help me. The hooded figure says, We can't help you. And I see its face. Three faces. On three heads. My mother. Brother. Father. And then Rosie pops out of my mother's mouth.

We wouldn't help you even if we could, she says.

But I'm just a kid, I cry.

I couldn't say how long I had been lying there in the hotel bed, sleeping and dreaming those dreams, shaking and shivering. I woke up screaming, expecting to see the hooded creature at the side of my bed. The room was black but I made out enough—a chair, an armoire, a carafe and glasses—to remind me where I was. And that I wasn't a kid at an inquisition, but a woman in a hotel, dreaming.

Clearly my fever had broken. And whether the dreams had dispelled the fever, or the fever had incited the dreams, I couldn't say. They were familiar dreams, nightly invaders once upon a time; then, for the longest time, since my father died, nowhere in sight.

I fumbled my way to the window and opened the drapes. The sky was gray. In dawn or dusk, I wondered. I opened the door and tiptoed to a discarded room-service tray next door. Toast crumbs. It was morning. At the next door there was a newspaper. It was the morning of December 9th. The day my brother was supposed to meet me. To find our father.

The fever and dreams had drained me. But my old dream trial, seeing my accuser and judge, then waking as an adult, not a mute child, had lifted something. I felt ready—or closer to ready than ever before—to hear the truth. Dead or alive. We'd find him one way or another, my brother and I.

11: Union Square

MY SEARCH
had left me thinner than I'd been since childhood, when our chronic worrying kept us hovering at scrawny; and after showering and dressing in clean jeans and a clean shirt that flapped on my bony body, I felt like the waif of that earlier life—half of the Betsy-Tom urchin team. Walking up the hill to Union Square now, I missed my brother as I hadn't in years. I couldn't wait to see his face, hear his voice. Skinny-ninny, he'd probably say when he saw me. And then we'd find a bakery and kill a bag of donuts. And then we'd face whatever there was to face. Together.

I tried to imagine how Tom would look. Would he be gray? Would he be bald? Would he be in his old student jeans or his new Third World outfits, in which he did *his* bidding for a new world. The last time I saw my brother was more than five years ago, when he was back in town for a UN conference on hunger. He sported tinted glasses and a Ché-style beard, by day a Caribbean-style guayabera, by night a black suit—both a shiny polyester making him look like a cross between a dentist and a bouncer. And watching him leave each morning in pastel see-through over-shirts, I had to quell the urge to call him back, to make him stay by my side, to protect him always from a mocking world.

My brother had no style, a quality I admired in him as much as I did his piercing righteousness and relentless energy for the downtrodden of the earth. But now, trying to assemble in my mind a picture of the brother who would meet me at ten, I couldn't. All I could call to mind were his knees. How my brother's knees jiggled and shook. Waiting to see Sam or hearing the voice of some crank caller on the phone or walking past the American Legion Headquarters where a WWI veteran, with a plate in his head, would boo at us, the knees would start going. Sometimes I took his hand, but he'd only scream, Take your mitts off me! If you looked at his face, you'd never know the anxiety below. You'd have to be right next to him to feel the nervous vibrations.

He will be late, of course. The question, I thought, as I sat on the bench in Union Square watching a mime imitate an old Chinese lady nibbling a bun, was how late. Except for goody-goody me, lateness was a family habit. No one in our family could make it anywhere on time. It was an odd behavior, I'd often thought, in men who built their lives on routing out "self-indulgent excess" in the world. Was it a sign of arrogance? I'd wondered. Or an odd moral stance? Was my chronically late family just showing their rejection of the rules of *this* world as they tried to make a new one? Or maybe it was just the result of a minor learning disability. I heard my father saying, Honey, time just flew. I'm sorry. I heard Tom's voice: No one wants to be late, dummy. It just happens. What was the truth—about my father and my brother and time, about my father and the time of the last twenty years? Would I ever find out? I looked at my watch. Tom was already half an hour late. People were smiling at me and for a moment I thought they were my brother's new posse and I began searching for his face among them. For the dark eyes, the long nose, the curly black hair. But then I realized they were laughing, not smiling—that the mime had changed his focus. *To me.* He was biting his lips and biting his cuticles and I tried to laugh it off but he only covered his mouth and laughed back at me, which made the crowd laugh still harder. But then a fat kid waddled across the path, winning the mime's attention, and saving me.

He could be an hour late or two hours late. He could come at three with a half dozen of his cohorts. Sitting there, I thought of all those bodies marching in and out of our lives. The body guards, Aunt Elsie used to say, when Tom trekked in with his gang. Or, the liberation army. An army whose membership was always changing, depending on the group my brother was be-friending and defending at the time.

When Tom was six or so, he was a friend to the American Indian, his first major minority. He was too young yet to walk the city, gathering his people to bring home for supper; the Indians he brought home, therefore, were scaled down—painted cast-iron miniatures from the Museum of Natural History gift shop, lean coppery bodies scooping fish, riding horses, tending children and fires, hundreds of Indians covering his bureau, his desk, his floor, his bed. His walls were covered with Indians, too, stern portraits, haunting sepia photos. Chief Joseph, Sitting Bull and countless unnamed men on horses—my brother's earliest heroes.

Sitting cross-legged on his bed under our father's army blan-ket, he would greet me in any number of Indian tongues. Then breaking into an arched English, he'd say, Watch out for the rushing brook. Or, Do be careful—the deer are crossing. Taken up by the game, I'd say, Oh, boy this water is freezing. Look at that baby deer. And with the authority of one of the chiefs on his wall, he'd say, The white men have killed all the fawns. And you've scared off all the fish in the silver stream, young fool. Once he found a real Indian wandering along the beach at Pel-ham Bay, where we lived the years before Mexico. He'd come down from Canada to help build the Throgs Neck Bridge. Tom brought him home and he lived with us for a few weeks. Sam tried to get him to organize, expanding minority representa-tion in the ironworkers union. Marie tried to get him to teach her Indian dances. Tom tried to get him to change his name from Bob to Mountain Peak. Because Tom and I had to share a room when guests stayed, and I was tired of getting yelled at for destroying Indian villages, I tried to get Bob to leave by asking if he didn't miss his family. Apparently what I said got to him most—for one night he walked out to buy a pack of cigarettes and never came back.

When we lived in Mexico City, it was the Mexicans, of course, whom my brother befriended, ultimately choosing to attend the local Mexican school, at night wandering the plaza, following the mariachis. I attended the American School that was also attended by a few other political renegades' children but mostly by the children of American diplomats and industrialists. I got As in all subjects, and trophies for tennis, basketball and squash. I was a cheerleader until Tom gave my gold baton and red pompoms away to some Mexican children down the block, "who had not a toy to their name."

Once back in the States, my brother had a Puerto Rican phase, a Filipino phase, a West Indian phase. During a brief East Indian phase, during which he brought home a dozen Indians for Thanksgiving. Aunt Elsie and I had cooked turkey and stuffing. As they all marched in, Tom announced they were vegetarians, and we scurried to the kitchen to wash the stuffing, which was all they ate that day, the Indians and Tom—washed stuffing and yams. None of the turkey, none of Aunt Elsie's chopped turkey liver. They were a friendly group and I think one or two would have lived on the couch or floor for a while, but from the discussion at dinner, learning that they were Brahmins, Tom stopped talking. They all left quickly after that. Tom was pale and twitching all over when the door finally closed behind them. His knees were jumping—his whole body vibrating. He said, I thought they were untouchables, and ran off into his room.

Untouchables for bodyguards, untouchables in your army, Aunt Elsie laughed. That's a good idea. Who would go near?

Remembering, I was laughing. But the mime was eyeing me again, so I stood up and walked around the park. I must have walked each of the paths a dozen times, zig-zagging nervously back and forth like a hamster in a maze. When I finally sat down

I was exhausted and the mime and the crowd were gone. From the next bench someone said it was going on one. Three hours late. Three hours late was too late, even for a Vogel. Then I thought, not late. Just not coming.

Then a deep voice called, "Waiting for someone, girlie?"

And I raced into his arms.

How long did we sit on the bench, saying nothing, cuddling, then holding each other at arm's length to look, then collapsing on each other again in joyous relief. "Ain't love grand," an old woman called from a nearby bench. And we laughed. Love *was* grand.

Arm in arm, we walked without a plan. We wandered through Chinatown, nibbling egg rolls from bags. We jumped on a cable car and rode it down to the Wharf. We walked out onto the pier and watched the boats load their cargo. I rubbed his head, finding a copse of gray under the black. He poked my hip bones and called me Skinny-Ninny. Mostly we said nothing but just marched up and down hills, side by side. And then, tired, we settled into a booth in a North Beach bar. We had to talk seriously, though neither of us really wanted to.

What had our father done? Had he really gassed that building with poison? He was of the old school of organizing, always talking about the stupidity and cruelty of desperate measures. What could have changed him so? The murders at Kent State? And if he did the deed, why was there only one article in the *San Francisco Chronicle* and then not a word more? Maybe it was just a tear gas bomb, to call attention to all the tear gas fucking up kids' eyes at demonstrations. Maybe it was just a bomb of dust and dirt, to make a point about the U.S. presence in Southeast Asia—how it's really dirty. A stink bomb, Tom said, to say, This war stinks. On and on, we theorized, feeling like we were kids again trying to make sense of all the eruptions and explosions in our life.

And what had he done before the San Francisco action? Horowitz had said that people believed something about Sam that he,

171

Horowitz, didn't. What was that? And if whatever he had done had turned all his friends against him, why hadn't he turned to us? Side by side in the oak booth, we sat, downing shots of vodka, mustering the courage we needed to review a panel of possibilities, each worse than the other. He'd been killed. He'd killed himself. He was alive, but mad. He wasn't mad but had amnesia and had forgotten us. On and on, we wove our theories. And then there was no escaping the fact: We knew nothing and had to find the one person who might know. Doreena Jones.

But face to face with the San Francisco phonebook, which the waiter was kind enough to bring us, we both froze. I looked up a hairdresser on Clement who had tried to shave my head the last visit—curious to see if he'd managed to keep enough customers to still be in business. I looked to see if North Beach Leather was still around—since it had opened and closed in New York. Like I'd done the day this whole thing started, the day I went to see Sam's grave, I stalled. Did I really want to find Doreena, find her number, say, Hello, it's me, Sam's daughter? With my brother, Sam's son. Now tell us the whole story! Tom stalled too, looking up his college roommate, calling from his cell, leaving a long update for a message.

Then we made deals. You do it, no you. Like our old volleys back and forth for who would make the scary grown up calls. To doctors and prison wardens, to funeral directors and school principals. Tommy would call the first five, we decided now, and then it would be my turn. But seeing that vodka had only made my brother more jittery, his knees more jiggly under the table, I breathed deeply, made my mind blank, and dialed. There were six D. Joneses in the San Francisco phone book, and three of them were home—Diane, Dolores, and Dot respectively; four Dorothy Joneses, all of whom were home but never went by the name Doreena; two Doris Joneses, one wasn't home and the one who was used to be called Dorrie but never Doreena by a step-mother in Baton Rouge, but her name only recently be-came Jones because she married a Richard Jones only eighteen months prior after knowing him only a month; one Dee Dee who said, "Doreena, that's not a real name."

The waiter walked by with some nuts.

"How about Berkeley and Oakland?" he said. And he handed me the books for Berkeley and Oakland, and there, right in the middle of the directory, at Devon Street, Oakland, was Doreena Jones.

Then I was dialing and then *I* was shaking, more than Tom even. For there it was, a woman's voice on the other end—and here I was with no idea of where to begin.

"Is Doreena Jones there?"

"This is Doreena. Doreena Jones."

"This is Betsy. Betsy Vogel."

There was a silence.

"Sam's daughter," I said.

"Uh, huh," she said. Then nothing.

Indifference? Hostility? Fear? I couldn't tell.

"I'm in San Francisco. With my brother."

"Uh, huh," again. Then, "Is there something you want to tell me?"

And now I could hear that it was fear. "Something . . . that happened?"

I said, "We don't know anything that happened. . . . We thought you could tell us something. . . ."

"Oh," she said. "I thought you were calling to tell me. . . ."

And then she laughed as if she'd just told a joke. And then she sighed and you could hear the huge relief.

"Nothing's happened. But we need to see you," I said.

By now it was almost nine, but we found an open car rental on Van Ness and before I knew it we were driving through the foggy park and then over the misty bay to Oakland.

"Berkeley," I called to my brother, who dozed in the passenger seat.

"Hail to thee, alma mater," he mumbled.

"Little men power," I said. And we both laughed.

How many years since I thought of that speech, which my brother had delivered on the steps of the administration building, and which I read alone in my Ann Arbor dorm room, in a *Ramparts* magazine someone gave me. Whoever introduced Tom had called him a big hero for lying down in front of a munitions train on its way to San Diego. And Tom's speech went on about how there were lots of *little* heroes out there, who needed to be appreciated and given power. *Little men power*, he said. They were white and brown and red and black. In Vietnam, in South Africa, in Mississippi, in the factories and offices and streets of Chicago and L.A., Detroit and New York. The little men needed jobs, education, healthcare, peace, justice. Across the nation, they were staking their claim to America. Hail to the little heroes, the little men, he called.

Reading the speech, seeing my brother's words marching on the page, I had tingled with pride. But then I started smarting. How about little women—you asshole! And now I remembered, too how spooked I'd felt—for Tom had sounded just like Sam. Not just the total comfort in being called a hero, a big hero, but the way Tom said, little hero, little men, admiring and patronizing at once. And now years later with my brother at my side, searching for our father, I am laughing wildly again, because it had been such perfect "Son of Sam" talk.

When we were growing up and Sam was around—between trials or out on bail—he'd call every other shopkeeper "the little man." Not surprisingly, we were not allowed to shop at the supermarkets that were just sprouting in our Bronx neighborhood, but had to buy butter from this little man, cheese from another, vegetables and fruit from another little fellow with a little store. But our father was so preoccupied with his work and troubles, and so intent on the general principle of little shop owner versus giant corporate supermarket—and the sympathy and rhetoric due the former as a group—that he never distinguished among his little men. *Go to little man and pick up the order,* he'd write in a note and we'd go from little store to little store looking for the right little man. When I was very young I thought Sam called them little because they were short; at least they appeared that way seated behind their scrubbed marble counters.

Out in the water was Alcatraz, a black shadow asleep in the darkening bay. He'd been at Sing Sing and Attica, Leavenworth and Lewisburg, my father. Why not Alcatraz now—when it was closed down and dead to the world? I mused as my brother dozed. The Missing Man of Alcatraz? The Dead Man of Alcatraz? I studied the outline of rock against the open water, remembering the wide flowing Hudson behind the Sing Sing bars. And then we were there—on the other side of the bay.

As we looked for her street, we distracted ourselves from our growing dread with shtik, as we'd done so many for so many years.

"How much you want to bet," I said, "she opens her arms for a big, showy, left-wing 'I love all humanity' hug or we get a serious 'a people united will never be defeated' handshake?"

Tom said, "I bet she kisses on both cheeks. To show she's spent considerable time in Europe. I'm not kissing her back! I can tell you that much."

"Me, neither," I said. "I'm not touching her for anything."

We suppressed nervous giggles as we found her street up above Jack London Square.

Doreena had the yard and porch lights on, and we found the house easily. It was a gray Victorian up on a hill, and coming upon it perched above the bay, I felt like I'd gone back to our childhood home. With its gables and turrets, its verandah and precarious steps, its dangling shutters and peeling paint, its tall windows reflecting the water, it looked like our old house near Pelham Bay—the top floor apartment we rented in an old clapboard house, those years before Mexico. From the car I could see her on the steps—tiers of silver hair, silver earrings, a fringed shawl draped over an embroidered floral blouse and flowing peasant skirt.

"Hello, Betsy and Tom," Doreena said, when we reached her. No hugs or handshakes or showy kisses. Just a simple hello.

"Hello," we said.

She led us into a small living room with dark oak furniture, a carved mantel, a fire in the hearth. Her face was lined all over, like fine old lace. I guess I was staring at the delicate network of lines, for she said, "I'm sixty-five. I know I look much older."

I shook my head, no, but it was true. Except for a wide, girlish smile, she looked ancient. I began to search for the face that had gone with the smile, the face that had been there, long ago, beneath the lined veil.

And she must have read my eyes. For she said, "I was never truly pretty. I was what they called 'vivacious.' And I qualified for that more by my screaming costumes than by anything in me, I think. I guess 'vivacious' turns to 'frisky' when you get old. Anyway, I was never a beauty. Your mother was the beauty."

I pictured my mother's blond curls, her peachy skin, her coal eyes, and nodded.

"You have his dark skin, Tom. You, Betsy, have his eyes." She lifted her hand to touch us, but then held back.

"Don't hate me," she said, reading my mind.

I shook my head, no, I don't hate you.

"Yes, I can tell," she said. "Your eyes just turned yellow. Like his, from green to yellow, in anger. It's OK."

We were hideous, Tommy and I—pre-adolescent at most. "Thanks for giving me permission," I think I said, spouting proclamations of petty defiance I'd never tried before in my life. "I don't know what I'd do without your permission."

Tommy said nothing. He sat on the couch, looking out at the black bay, tapping his finger impatiently on the couch's arm and working his knees.

"Maybe you both have a right to resent me. But not for the reasons you think. Not because of Marie."

"You have no right," I heard myself say, "to talk about Marie as if she's your pal. When you took our father. You ruined our life."

"Ruined your life," she echoed, and I nodded yes.

My brother, the great organizer of movements and campaigns, strategies and language to advance social causes, is a poor organizer of simple words for simple conversation. But hearing the word "ruined," his political instincts kicked in.

"Jesus, nothing's ruined, Bets. We have a lot to do . . . for the future. So let's get this over with. . . ."

"You two really don't know anything, do you?" Doreena said.

I shrugged. "Not about him. Not recently."

"Not the past twenty-five years," Tom said, laughing.

"What do you want to know? Just ask me."

With her shawl and earrings, she looked like a gypsy fortune teller, and sounded like one, too, bold and commanding: "Ask me and I will tell you anything you want to know." But one of her eyes was twitching under the lavender shadow. Poor Doreena. She was as scared as we were, suffering her own ghost and now me, her ghost's brat with the self control of a twelve-year-old.

"I'd like to know how he ended up with you," I said. "Our father."

She said, "Well let me start at the beginning. We met in Washington. I was an actress in Washington for a production of *Romeo and Juliet* at the Folger. I was totally apolitical then. A lawyer friend took me to a hearing, claiming it was the best show in town. And there was Sam. We entered as he spoke: 'Betray friends? The proposition is revolting, nauseating, utterly contemptible. I hold this committee in utter contempt.' It was thrilling to be in the same room with such fearlessness. He was the least afraid person I'd ever known."

"Love at first sight," I said.

"Not at all. After your mother was away for a long, long time. After he started his *new* life. Before that I'd met him again in

177

Mexico. I was down there for a film. I met the two of you, too. At the Shawns' pool. But it wasn't till much later that we linked up."

"I remember the pool," I said, as if to say I do not remember you. And I did not hear you say "linked up," like a trashy cheerleader.

"I hated that pool," Tom said.

The Shawns. Jake Shawn, the blacklisted Hollywood director. The Shawn swim parties as lavish as anything in Beverly Hills. I remembered our confusion, for wasn't this the enemy—rich people with big swimming pools? And Sam saying, They're "progressives." I don't go for the big style, either, but they're progressives, they're on our side. And things go cheap down here. So they can make believe they're still big shots.

"I used to go there to the Shawns' to do laps."

"I only went there once," Tom said.

"I remember," I said. "And you told Jake Shawn that you wouldn't be coming back. 'I object to this luxury. It's built on the backs of small, dark people.' And Shawn said it bothered him, too, but one had to go on."

"I can hear it now," she laughed.

"You weren't there," I said.

"I hated how they pretended not to notice that they lived in a villa," Tom said. "I had to get out of there. . . . Dad understood why."

Then another memory—away from the Hollywood heavies, our father with a hammer in his hand, a fistful of nails in his mouth, bent over a coffin. Back then Americans could work in Mexico if someone would sign that no Mexican could be found to do the job; someone with a coffin factory felt sorry for Sam and signed papers saying his skills were needed to make his coffins. In Mexico, my father built coffins six days a week. Marie made it to Mexico with us, but then went back—to a hospital in upstate New York, where she received electric shocks to stop her sense of steady persecution.

"Your father was very proud of you, Tom . . . Tom Paine," she laughed.

My brother beamed.

"I've followed your campaigns over the years. At Berkeley. Now with End Hunger. Hunger. Wasn't that supposed to be passé by now?" she laughed.

And just as I was thinking, Who can compete with Tom Paine—great man with his sword of a pen? Certainly not little Betsy Ross with her puny needle and kindergarten stars! Just as hideous old jealousy started to uncoil inside me, and I thought, Hey, Dorito, this trip was all my idea, not his, she said, "Proud of you, too." Her voice soft, pliant with something like pity.

"Me?" It came out like a squeal.

"Yes, Betsy. Betsy Ross. He was never without that picture of you carrying the flag. You really don't know about him."

"How could I?" And again it came out angry, an angry bark. "He never told us anything. And then. . . ."

"And then he left you."

"And then he left us."

When I looked up *she* was crying. Because, of course, he'd left her too.

Then Tom was patting her hand. And then the three of us were sitting side by side on the worn mohair couch, holding hands, like we were watching a movie and had come to a part too sad to view without holding onto someone.

"The only thing he feared back then was jail," she said. "He thought he'd never live through jail again. I don't have to tell you what happened. He was convicted three times. It's like they shot him and kept shooting. The last time they arrested him, it was just too much. He'd already been in jail ten years on and off. His heart was bad. He was sure jail would kill him. And he wanted to live so much. For his cause. For his kids. For all the reasons people hold on to life—big and small, I guess. Long after Washington, long after Mexico, I met him at some fundraiser in New York. He'd just served six months on another contempt charge. You kids were there, I remember. You collected the envelopes with Dr. Horowitz."

"I don't remember you," I said, instantly regretting my lingering spite.

Doreena nodded, patting my hand. "You were little, Betsy. Ten, or so. You and Tom looked like those kids painted on velvet. Giant black eyes staring out."

"Go on," I said. "About you."

"Please," Tom said.

"I'd been blacklisted a few years before because a man I had lived with, who later went nuts and walked himself off a bridge, had been in a lefty theater group. The theater and movies were full of wide-eyed people—communists, socialists, New-Dealers with all these good-hearted scripts about good guys making a good world with no malice or prejudice or greed. Sam sat down at my table and said, 'You have kind trustworthy eyes. If I need to go away somewhere, will you help me?' I said, 'Yes.' I'd met him only twice. He said, 'It may mean giving up your present life.' I said, 'I know.' I had very little of my life left. I hadn't worked in three years. I did some voice work for ads under the name Della Dayton. I gave him my number. He said if he was arrested again, I'd hear from him. The plan was for him to jump bail. I'd help hide him. In Chicago. I knew people in Chicago. That's where I'm from."

"I didn't know about you."

"You said that already."

"I mean, I didn't know you were the one who was hiding him. . . . We visited him in Chicago, in Detroit, in St. Louis. And then we didn't. Aunt Elsie said he died. And now she says he didn't die. At least not back then. If he didn't die, why didn't he come back—or let us visit him?"

I missed him terribly, suddenly, and I started crying. Tom put his arm around me, but I could tell he was somewhere else. Or at least trying to get there, as if his knees were engines that could propel him away from all this old misery.

"What does it matter, Betsy?" he said distractedly. "What matters is now. And tomorrow."

Doreena looked away. "I want you to understand as much as I understand," she said. "He was in anguish because he couldn't come back. But everything had unraveled. Everyone on the Left admired him when he jumped bail. They admired everything he ever did. He acted very independently but that seemed to go with his special dynamism that could win people over. So even the most rigid old-timers adored him. But then everything changed. At first, when he took off, lots of people around the movement helped him. Then later they stopped helping to arrange safe houses, stopped talking to him, or me. No doors were open. The world he knew was closed to him. Everything he'd ever done became suspect. He was on his own. Except for me."

Except for me. I looked at her face for signs of self-congratulation. But all I could see was that twitching eye, signaling terror and isolation.

"What about us?" I said.

"I'll get to that. I'm still back then. You have to remember how things were back then. How scared people were. A lot of people ended up informing. They were threatened, terrified. They ended up making deals, doing different things. Sam had always done things a little differently. Refusing to sign. Then refusing to step down from union leadership. Then refusing to shut down the union after its charter was rescinded. Then refusing to go back to jail. Everyone in our world loved it. Then later on, they pointed to his flagrant independence as the first sign that he was questionable. Those were crazy times!"

Tom said, "*Questionable?* What? What's going on?"

She was holding our hands hard, like Marie and then Elsie used to before the verdict would be announced. "They questioned his loyalty. And then they stopped questioning. They said they had proof."

"Loyalty to what? Proof of what?" I said.

"Loyalty to the movement. Proof that he was working for *them*."

I had a photocopy of the *San Francisco Chronicle* article in my bag, and I pulled it out. "*Them?*" I said, pointing to the man who looked like Brown and Gray. "Is he *them?*"

And she nodded.

When my father's friends stopped talking to him, he had only her to talk to, Doreena said. And, in time, when he thought that she, too, doubted him, he talked aloud to himself, walking back and forth from room to room, and silently, at night, sitting at his desk, writing in notebooks he kept hidden even from her. We followed Doreena into a small study, where a dozen pebbly black and white notebooks were stacked on a battered oak desk.

"He left them behind. It took me a year before I found them and another year before I could read even a page. I took them out for . . . whenever you're ready."

I huddled near the door, afraid to cross the room to the notebooks, as if they would go up in smoke.

Then Tommy pulled me with him.

There was a view of the bridge from the window, a frilly lampshade on a milk glass lamp, an Indian bedspread with tiny mirrors on a single bed. I think I remember that. But it's the notebooks, of course, that have stayed in my mind. Touching them, as if each page were a piece of him.

Side by side, we divided the volumes, eight in all, each for a year. From 1963, when he went away, to 1970, when he *died*. And then one that wasn't really a notebook, but a scrapbook. What he did and why, where he went and when, where he was now, how he was if he was alive? With our questions spinning in our minds, we opened the notebooks. But first, like kids or young lovers, we skimmed for any mention of ourselves, and when we'd find it, we read it out loud, as if to tell the whole world that our father never forgot us.

1963. Visited with the children at B's in Detroit. Betsy appears to be developing, Her waist is as slender as Marie's when I first met her and you can see she's practicing a brand-new grown-up walk. Tom has fuzz on his cheeks and when I touched it I got goosebumps. Will I get to see my children grown with breasts and beards?

1965. Betsy and Tommy need to meet other progressive kids. But living with my sister limits that. They try not to complain, but I know the neighborhood kids ride them hard for my politics. And I'm not there to help them fight back. I saw a black and blue mark on Tommy's face. He said it was nothing. Betsy said, They called him a Red and kicked him in the head. Tommy said that he "got them back good . . . where it really hurts"

1967. *I hope they don't take it out on the children. The children need all the friends we have.*

1969. The best thing about the plan with T is that it will restore trust. With friends of course. And with the children. They will understand who I am, and what I stand for.

1970. My sister has told the children that I died. She's correct. The best thing for them is for me to 'die.' I have only brought them sorrow. And pain. Pain and sorrow. And now this fiasco on top of all the others. No more if I'm dead.

In every volume we were there. But we're surrounded by a blur of strange people and stranger events, like we were in our childhood. What happened in 1967 to make our father think we might lose our friends? Was it the something that made his friends *question* him? Was "T" Terence Lutman? Our father didn't die when our aunt said he did, but later?

Tom read aloud: *March 3, 1967. I ran into R today in the street where we usually meet. I had asked for a meeting but I hadn't heard from him and was glad I ran into him. I wanted to know how P and the other war resisters were doing in Leavenworth. But R wouldn't talk. He just stared at me like he'd never seen me before and said, We won't be meeting again. I'm sure you understand. And when I said, No, I don't, he said, Don't you? And walked away. I called after him but he wouldn't turn around. I ran all the way down Lake Street but he had disappeared.*

And then a few weeks later: *I called V to arrange for a meeting to discuss what happened. But he said he wasn't interested in any meeting with me. I said that I'd settle for the briefest conversation, just long enough to figure out what was going on. He said, You know better than the rest of us what's going on. I said, What the hell's going on? Just what the hell is going on? I was screaming in the phone booth, which was really stupid. I could have gotten picked up then and there.*

"They think he's police?" Tom said. "For months he's trying to talk to his closest friends and contacts. People he trusted and relied on. Tries and tries. Month after month after month."

At the end of 1967, I found: *I discussed with D the possibility that they think I'm an agent. This seems the only explanation. I'm sure everything can be cleared up. But in the meantime it's painful. I can't wait till I reach a friend who's willing to talk to me and get this whole mess cleared up.*

Then at the start of the next year: *I woke in the middle of the night racking my brain for who could help me out. Clarify the terrible mistake. I came up with S. I've always found him open-minded and an independent thinker. In the morning when I reached him he said, I don't know you anymore. I said, You know me. It's me, Sam. He said, No, you're not the man I knew. You're someone else now.*

April 1968. Tom read: *D tries to talk to people for me but they avoid her too. C was a little more candid. She shook her head up and down when D said, Do they think he's an agent? She walked D out to her car and said, They say he accidentally left a note in a phonebooth. A report to the bureau giving names and dates of meetings and political actions, then a request for more money for his work. D said, That's insane. You know Sam. Besides, no agent would leave anything that obvious. It must have been planted. She asked C if I seemed like someone who would spy on friends for money. C said, Not till now. C said that some people aren't surprised. He was always doing things on his own. Some people say it all fits together now. And you? D asked C. What do you think? C said, I can't think straight these days. And walked back to the house.*

In the fall of 1969 my father almost died of pneumonia. In the winter he suffered bouts of angina day after day and felt death was imminent. In the spring of 1970 something happened to make him feel alive again.

April 1970. I met a guy at the Foundations Bookstore. He is a serious individual if a little somber, but then the world we live in induces that even in jolly souls. Like me he is following carefully the events in Southeast Asia, and is outraged by the widening aggression. Of course I didn't go into my personal situation with him. But without saying anything, I sensed sympathy—deep social consciousness and an earnestness on a personal level that I appreciate particularly at this stage.

"Poor Daddy. He sounds like a boy scout," Tom said.

"It's like he's writing for an audience. To show he's an OK person."

"He was desperate," I said.

"Desperate enough for a *device*?" Tom said. "I still don't get it."

In May 1970 there's an entry about Kent State, the National Guard killing unarmed students, some protesting the expansion of the war into Cambodia, some just walking to class. A few days later, there's an entry about "T and his thoughts," which then quickly becomes referred to as "T and his plan," which is part of their joint program of pamphlets and special actions. My father is not "comfortable" with T's tactic, and argues for an "alternative approach."

T said he was willing to be flexible because he'd come to think of me as his partner in conscience. Whatever we did, we needed to do it together. I knew what he meant. I wished to be partners in conscience with people once again. With T, but more especially with my old friends. They'd be impressed and realize how much they'd misjudged me and what a committed activist I've remained. Then we'd be together again.

"He's planning on doing something about the war to clear his name. Is that it? And he has a new friend to do it with."

June 1970. D does not approve of the program. She thinks T is juvenile. But then I have always been in the lead politically in our relationship, and agree with T when he says dramatic action is needed to bring attention to the situation in Cambodia. She says, You have never done this sort of thing, why now?

Tom and I were taking turns reading sentences now. For each sentence left us breathless.

I say, No one will be hurt.

It will be used, you'll see, she says.

I think it best not to share specifics with her.

My faith grows every day that this program will allow me to work again with those who have questioned me.

Would an FBI agent have conceived of this? I will my ask friends this question one day when my name is cleared and we are reunited.

We skimmed ahead to the time around the enactment of the plan, but found no mention of it. In an entry a week after the event, we read:

The chest pains come mostly at night and in the early morning.

My sister, when I called her, said, You're dead to us now, and when I wake in the dark with the stabbing on my side, I think she's right, I'm gone.

There was no more mention of T or Lutman. There was an article in the *National Guardian*. DENOUNCE FBI WAR ON OUR EFFORTS FOR PEACE. The text said that FBI agents had taken to initiating destruction of property and people in an effort to discredit the peace movement. An undercover agent had admitted to being at the Kent State rally with his gun. Had he fired a shot to discredit the protestors? Had his shot incited the Guardsmen to shoot? The agent said he never fired his gun. But ballistic tests showed that it had been fired. And what of the event in the San Francisco recruitment office? It was in fact not a bomb but a spray can—a roach bomb that had been refitted to emit ammonium sulfide and printer's ink, producing an unpleasant smell and the appearance of smoke. An action of "no lasting physical consequence." But in terms of the "political climate" it stimulated a scare and the round-up of peace activists on charges of potential terrorism. This was the work of FBI agents Terence Lutman and Sam Vogel, Lutman a career agent,

Vogel perhaps a relatively recent turncoat.

Ammonium sulfide and ink. A stink bomb! Tom and I stared at each other. "Told you so!" Tom said. "To say, 'This war stinks!'" We couldn't stop laughing, it was as hilarious as it was pathetic.

A final note. About Doreena. *D turns white when I come up to the attic. Hypothesis A: She too thinks I'm police. Hypothesis B: She thinks I'm pitiful. And if so, what then?*

Then no more entries.

"Permit me to summarize," Tom said, with mock officiousness. It was early morning and we were goofy from the long night of reading and laughing and weeping.

"They came to think he was an agent. A planted note from the FBI. On top of some crazy old suspicion in the movement because he's independent and unpredictable. To prove he's not an agent, he gets involved with an actual FBI agent, who ensnares him in a plan to stink up a government office. To prove he's true and not an agent, he becomes an agent's dupe. And then he's damned forever. In their eyes."

"And in his own eyes, too," I said.

"But was there a note?" Tom said. "And how do we know that Terence Lutman was an agent?"

"Read on," Doreena said, appearing at the door. She pointed at a file folder on the desk, thick with papers.

"He kept files, too?" I laughed, slap happy with fatigue.

"No, *they* did," Doreena said, appearing at the door. "The Freedom of Information Act opened up a secret world. That's his file. Too bad he never got to see it."

"This is his FBI file?"

"Just a sampler I put together," she laughed. "From his thousand-page dossier."

I opened the file. Department of Justice. Then my father's name and file number. Then whole paragraphs and pages blocked out with Magic Marker. Here and there some words peeked out from the squares of dark gray, like inscriptions on tombstones. *Samuel (Sam) Vogel. Under surveillance for his commu-nist leanings.* Here and there longer stretches of sentences and paragraphs about "subject SV," prepared by various agents, cov-ering three decades of "un-American" activity.

Agent reports about my father and mother being "Negro" defenders and "prematurely anti-fascist," indicative of "com-munistic sympathies." A report about my father at a union delegates meeting, giving a report on the post–War spiraling cost of living and the "explosion" of strikes around the coun-try. Lots of information, which the agent suspects is being fed by the Soviets since similar data appeared in the Daily Worker. A report claiming my father favors more integration of Ne-groes into building trades; the agent proposes that the bureau approach white carpenters about this orientation, and indicate to them how this will hurt their economic interests. A report about my father at an international peace conference, raising "communistic issues regarding war, class, profit, etc." A 1967 letter from the New York Office confirming that SV "uses only longhand for correspondence. . . ." *No need to undertake more time-consuming typing forgery. The office will provide the lab of the Document Division with SV handwriting specimens on the basis of which a letter from SV to the bureau will be generated . . . to in-clude notes on his private meetings with political allies and request for increase in bureau payment.* A 1970 agent report to the San Fran-cisco bureau: *growing communication and trust with SV, who is very motivated to restore his reputation and warming to the plan to be "partners in conscience."* An agent reports that "SV has left SF area." My father is deemed "neutralized": *SV isolated and prob-ably harmless in terms of future subversive Un-American activities. The Southern California office will be alerted as he probably will favor warm weather for reasons of poor health.*

When we were very young, Marie would sing a song her father used to sing, a Celtic lament that made its way to the Virginia mountains, about how castles were sacked and chieftains scattered, how truth alone was steady. "Truth is a fixed star," my mother would sing in a tremulous falsetto, and the rest of us would join in for a refrain. Truth was dangerous, sad, terrible, and it's all we had; somehow that sentiment had gratified our young souls. Now as we lay on the floor in the gray dawn, books and files all around, I found myself humming the song. Among the miserable documents of doubt and mistrust, trickery and treachery, we'd found it.

Tommy had fallen asleep on the floor.

"Do you think my father is dead?" I asked Doreena.

She shrugged. "Some of the old-timers talk to me again. I guess I've been cleared, him too, with people reading their own files. Anyway, someone said he was living in Santa Monica. On the street, they said. I don't know if it's true. I stopped putting too much stock in what people say years ago."

"I guess we can drive there."

"Count on it taking a day."

I said, "Won't you come?"

She shook her head. "Death can be an easier fact to face than some others."

"I know. It was easier in a way when I thought he was dead."

"You might be better off not knowing anymore. Assuming you can find out anything more. . . . But I see you know that already . . . and you're going anyway."

And I nodded.

"At least you'll have Tom with you. It's hard to go it alone."

We woke to a brilliant noon light and the smell of the salty bay.

"I'm feeling hopeful," Tommy said. "You know, Bet, I just had a kind of dream that he's still alive."

"He may be."

"And he was doing some important work somewhere, some important political work. He healed and moved on."

"Nice dream, sweetheart," I said. "But I'm not sure that's it,

Tommy. I think he may be pretty broken. Doreena said she heard he was living on the street."

"And you believe that?" my brother snapped.

"Tommy, we can get through this. Whatever it ends up being. Together."

That's how we'd gotten through the worst times, years ago. You and me will be together, we'd say. It'll be all right. Meaning, We'll sit together in the back of the courtroom together. We'll ignore the reporters together. We'll hold hands . . . and count to a thousand together till the crowd stops screaming.

"I don't want to find a hopeless bum, Bets. I couldn't bear that."

"We're looking for him. Whatever he is. Together."

"I have no use for *whatever*, Betsy. *Whatever* undoes me. I need to remember him a certain way. To go on."

"What way is that?"

"Strong. I can't follow your lead here, Bets. Not if there's nothing good to find. Not if it only gets worse."

"We'll be together," I tried one more time.

"Sweetheart, if he wanted us, he'd know where to look. He doesn't want to be found. Go back, Betsy. Go back home."

I said, "Which home? I gave up everything. The apartment. My job. David."

My brother shook his head. "I can't look at hopeless, Betsy. And you don't have to either. We have to move on."

"Not yet. We're so close. . . ."

"Betsy, you'll never find him. Even if you find him, it won't be *him* anymore."

"I need to see him if he's alive."

"Why, sweetheart?"

"Because he's our father. And. . . ."

"And what, sweetheart?"

"I need to see that he's OK."

"And what if he's not?"

"I need to fix it up. . . . I think I did terrible things. . . . It's

190

been so many years since I've thought about it. But I think I actually did terrible things."

"We all have those thoughts. . . ."

"Not *thoughts*," I said. "Even you knew what I was capable of. You called me Judas girl! You knew."

"We were little kids. Jabbing at each other. We were both proud of him."

"No, you were proud of him. I wasn't. I yearned for him, but I was ashamed of him too. . . . I wanted to belong. You always knew who you were. I was their daughter, but in my heart. . . ."

Then I couldn't speak. I just leaned on my brother—ashamed now of all my shame back then. For telling people my father was the Director of Construction for the City of New York, not a carpenter and champion of sweaty men in kiddie overalls. For saying his job had sent him to Chicago when he was really away in Leavenworth. For saying he didn't really like Negroes but just made believe. When was that? That night I pledged for the Puff Balls. I remembered my old dream. But it was worse than the dream. They made me sign a note stating my father was a communist and a spy. They promised to rip it up. But then when I signed, they denied me membership forever, and made me crawl out through the cellar door.

"You know, Tommy, I think I got him arrested once."

"With that stupid letter you wrote to the Governor and the other dopes? No one read your letter, sweetheart. What they sent you back was just a form letter. Have you been tormenting yourself over that all these years? I punished you enough for that," he laughed.

"Not with that letter. . . . Something else."

I sputtered a version of the Puff Ball story.

"And Eugenia Kabat's father really did have a big job. He was chief of all the token booths for the whole city. He probably took my letter to the Mayor, who took it to the Feds or God knows who. I never told anyone. . . . That's probably the reason they took him in that last time."

My brother is trying to hold me but I won't let him.

"I ruined everything for everyone," I cried. "I think Mommy knew what I did. That's probably what made her really sick!"

I heard my mother's voice: He's never coming back. You saw to that. Who'd want to come back to you?

I begged for forgiveness. Where were we? She must have been home from the hospital—for a short stay. I remember staring at something gray as my mother shouted. Gray marble. The kitchen linoleum.

This can't go on any longer, she cried. She banged my head, she bit my hands. She roared. And then she got a knife.

Mommy, I cried. Don't.

Don't Mommy me, she said. Come here, you traitor, and get the punishment you deserve. Then she started crying and went to the phone. Calling the police, to lock me up, I thought, as I slid under the kitchen table.

I need to be away, she said. Then she was whispering, You need to come get me! I'm dangerous to myself and others. Then she was pulling me across the floor like a fireman, shoving me in the closet. How long was I in there—till they came to get her—and me? A minute? An hour? It felt like years, crouched in the dark.

As I told him, my brother held me tight, and now I let him.

"Betsy, she was very sick by then. She didn't know anything about you and your Puff Balls. You were just the enemy of the day. She lined us all up all the time, friend, enemy. Even me. I was their clone politically, but that didn't stop her from calling me, Traitor Tom. Fear does that to people."

"She did that to you too!"

"Fear made her crazy. And you too," he said.

I shrugged.

"Say, 'I believe,'" he laughed.

"I believe…," I said.

"Say, 'I believe that I am innocent,'" he said.

"I believe . . . my big brother," I said. "He knows everything."

"But you probably think he's terrible now for not wanting to go with you. . . ."

I cuddled into his arms.

"Maybe that's what fear did to *you*?" I said. "Made you need to keep going all the time. Because there was no ground to stand on."

My brother looked at me blankly. "Interesting point, sweetie, but I don't know what the fuck you're talking about."

"Give me another week, Tommy. And then you can go."

"I have a meeting in Toronto. I can't miss it," he whined.

"You're afraid to see him?"

"Let's say that I've gone as far as I can bear, Betsy. Let's say that I have no stomach for tragedy. I never felt anything but honored to have him as my father. For me, all that mattered was his work. And then mine. And now I just pity him. And I don't do well with pity, honey. It dissolves me. I need things simple and clear and forward marching."

Ten minutes later he was in the shower. Half an hour later he was in a taxi on his way to the airport. I should call him if I found out anything new. If he was busy in a meeting, he'd call me back.

It wasn't easy to say goodbye to Doreena. Before I left, she took me into her studio, a vast attic room at the top of the house. Canvases were stacked everywhere—in wooden cradles, on the floor, against every wall.

"Forty years of D. Jones." she laughed. "I couldn't act . . . so I tried to paint. Nothing much. But it kept me going."

"Do you show?" I hated how I sounded. Remnants of the *Big Apple* interviewer.

"Now and then. It helps the pocketbook and the spirit. A few small galleries sell my stuff and I give paintings to the local peace groups to help them raise funds. But you know, I'd paint anyway, even if no one ever saw. I can't seem to stop, even when I've thought I'd be better off."

"Betsy, they don't ever leave you, those years," she said. She pointed to the canvases again. "Here are the HUAC years. The McCarthy Hearing Years. The Traitorous-Commie-Under-the-Bed Years. In Labor. Movies. Government. Schools. Here are Kill the Spies Years. The Scared to Death Years. Destroy the Panthers Years. Destroy the Peaceniks Years. Here are the Nothing Left Years. The Gone Away Years. The Runaround Years. The Left Alone Years."

I looked around the room. Skeletons on every canvas. Taunting, dancing, kissing, hiding.

"Like those Mexican skeletons," I said. "I had a skeleton doll. Dressed as a bride. Tom had a skeleton bandit puppet."

"People got broken by those times, Betsy. And, of course, I don't just mean the Fifties. Hoover's counterintelligence program ran secretly into the Seventies. They spied on thousands of people. Spread miserable rumors. Destroyed reputations. Planted provocateurs. They taped Martin Luther King with women for years, then sent him the tapes and told him to commit suicide or face disgrace. They persecuted Einstein. Spread stories that he was a dangerous anti-American subversive. Tried to bar him from the U.S., get him fired. They broke a lot of people. Some never got put back together again."

Silently we walked out onto the verandah, then through the grass onto the gravel driveway. I thought of my father's slender feet in those cordovan boots he used to slip on after work. I imagined the boots crunching the small stones as he walked back and forth, telling himself whatever it was he had no friends to tell.

"Maybe I'll find him." I looked down, as if to find footprints.

"Maybe you will."

"Doreena," I said. What did I want to ask her? To change her mind and come with me? To not let me go? I said, "Doreena . . . should I call you . . . if . . . ?"

But before I could finish, she shook her head, no.

12: The Carousel

I TOOK THE OLD COAST HIGHWAY, bypassing the Freeway trucks and traffic, and made it to Santa Monica by late afternoon. At the north end of town, I found a hotel on the beach, and I checked in and showered, then forced myself out the door. It was December and going on six, but the sun still blazed as unforgivingly as a summer noonday sun back home. In short, there were hours of daylight left and no excuse, besides my dread, not to face this last leg of my sorry search.

I had only the old snapshot that Doreena had given me to go on, an early color photograph, so intense in its rendering that my father looked like he'd stepped out of an old MGM technicolor movie—with blue-black hair, skin the color of a penny, eyes the color of a tree frog. I made my way along the beach to Ozone Park and back, showing my picture, explaining, as Doreena had explained, that the hair in the front was now a shock of white. But he looked familiar to no one. After a couple of hours I moved onto the pier, eyeing everyone I passed. Tourists with mirrored sunglasses, pensioners in white overshirts, bums whispering and smoking and coughing. Inside the arcade I showed some boys the photo, but no one knew him. At novelty shops, hot dog stands, benches, I stopped to talk to anyone who looked my way. But got only no's or shrugs, or scared stares—as if I were a thief or a cop.

Santa Monica was my only lead, though, and I wasn't ready to give up on it. Besides, there was something about the pier itself that held me. The way it was framed by the brilliant blue of sky and water. And indeed it was in such splendor that I'd always imagined reuniting with him, running down a long shimmering pier or bridge into his open arms So, though a full day of walking and talking had brought me no new information, I roused myself and walked the pier again, stopping at stand after stand. Then, too tired to go on, I made my way back to the hotel to sleep. Rested, I'd give it one more day.

In the morning, I drove to the city's outskirts, down toward Venice Beach and up to Santa Ynez Canyon, from boarding houses and motels, to community centers and shopping centers, showing the photograph. At a bingo game at the North Santa Monica Senior Center an old woman thought he looked familiar and passed the picture around. Every person said he looked like someone she knew. A brother. A husband. A son. And soon another day had passed. It was time to give up.

The pier again. I had to see it one more time. Driving back towards the water, I planned how it would be. The place I imagined for our reunion would be the site for our goodbye. Maybe I'd tear up the photograph and toss the pieces in the water as if they were his ashes, then watch as they floated out to sea. Maybe I'd sing a song. That song about truth. Because I hadn't found him, but I'd found some truth?

"You again?" "Still looking?" "No luck?" some vendors called as I walked down the pier, his photograph clenched in my hand. Slowly, ceremoniously, I made my way past the arch toward the end of the pier. But then something stopped me. The sound of an organ playing "You Are My Sunshine"—my father's favorite song? The pungent, hopeful smell of the freshly painted carousel? The rays of the late afternoon light flashing off the water?

And then the carousel man, a cigarette dangling from his mouth, his eyes half closed against the smoke and sun, was standing before me.

"Do you know him?" I said.

He studied the picture. "What do you want?" he whispered. "Why are you hounding me?"

"I don't mean to bother *you*. I just want to find *him*."

He pushed me away to look at my face, not at the face in my hand.

"Why won't you let me be? Won't you people ever stop?".

His hair was white, his skin leathery brown, his eyes black behind black glasses. One top and two bottom teeth were missing. With the sun shining from behind him, reddening him, he looked like a jack-o'-lantern. I searched the face to understand.

I lifted my hand, lifted off his dark glasses.

"It's you. . . ," I said.

Then I took off my sunglasses. "It's me, Daddy," I said.

He stood me at arm's length to study me. Then opened his arms wide.

I told my father a hundred things.

How I'd gone to the grave. All the people I'd gone to see.

I told him about Aunt Elsie and the bridge of love. He told me he never stopped thinking about any of us, not for a day.

I told him about Grandma Alice and the money and junk. The money was for my mother and us, he said. He'd left a note with the money, for Doreena to send; but Alice probably turned the note over to the you-know-who, he said.

I told him about Leo and Rosie. Doreena. Even Cousin Arthur. "That fat little shit," he laughed. "Some things never change."

We'd walked down to the end of the pier. "Well, you saw Doreena. So you know. About how bad I fucked up. Betsy, I was a fool. I let myself get set up. Not once but twice. But I can't ever prove that I was set up. So I just live knowing that people I love hate me.

"I know what happened. I read the notebooks."

"So you know. . . ."

"And I read the file."

"The file?"

"Freedom of Information Act."

"Never heard of that. I haven't kept up with the news much the last decade or so."

I told him about the FBI letter and the handwriting lab, the report from his "friend" in the bookstore. As I spoke, my father's bronze skin turned pale green, and he staggered over to a bench and sat down.

"Oh, Jesus!" he whimpered.

"You OK, Daddy?"

"No," he said. Then, "Yes. . . . Oh, shit, I don't know what I am."

"This means you could come back, Daddy. We could tell everyone. They'll all understand." I rubbed his hands and arms and cheeks, to bring back his color.

"They will? You think so?" he said, sounding like a five-year-old. Then he said: "I couldn't serve time now. I'd die in jail. I think I could make a deal. Do you think I could make a deal? They had me on something minor. It was very minor. I spoke at a rally. I was out on parole. Which revoked my parole. Wasn't that it? It was minor. But they were going to put me away. I couldn't go away. I couldn't serve time. I would have died. I didn't want to die. I was wandering a long time. I have so little time left. They took all my time. . . ."

I had my arms around him as he babbled, and I could feel when he started to cry, and I began to cry too.

"They played tricks on thousands of people, Daddy."

"Anyone else I know?" he whispered. "Did they get anyone I know?"

"Hoover hated Einstein, too for being a socialist and a pacifist." I told him what Doreena had told me.

"Einstein. Now *he* was no fool. But they got him, too?" My father was smiling his jack-o'-lantern smile. Proud to be in the company of a genius?

"And they hounded Martin Luther King for years. I guess to Hoover, civil rights was Un-American. And I guess him becoming anti Vietnam War . . . and starting that campaign for poor people made him a total traitor." I told my father about the tapes and their threats.

"What did he do?"

"Some people think that when King wouldn't kill himself, Hoover had him killed."

"Oh, Jesus, what a thought. . . ." My father bowed his head.

"Tommy said that someone's writing a book about King and the FBI and the CIA."

"Does my son know . . . about *me?*"

And when I nodded, he said, "Good. And my sister?"

"Soon," I said. "Soon."

I stayed at the entrance, as my father strode into the carousel house to get back to his shift. He extended his arm and straightened out the line of children coming through the gate. A small child cried as he strapped him on a horse. "Sorry, buddy. House rules," my father said. "You'll be fine."

I watched my father making the rounds of horses and ponies and golden chariots, lifting kids, strapping them in. My rebel father subdued—playing by the rules.

"You'll be fine," I whispered. Like he'd told me a million times back then.

My father's worn jeans flapped against his bony ass. I'd make sure he ate, get him new clothes. Check on his heart.

The music stopped and my father walked to the gate.

"I'll be a while," he said. "You stay here."

I wanted to run after him, so he could lift *me* up. Hey, you. You come here. Up here on my best horse, you. How I wished it could have been like that all those years. You come, instead of, You stay. You stay while I go away.

I bought a ticket and walked through the gate, climbed on the platform. A snow white horse with a silver mane and a gold saddle stood empty and I ran for it, climbing on just as the music began.

Up and down I went. Round and round. On the central column was a laughing clown, then a mustached bandleader with a jeweled baton, then a smiling ballerina on a tiger, then the clown again. The late sun was slanting through the entrance arch and each time I passed there, my horse's mane glistened and I waved as if my father were waiting with the other parents.

The third time around, he *was* there. How many years I had waited for this. It was crazy—he was old, I was middle-aged. And there I was, waving like all the kids. Here I am. Daddy, here I am.

Each time I left the entrance for the dark interior, I wondered if he'd be gone by the time I reached the front again. But each time he was there, his head bathed in light, his hand in the air.

The music stopped. My father stood beside me as I climbed off my horse.

"Nice ride, honey?"

I nodded. "Really nice, Daddy," I said.

When my father's shift on the carousel was over, we sat on the beach and built a fire. He told me more about his life now. He lived in a rented room in town. In the morning he worked on the pier. "I wake up the derelicts. When it's cold I drag the sick ones to shelters. Afternoons and evenings I work the carousel. Round and round we go," he laughed sadly.

I told my father about my life. David. Journalism. My plan to freelance. My old job at *Big Apple*. I did imitations of Alan. He said, "Good you got rid of that 220 hitter, honey." I told him about Yukio. "Glad you found someone who could use that old junk." I told him about Tommy. His work with End Hunger. About my mother.

It was my mother, he said, that he felt worst about. "I should have protected her more. She was a frail girl."

"That wasn't you, Daddy. It was the times. You didn't do that."

"I fucked up, honey. That's why I had to stay away, honey. I really fucked up. I couldn't inflict any more on you kids. I'd already destroyed my wife."

"That wasn't you, Daddy," I said again, drawing him close, remembering Tommy the other day in Doreena's study, holding me as I writhed.

"Nice of you to say that, sweetheart," my father said into my hair.

While he was working I'd bought hotdogs and marshmallows in a convenience store on Pacific Avenue, and we cooked them now on wire hangers we found on the beach.

I told him I had plans. First to fatten him up. Then to get him to a doctor.

My father laughed. "And then what?"

"Never let you go," I said. On the carousel, I'd figured it out. How I'd keep him with me. Smuggle him into Mexico somehow. Then Guatemala.

"I'd fuck it up for you, Betsy." There was no way he could get out of the country. But that wasn't all. "I'm not all here," he said.

"All there?" I said, pointing to his head.

"That, too," he said. "And all *here*, too. I'm back *there* a lot. Remember your mother once painted the ceilings sky blue so we'd feel we were outside when we were inside hiding?"

"And she'd put blankets on the floor and we'd have picnics."

"Lots of days, I feel as if I'm still back there, locked into that time."

"I could fix that, I know I could. I want to be with you."

My father smiled. He needed a good dentist, too, then off to Mexico.

Then it was late. I made him promise to meet me first thing in the morning. To make our plans. There was so much to organize.

"Both my children are *organizers*. . . . I'm very proud," he said, kissing me goodnight.

I barely slept. At midnight I reached Mitzi and got David's number in Cuernavaca. I left a message at the hotel that I'd found my father, and needed just a little more time. Somewhere before dawn I showered and dressed and went out to sit on the balcony, watching the little pink lights on the pier flicker and then fade as the sun seeped into the sky.

I pulled my hair back into a ponytail. I put on my white shirt and blue skirt, the schoolgirl outfit I'd dressed in to *see* him that day it all started. All I need is a flag, Daddy, I'd say as I approached him later. Or he'd say it to me.

I put on penny loafers and took a navy cardigan from my suitcase in case it was cool. Maybe we'd walk along the cliffs until we found a place to have breakfast. I'd order him a huge breakfast. Sunny-side up, crisp bacon, home fries. It was windy on the hill down to the pier. I felt in my bag for my credit cards. I'd buy him something warm. A lumber jacket, a flannel-lined jean jacket, a down vest? A white shirt like mine, so we could match? We wouldn't even go back to his room. There couldn't be anything worth keeping.

The gate was locked when I got to the carousel, and corrugated metal doors covered the arches of the carousel house. He wasn't there but what did that mean? We weren't supposed to meet till six; and he was never early, he was always late. I walked down the pier to an all-night diner. Inside men were busy changing the place from a night place to a day place, dumping greasy clams, wrinkled hotdogs, setting up vats of coffee, cartons of donuts. I busied myself watching them. Then I turned to leave.

"Looking for Whitey?" one of the men behind the counter said. "You his kid? I see you got his eyes. What's your rush? Cup of coffee?"

"I have to go meet him."

"It's funny. He should have been down here by now. We hose down in the morning. He usually has the dock cleared by now."

"He's always late," I said as much to calm myself as to quiet him.

"Whitey? Late?"

I walked out onto the pier, walking quickly to escape the man's gargly laugh. The arcade was open and empty except for two boys at the Space Invaders game. I walked up and down the aisles, until I came to Asteroids. I won a game. A good sign, I told myself. He'll be there. One more game would guarantee it. I won a second game. And then it was six.

He was nowhere. I circled the carousel again and again. Yesterday he'd watched me go round and round. For one hopeful moment I imagined him watching me from some secret hiding place, getting ready to emerge. I looked up and down the pier but all I could see in either direction was dark sky and dark planks, and the blur of bodies on benches. One body wore jeans, a plaid shirt. Had my father slept down on the pier so he wouldn't oversleep and be late to meet me?

"Wake up, you lazy bum," I whispered as I walked towards him. Wasn't that what we used to say way back? When he was home, when she was home. When we'd jump into their bed early in the morning. Wake up, you lazy bum.

But up close I saw he was a stranger.

At a phone booth where the cliffs and the dock meet, I dialed his number. Let it be the wrong number, I thought. I told myself that if it was the right number, he was gone. After the fourth ring a sleepy woman's voice said, "You want Whitey? He's gone."

"When did he leave," I asked.

"Early this morning. He left his keys and a note saying he wouldn't be coming back. I could rent the room to someone else."

I walked back to the hotel. Maybe he'd been confused and thought we were meeting there. Maybe he'd checked out of his room to stay with me.

"Ms. Vogel?" the woman at the desk said.

"Yes," I said expectantly.

"This is for you," she said, handing me an envelope. I saw my father's script on the front—angular, upright but in miniature, all the letters huddled together in the middle of the white empty space. I touched each letter as if it were part of him, shrinking away from me.

For Betsy, the envelope said. *From Daddy*. I tore it open.

Dear Betsy,

When you get this, I'll be gone. I knew if I told you in person what I was planning, you'd try to change my mind and maybe you would so I'm doing it this way because I'm convinced this is the right decision.

I stayed up all last night thinking hard about this and about you. I can't believe you came all the way across the country, in a bus no less (the people's transportation, ha ha) to find your old pop. It was beautiful to hear you ask me to come with you and go to doctors and all that. What a terrific girl you are! But I am certain that I'd only bring you more pain. You need to live your life. I had mine.

Here are some specifics that went into my decision:

1. Like I told you yesterday, you'd never get through the border with me. So I'd screw up your plans.

2. Also, no matter where we were, I'd ruin things for you. I mean, it could begin all over again. There could be another Hoover one day. Then I'd be a real liability, for you and your guy and your family when you have your own. You never know when another bad period could start up. We're the only superpower now and I read that certain powerful elements don't think we went far enough last year in that Desert Storm. So there could be more damn wars and maybe more un-American hunts. In which case being associated with me would be big trouble, honey.

3. That's not all. I'm not who I was. I mean I am but I'm also not. I lost the knack of living in one place. Remember I said I wanted to go around and organize in bus stations? I could tell that you thought I was meshugga. That's me now, more or less, working here and there with my bums. I'm a little bit of a bum, I guess, which helps them to trust me. It's not anything much, I know. But it's all I can do at this point in time. So I should keep on doing what I do. I wanted to move on, anyway. To a new venue. Isn't that what everyone says these days? Venue?

Maybe if you tell my sister what happened, I could call her soon. That way we could be in touch like in the old days, and maybe even meet now and then if it's safe. It was definitely not a mistake for you to have come. Don't think that. You are a good journalist and you found out the truth. You enlightened me with that whole Hoover deal. I feel so much better now that I know that others will know what happened. To me and Albert Einstein and Martin Luther King.

Cheer up, honey. I have a feeling things are looking up for you! You got rid of that deadbeat Rotten Apple magazine and can write about something substantial. Hey, you could write this whole story maybe, about the union, the Red scare, the Hoover stuff, everything in the notebooks and files. Don't feel pressured. It's just a suggestion, though I do think the objective conditions might be right for such a public discussion.

Now I need to ask you a question. Are you pregnant? You didn't eat your hotdog and you told me you were sick on the bus trip. Also, you looked pale. Both times with Mommy, her skin was what gave it away. You know, when you were little, I could tell things about you right away. When you rubbed your ear, it meant you were tired. When you were going to throw up, you rolled yourself into a ball. Wouldn't it be something if I was right and could tell things about my child without either of us saying a word. Last night since I couldn't sleep I gave some thought to names. For a girl, I like Susan B. Anthony, or just Susan B. if it feels too much. For a boy, I like Eugene V. Debs or again just Eugene V. Or Frederick Douglass but not just Frederick D. Again, don't feel pressured but keep an open mind. Remember, I came up with your and Tommy's names and they were very substantial and effective.

Please don't try to find me and change my mind. I promise I will contact my sister. And as I said, via her we can keep in touch. If you decide to write about us, you could send me chapters for commentary.

I could fill in certain historical material, which I used to have a good grasp of and still do when I put my mind to it. You'd have to change the names. Again, don't feel pressured. But the time may be right for such a volume

I love you, Betsy. Tell Tommy I love him, too. And Mommy if she remembers me, or actually even if she doesn't. Send love to Doreena too. And everyone whose heart I broke and who broke mine back. Tell them I never stopped being their friend.

One more thing. I notice it's your birthday. Imagine that, you're forty today! I remember the day when the warden called me to his office to say my little girl had been born. Happy birthday, Betsy Ross. Happy birthday, my big girl.

Daddy

The road out of town was slow. Twice I thought I saw him walking south in a dust cloud. But I just held the steering wheel tight, forcing myself to keep on driving. The radio was broken, which was just as well. I wanted to be alone with him still, with what of him I still had with me.

When I reached the Freeway, I started to sing. The songs we'd sung on the beach the night before, which were the songs we used to sing, all of us together, all those years ago. I sang "Joe Hill" remembering how my father crooned, "'I never died,' said he," his voice sounding sweeter and lighter than in the old days, like a cross between Harry Belafonte and Patti Paige. I sang "Strangest Dream," remembering how, when we got to the part about men in a mighty room signing a paper that "put an end to war," my father said, "Now, *that's* something worth signing, not that shit they gave me," and I said, "Damn right, Jack." Which is what I used to say to show him I was on his side.

Then I sang the last song we'd sung at the end of the night as we waded in the ocean, our eyes fixed on the dark sky. Driving down the highway, I imagined I was marching down the aisle of the auditorium and my father was watching, calling "Atta girl. Go, Betsy, go."

JUST THE WAY YOU WANT ME

Oh, say, does that star spangled banner still wave
o'er the land of the free and the home of the brave?
I it sang at the top of my lungs, as if my life depended on it,
pushing the gas pedal hard as I made for the border.

THE AUTHOR

Nora Eisenberg is a professor of English at The City University of New York (LaGuardia) and Director of the University Faculty Publications Program. Her short stories, essays and reviews have appeared in *The Partisan Review, The Village Voice, Tikkun,* and *The Los Angeles Times*. Her first novel, *The War at Home,* was named a Book Rave of 2002 by *The Washington Post* Book World and nominated as a Best Book of the Year by *ForeWord Magazine*. She lives in Manhattan.

About the Type

This book was set in Bembo, a typeface modeled on typefaces cut by Francesco Griffo for Aldus Manutius' printing of *De Aetna* in 1495 in Venice, a book by classicist Pietro Bembo about his visit to Mount Etna. Griffo's design is considered one of the first of the old style typefaces, which include Garamond, that were used as staple text types in Europe for 200 years. Stanley Morison supervised the design of Bembo for the Monotype Corporation in 1929. Bembo is a fine text face because of its well-proportioned letterforms, functional serifs, and lack of peculiarities; the italic is modeled on the handwriting of the Renaissance scribe Giovanni Tagliente.[*]

Composed by JTC Imagineering, Santa Maria, CA
Designed by John Taylor-Convery

[*] Type description courtesy of Adobe Systems Inc.